"I slept with my ex-wife."

Suddenly everything—except Kurt's voice—seemed louder than normal. The ticking of the clock. The drone of voices outside the office. Then the smell of coffee from the waiting room turned Zoe's stomach. She grabbed the back of a chair.

"Where, Kurt? Where did you sleep with Elizabeth? In the bed where we made love last weekend?"

The color drained from his face. "Zoe, please don't—"

She stared at him. A cold feeling of dread seeped into her. "There's more, isn't there?"

"She wants a reconciliation. Our daughter—"

Oh, God. He hadn't told her no. Zoe covered her mouth with her hand, afraid she might be ill.

"Zoe, I'm so—"

She stood abruptly. "Please don't say you're sorry. Obviously you're considering going back to her."

He swallowed hard. "Yes," he said softly.

In that moment, everything changed. Nothing would ever be the same again.

Dear Reader,

It was a joy to return to Bayview Heights High School for the setting of my twelfth Superromance novel. A spin-off from *Cop of the Year* and *Because It's Christmas*, this new story, *Count on Me*, tracks the lives of Zoe Caufield and Kurt Lansing, both of whom we met in those first two books. Now they're involved with each other and searching—just as Cassie and Mitch did, and Seth and Lacey did—for a way to make a life together.

Kurt has betrayed Zoe in the most elemental way a man can betray a woman. Now he's learning just how hard it is to win back the trust of the woman he's never stopped loving. Zoe learns that her feelings for him haven't diminished despite the mistake he made and that she can, indeed, count on him this time.

Part of what happens to change her mind centers on a group of her students—five girls she's come to know and love during the course of their high-school years. Five girls who volunteer in Kurt's clinic. As I entered my thirtieth year of teaching, I found that writing this book caused me to remember the many students I've taught—the joy and heartbreak of getting close to them and sharing their problems.

The message of this book is clear: with enough concern and caring, any problem—between men and women, between teachers and students, among friends and family—can be overcome.

I hope you enjoy Zoe and Kurt's story and I hope you enjoy meeting their students.

Please write and let me know what you think. I answer all reader mail. Please send letters to Kathryn Shay, P.O. Box 24288, Rochester, NY 14624-0288, or e-mail me at Kshay1@aol.com. Also visit my Web sites at http://www.home.eznet.net/~kshay/ and http://www.superauthors.com.

Kathryn Shay

Count on Me
Kathryn Shay

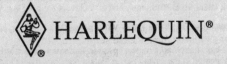

HARLEQUIN®

TORONTO • NEW YORK • LONDON
AMSTERDAM • PARIS • SYDNEY • HAMBURG
STOCKHOLM • ATHENS • TOKYO • MILAN • MADRID
PRAGUE • WARSAW • BUDAPEST • AUCKLAND

ISBN 0-373-70976-5

COUNT ON ME

Copyright © 2001 by Mary Catherine Schaefer.

All rights reserved. Except for use in any review, the reproduction or utilization of this work in whole or in part in any form by any electronic, mechanical or other means, now known or hereafter invented, including xerography, photocopying and recording, or in any information storage or retrieval system, is forbidden without the written permission of the publisher, Harlequin Enterprises Limited, 225 Duncan Mill Road, Don Mills, Ontario, Canada M3B 3K9.

All characters in this book have no existence outside the imagination of the author and have no relation whatsoever to anyone bearing the same name or names. They are not even distantly inspired by any individual known or unknown to the author, and all incidents are pure invention.

This edition published by arrangement with Harlequin Books S.A.

® and TM are trademarks of the publisher. Trademarks indicated with ® are registered in the United States Patent and Trademark Office, the Canadian Trade Marks Office and in other countries.

Visit us at www.eHarlequin.com

Printed in U.S.A.

To my son, Ben—actor, singer, scholar, athlete
and all-around good kid.
I love you, buddy.

PROLOGUE

LIFE DOESN'T GET any better than this, Zoe Caufield thought on the thirty-minute drive into New York City, feeling a little like Cinderella going to meet the prince. Through the open windows of her car, the air smelled of early fall and newly mowed grass. Soon she turned onto the expressway, and the country sights and scents gave way to honking horns and the smell of exhaust; traffic was heavy today, too.

But nothing could darken her mood. She was on her way to celebrate her birthday with the man she loved, and she'd just come from doing a job she adored. She smiled, thinking of how six of her favorite students had surprised her with an impromptu party after school today.

Zoe had taught science to At Risk kids, as well as regular health classes, at Bayview Heights High School for most of her professional life, but three years ago, armed with her certification in health education, she had volunteered to design and implement three health-education courses: Leadership, Women's Concerns and Life Issues. A broad spectrum of students had signed up for them, including this core of bright dedicated girls. While careful to keep their relationship professional, Zoe often spent time with them outside of school. Now they called themselves Caufield's Chicks.

Though politically incorrect, it was an affectionate term.

They're the daughters you never had, Kurt had told her.

Still smiling, she thought about Dr. Kurt Lansing, her best friend Cassie's brother-in-law. She had high hopes for the upcoming weekend with him. His green eyes had sparkled like rare jade when he'd held her close last weekend and whispered, "I've reserved a suite at the Marquis Marriott Friday night. Meet me there at six."

Her heart fluttered, remembering his next words. "I have some things to say to you, Zoe. Important things. Your fortieth birthday is the perfect time."

She'd stilled. Their yearlong relationship had only gotten better over the months, though Kurt's initial reluctance to get involved—he'd been badly hurt by his ex-wife—had slowed it considerably.

"Are they, um, good things you want to say to me?" she'd asked.

"Oh, they're good, sweetheart. They're really, really good..."

"He loves me," she said aloud in the car. She knew it, even though he hadn't spoken the words. Neither had she, not that she didn't feel them, but she didn't want to put pressure on him. Yet she sensed his feelings every time he brought her tiger lilies, every time he sat up late with her to discuss a problem she was having with a student or share a fear about his clinic, every time he slid his hands over her body.

Thinking about the fire-engine-red lingerie she'd stuffed in her bag, she glanced at the dashboard clock. The clinic was just off the expressway. Maybe she'd stop there first, entice Kurt to leave early and have plenty of time to talk before their eight-o'clock reservation at the revolving restaurant at the top of the hotel.

After all, it *was* her birthday—the big four-0 no less. And Kurt had been making progress in controlling his own personal demon—workaholism. He'd once confessed to Zoe that his work habits had been partly responsible for the breakup of his marriage to his childhood sweetheart, Elizabeth. Zoe had met her a few times at events for Kurt's daughter, Lauren, and had seen with her own eyes the pull the woman had had on him. Zoe sensed a calculating coldness in Elizabeth, which was why Zoe had been happy when, after about six months, Kurt confided that she had brought him a long way toward getting over his ex.

When the clinic exit came into view, she veered off the expressway and in no time found the medical building Kurt operated with two other doctors. As usual, the parking lot was packed. People needed help and Kurt wanted to save each and every one of them. He felt about doctoring as she did about teaching.

Exiting the car, Zoe hurried into the clinic, breathing a silent prayer that the town board of Bayview Heights would accept Kurt's proposal to open a clinic for teenagers. There had been opposition from newly elected officials, so the proposal had been stalled, which was crazy since Kurt's two city clinics were so successful he'd been approached by medical organizations all over the country—and beyond—to consult on setting up similar facilities. Surely the town would give approval and then Kurt could move to Bayview and maybe...

Zoe entered the building, humming a song from the upcoming school musical this year. After greeting the receptionist, who told her Kurt was in a meeting, she strolled into the waiting room outside his office, adja-

cent to the front desk. Pouring herself a cup of coffee—
its strong aroma permeated the whole room—she sat
and perused the area. The chairs were somewhat worn,
and the walls could use a new coat of paint. A little
plant in the corner drooped from neglect. But good
medicine was practiced in this clinic, she knew.

Fifteen minutes later, the door to Kurt's office swung
open. Zoe looked up from the magazine she'd been
flipping through to the man she loved; he was dressed
in a white shirt, the sleeves rolled up to reveal muscled
forearms. His dark hair was disheveled; she knew he
ran impatient hands through it when he was upset. He
was gazing down at a gorgeous blonde, outfitted in an
expensive-looking suit and fashionable heels.

His ex-wife, Elizabeth.

Zoe's mouth fell open as the woman reached up and
encircled Kurt's neck with her long, slender arms.
Bringing his head down, she kissed him thoroughly on
the mouth.

Zoe's stomach lurched.

Elizabeth drew back and soothed a palm over Kurt's
angular cheek. "I'll wait to hear from you."

Without even seeing Zoe, Elizabeth floated gracefully out the door.

Leaning against the doorjamb, Kurt stuck his hands
in his pants pockets and watched Elizabeth go with a
torn expression on his face.

Finally Zoe stood.

It was then that Kurt's head snapped toward her.
"Oh, my God. Zoe?"

*Keep cool. Don't overreact. A show of temper will
not get you what you want.* "Hi."

"We were…" He glanced at the clock. "I thought
we were meeting at the hotel."

She just stared at him. His face reddened, the way it did when he got too much sun on his boat.

"Come inside," he said, standing back from the doorway. She tried to deny the guilt in his voice.

Woodenly, Zoe crossed the worn floor and entered Kurt's office. Everything seemed the same—two big windows, a battered oak desk, mismatched filing cabinets, the picture of her and Kurt smiling on the deck of the *Lady L.*

"Have a seat," he said stiffly.

She sank onto a padded chair, glad for the support.

He leaned against his desk, his hands digging into his pockets. "I don't know what to say."

Releasing a heavy breath, she studied him. Damn it, she wasn't giving in to insecurities and hurt pride. "I trust you, Kurt." Though they'd made no commitments to each other, about four months ago he'd asked her not to see other men and had promised not to see other women. "It didn't look good, but I'm sure there's an explanation."

His throat worked convulsively, but he said nothing.

Zoe fidgeted like her kids before a test. "Kurt, you're scaring m—"

"I slept with Elizabeth."

At first everything seemed accented. The ticking of the clock was louder. The drone of voices outside the office rose in volume. The coffee smell that wended in from the waiting room turned her stomach. She grabbed on to the edge of the chair with both hands. "When?"

"It doesn't matt—"

"I asked when."

"Last Monday night."

Zoe tried to remember where she'd been Monday

night. She'd been playing volleyball on the high school teachers' team; before she'd left for the game, Kurt had called and teasingly ordered her not to flirt with Alex Ransom, one of Bayview Heights's vice principals, who'd had a crush on her ever since he'd been an eighteen-year-old student in her class.

"I don't understand," Zoe said, struggling to stay calm. "Did she come to see you? Or did you go to her?"

Kurt stared back at her, his green eyes bleak. "She came to my apartment to talk about our daughter. Lauren's gotten into trouble already this year."

"Where, Kurt? Where did you sleep with her? In the bed where we'd made love the weekend before?"

The color drained from his face. Finally he said, "Zoe, don't."

She rubbed her hands across her face, willing herself to think clearly. So much was at stake here. But all she could see was the man she'd been more intimate with than anyone in the world, naked and entwined with the beautiful Elizabeth.

Could she ever live with that?

Did it even matter? A cold feeling of dread seeped into her. "There's more, isn't there?"

He nodded. "Yes." His voice was gravelly. "She wants a reconciliation."

I'll wait to hear from you.

Oh, God, he hadn't told her no. Zoe covered her mouth with her hand, afraid she might be ill.

"Zoe, I'm—"

She stood abruptly. "Please, don't say you're sorry." She lifted her face to take this on the chin. "Obviously you're considering going back to her."

He stared at her. Swallowed hard. "Yes."

In that minute everything changed.

And could never, ever be the same again.

CHAPTER ONE

"I MADE A MISTAKE." Twilight peeked in through the kitchen window as Kurt faced his older brother and willed himself not to shrink from Mitch's icy green gaze. They'd had several volatile discussions over the past eleven months, three days and several hours. Their disagreements had rivaled those they'd had when Mitch had first gotten back from Vietnam twenty-five years ago, when Kurt had tried to keep his brother off a downslide to nowhere.

"A mistake. I see." Mitch shook his head, stretched out his jean-clad legs and clasped his hands over the Bayview Heights Police Department T-shirt he wore. "You know it's too late, don't you?" he said pointedly.

"You mean with Zoe." Just saying her name brought on angina-like pain.

"Of course I mean with Zoe."

"I know it is." He stared at his brother. "How is she?" Over the course of the past months, at Zoe's request, Mitch had refused to give Kurt any information about her. So Kurt had resorted to eavesdropping on her life—listening to Cassie talk on the phone to her from Boston where Zoe had gone for the holidays, observing her at Lansing gatherings, usually accompanied by Alex Ransom, overhearing Seth Taylor, the high-school principal, discuss her latest projects at school.

"She just got back from Paris last night."

Ah, Paris. And Pierre.

Tell that Frenchman to stop calling you, lady, and trying to lure you back to France. Kurt had been poised over her in bed; her short thick chestnut hair had been wild from his hands, her mouth swollen from his kisses, her sexy perfume filling his head. He'd teased her mercilessly about the boyfriend she'd had when she'd studied in Europe and still kept in touch with.

"Isn't that cutting it a little close? She starts school tomorrow."

"It's teacher prep day tomorrow." Mitch studied him and Kurt tried not to squirm. Finally Mitch went to the fridge and retrieved two beers. He handed Kurt one. "In any case, you gave up your right to be concerned about her when you went back to that shrew."

In his heart Kurt knew that Mitch had taken Kurt's reconciliation with his ex-wife so hard because Mitch had never liked Elizabeth. The fight with his brother over Kurt's decision to give his marriage another try had cut like the sharpest scalpel...

"You're *what?*" Mitch had asked, dumbfounded.

"I'm reconciling with Elizabeth."

"But you and Zoe..."

"Look, I've loved Elizabeth all my life. If there's a chance I can make it work, I owe it to her and Lauren to try. I hate that I failed at my marriage."

Mitch sighed, exasperated. "I know you hate to fail at anything, but this time you're being a fool. It'll never work. Elizabeth treated you like dirt for years. Then she cheated on you."

"I brought some of that on myself by sacrificing my family for my work."

"She's a siren. She's always had some weird control over you. You're going to get hurt big time—and lose Zoe in the process..."

Once again, big brother had been right. After only a month, Kurt realized he'd made a huge mistake. After three months, life had become a living hell. He'd waited until Lauren went to college to leave again.

Sipping the beer, he sank onto a chair by the window. "Of course I gave up all rights to Zoe. That doesn't mean I stopped worrying about her." *Or loving her.*

Mitch raked a hand through his dark hair. "You're not thinking of trying to get back with her, are you?"

"Of course not." Please, God, don't let him think that. "I hurt her too much."

"Good. Because I'd hate to have to scrape you up off the floor once Cassie got finished with you if you tried anything that stupid."

Mitch glanced up as his wife of five years entered the kitchen; she wore rumpled jeans and a Bayview Heights sweatshirt, and a weary expression on her face. As always, several strands of hair escaped her braid to fall onto her cheek.

"Speak of the devil," Mitch said dryly.

Cassie's smile bloomed at the sight of her husband. "The *devil* is now asleep."

"Which one?"

"The little one."

In spite of the blanket of tension in the room, Kurt smiled at the mention of his younger goddaughter, six-months-old Camille, whose conception had been a surprise to everybody—including Cassie and Mitch. Not only that, but both she and her four-year-old sister, Alexandra, showed signs of their mother's innate rebelliousness. Mitch claimed that was why he loved his daughters so much.

Cassie's gaze traveled to Kurt and turned steely. It was the same look she'd been giving him for the past eleven months. "Hello, Kurt."

"Cassie."

Crossing to Mitch, she took a sip of his beer. Then she focused back on Kurt. "What are you doing here?" The edge to her voice was marked.

Mitch slid his arm around her waist and pulled her close. "Cass," he said, softly chiding her.

Cassie swallowed hard. Both she and Lacey Taylor, Seth's wife and another of Zoe's friends, had frozen Kurt out when he'd gone back to Elizabeth. He didn't blame them a bit.

"I came to tell Mitch—and you—a few things."

When Cassie stiffened, Kurt saw Mitch's hand squeeze her waist in warning. "Fine. I've got about, oh, ten seconds, before Attila the Hun wakes up and realizes she's alone."

Without preamble, he said, "I've left Elizabeth."

Cassie's mouth dropped open, and she gripped Mitch's shoulder. Kurt's heart ached, watching the woman who'd once been like a sister to him. He'd lost her, too, when he'd made the worst decision of his life.

Before she could berate him, he added, "And there's something else." His eyes darted to Mitch's. "The teen clinic in Bayview Heights has been approved." He jammed his hands into his pockets. "I'm moving to town to open it."

"What?" Cassie's eyes were like heated mercury now. "You can't do that, Kurt."

Mitch scowled. "I don't think it's a good idea, either."

Kurt raked his fingers through his hair. "Of course it's not a good idea. It's a *terrible* idea. Do you think I'd do this to Zoe if I had any choice?"

"There's always a choice," Cassie said.

"The clinic has been approved, based on my running it. Not only was my success with the other two part of the town council's reasoning, but the federal grant I wrote for the one in Bayview Heights specifically names me as the operator." He held up his hands in a gesture of defeat. "The government was clear on that, as was the council. You know some of them aren't crazy about having a clinic here, but Philip Cartwright and his group of senior citizens finally got it passed." Philip was the former editor of Bayview's newspaper and Lacey Taylor's grandfather. "I tried to sway the officials, but they were firm that without my participation, the decision would be rescinded."

"Damn it," Cassie said. "First Jerry Bosco gets on the council and then the school board, and now you're coming back to Bayview." Kurt knew Jerry Bosco was a retired teacher who had given the high school a lot of grief when he worked there. "Could things get any worse in this town?"

Kurt winced.

"Cass..." Mitch said again.

"I'm sorry. I don't mean to hurt you, Kurt, but I won't let *you* hurt *her* again." Cassie put her hands on her hips. "Do you have any idea what you did to her a year ago?"

"Yes, I do."

Pacing, Cassie acted as if she didn't hear him. "She cried for days. She missed school. You know what a

Pollyanna she's always been. But she was depressed for a long time, and so sad it broke my heart.''

Each detail pierced him deeply. ''I'm sorry.''

''Yeah, well, sometimes sorry's not enough.''

There was a wail from upstairs. ''Oh, hell,'' she said, and with one scathing look which encompassed both brothers, stomped out of the room.

Silence became a brittle presence in the kitchen.

Finally Mitch spoke. ''Like she said, buddy, she doesn't mean to hurt you. She's just protective of her friends.''

''I know. I reveled in it when she felt that way about me.''

''I'm sorry. I haven't been there for you, either, have I?''

''It doesn't matter.''

''Of course it does. I think it's...'' Mitch peeled back the label on the bottle. His brother still sometimes had a hard time expressing his emotions. ''I think we all felt a little abandoned when you went back to Elizabeth.''

Why wouldn't they? The Lansings and Taylors and he and Zoe had become close friends during the time he dated Zoe. They'd enjoyed countless dinners and attended school events together, and even took a group vacation to the Bahamas. Kurt had broken up more than a relationship. He'd broken up a close-knit family of friends.

That Elizabeth had disliked Mitch from childhood and grown to hate Cassie added to the difficulties between the brothers.

Kurt shrugged. ''I'm sorry,'' he said again.

''Me, too.'' Mitch studied him. ''Look, where do you plan to stay here in town?''

"It doesn't matter."

"Cassie and I are moving into the new house in a few weeks. This place hasn't sold."

"Really? This is a great condo. I'd buy it in a second."

"Then it's yours."

"Thanks. I'll move in after you're in the new house."

"No, you'll move in now."

Kurt shook his head firmly. "Cassie won't want me under her roof."

"Cassie'll do what's right. You're family, Kurt."

Swallowing the lump in his throat, Kurt stared at his brother. "Thanks, bro. What about Zoe? Would it be best if I told her about all this?"

"No. Let Cass tell her tomorrow." Mitch glanced at the clock. "Zoe just got back from Paris this morning and she's probably sound asleep."

An image of Zoe, rumpled and warm in bed, pole-axed him. He could still remember what she smelled like, what she tasted like. He stood up to diffuse the feeling. "Fine. I'll do my best to make this as easy on her, and you, as possible." He headed out of the kitchen to exit through the garage. When he reached the side door, he heard behind him, "Kurt?"

He pivoted.

"It'll be nice to have my brother back."

Emotion swirled inside him. "Will it?"

"Yeah."

"Thanks." He left then, walking out into the chilly September air. Alone.

"'I WANT TO BE happy...'" On her way to the principal's office, Zoe sang the words to the famous song from *No, No, Nanette* in French; she'd seen the show in Paris with Pierre just a few days ago.

And it felt good. She *did* want to be happy; she *was* happy, truly happy, for the first time in months. Kurt Lansing's absence had put a gaping hole in her life for too long. Though she missed him desperately, she'd learned she could indeed be happy without him.

Seth's new secretary, a sweet young woman named Naomi, smiled up at her when she entered the office. "Well, if it isn't the world traveler."

"Bonjour, mon amie." Zoe turned to Nancy, the financial secretary. *"Mes amies. Comment allez vous?"*

Both women chuckled.

"You look wonderful, Zoe," Nancy said, eyeing her black French jeans, red top and high black sandals. "Paris must have agreed with you."

"Oui, oui."

"Meet any interesting Frenchmen?"

The door had opened on Naomi's question. "She's stringin' one along and breakin' my heart," Alex Ransom quipped from the doorway. Handsome as sin, he had disheveled dark hair that fell across his forehead. "Tell me Pierre didn't talk you into going back to France anytime soon."

"No, he didn't." She reached up and hugged Alex. He held on tight.

Over his shoulders, she saw the door to Seth's office open. Letting go of her friend, Zoe sidled around Alex with her grin still in place. "Hi, Seth. How's the father of the year doing?" she asked archly. Seth's wife, Lacey, had given birth to twin boys last year, bringing the total number of children in the Taylor family to five. Seth's son from a previous marriage; their adopted son, Josh; their own little Philip, who was now almost two years old, and the twins.

When Seth didn't answer, just stared at her blankly, she cocked her head.

She was totally unprepared for the man who stepped to the doorway, and she froze, along, it seemed, with everyone else.

Alex's strong hand on her shoulder broke the spell. Though her smile faltered, Zoe straightened and said evenly, "Hello, Kurt."

His beautiful green eyes were dark with fatigue. His sculpted mouth was bracketed with lines of stress. She hadn't seen him in five months and wondered how someone could age that much in so short a time. His meticulously cut navy suit and striped shirt were ill-fitting. He reminded her of an exhausted, overworked intern. When he gave her a weak smile, the cleft in his chin became visible. She would *not* think about the times she'd kissed that cleft.

"Zoe." Even his voice was tired. Her heart ached with the knowledge that Kurt, the man she'd once loved more than any other man in the world, was not doing well.

Apparently Elizabeth wasn't taking very good care of him. The thought hurt, though she chided herself for having it.

Seth stepped between them and hugged her warmly. "Zoe, welcome back." He whispered in her ear, "I'm sorry."

She squeezed him to let him know she was all right. "If you're busy, I can come back. Cassie's hot to talk to me about something, anyway, so I—"

"You haven't talked to Cassie today?" Seth asked.

"No. We had the faculty meeting this morning and

a department meeting after that. I just stopped in here to check on the volunteer placements for my Life Issues course, then she and I are going to lunch.''

Zoe recalled Cassie's excessive nervousness today and had chalked it up to her leaving Camille with a sitter. Even if it was only for half a day—Cassie was teaching mornings this year and Mitch was working afternoons at the police station—Zoe knew Cassie had a devil of a hard time leaving her child. Zoe cast a worried glance at Kurt. ''What's going on, Seth?''

Quickly Seth pivoted to face Kurt. Some silent signal passed between them. ''Come into my office for a minute.'' He glanced behind her. ''Alex, can I do something for you?''

The vice principal was throwing visual daggers at Kurt. ''No, I'm going to wait for Zoe.'' He squeezed her arm. ''I'll be out here.''

Kurt stiffened visibly. At the display of Alex's affection?

Seth herded her and Kurt into the office and shut the door. For a minute Zoe couldn't breathe. She hadn't been this close to Kurt in months. Even at Lansing gatherings, she'd given him wide berth. But now she was forced to sit next to him, and the first thing that assaulted her senses was his scent.

God, I love the way you smell.

Yeah? I think I put on Aramis…

It's different on everybody. Hmm…the best on you.

Nervously she clasped her hands in her lap, her ruby ring digging into her finger.

''Do you want to tell her or should I?'' Seth asked Kurt; there was definite anger in his voice. She rarely saw the principal angry, but it was clear that something was upsetting him.

"I will." Kurt shifted in his seat. She was forced to face him. Up close the lines around his mouth were deeper. "The teen clinic has been approved by the town council."

Forgetting what was between them, she said, "Oh, Kurt, what good news. We need it so much here. I thought it was a lost cause." But wait. What did that mean in terms of... She addressed Seth. "How does that affect us?"

"One of the things that got the clinic okayed was that our kids would be doing their volunteer work there."

Well, that was good. It would be hard for her to supervise her students at the clinic, given that she'd once anticipated working there with Kurt, but her discomfort was a small price to pay for such an important facility; she could get along with whomever was in charge. "That's good, Seth. We need more placements."

Seth watched her. "There's more."

Her heartbeat accelerated. "What?"

Again Seth looked at Kurt.

Kurt said, "I'm going to be running the place."

"You?" That couldn't be true. "All the way from Southampton?" Which was where Elizabeth lived. Correction. Where he and Elizabeth lived.

Drawing in a deep breath, Kurt shook his head. "I'm moving to Bayview Heights."

No. No. She couldn't possibly handle living in the same town with him and his wife, seeing them together, seeing their daily life. She'd gotten over him, but she wasn't strong enough for that yet. "I..." What could she say?

Kurt faced the principal. "Can I have a minute alone with Zoe, Seth?"

Seth looked at her. "Do you want me to stay?"

From the corner of her eye, she caught Kurt's wince. Before he'd gone back to Elizabeth, he and Seth had become as close as brothers. Seth's desire to protect her from him must hurt.

And why the hell did she care? "No, I'm fine."

Rising, Seth circled his desk and, passing by Zoe, squeezed her shoulder, then left them alone.

Kurt was still reeling from the third degree he'd gotten from Seth earlier about his situation and its effect on Zoe. That Seth had hesitated to leave them alone together hit an already weakened defense system. But the look on Zoe's face gave him the strength to suppress his feelings. "Zoe, I've left Elizabeth."

She looked at him blankly.

"It didn't work out."

Still she didn't say anything. Then she lowered her head, wrapped an arm around her waist, and dug the thumb and forefinger of her other hand into her eyes. "So much wasted," she murmured. "So much lost." Finally she looked up at him, her dark exotic eyes passionate. "All for *nothing*."

He nodded. "I made the wrong choice."

Swallowing hard, she shook her head. "I'm sorry."

"I don't deserve your compassion."

She shrugged. "So what does all this mean?"

"That I'm moving here alone to run the clinic."

For a second pure panic lit her face. "I wish you wouldn't."

He raked a hand through his hair. *God, let me make her understand.* "I have no choice, Zoe." He told her about the grant and how the council's decision was based on his success in New York. "I have no choice," he repeated when he finished.

She drew in a deep breath. "I see." She rotated her shoulders as if trying to relieve them of a burden. The silk of her shirt hugged all her curves and made him yearn to touch her. "Am I...are my kids... You'll be working with my students, won't you?"

"I'm afraid so."

He could see her mind clicking into gear. How was she going to deal with this? One of the things he'd loved most about her was her ability to deal with life's blows. Her optimism had always been the best kind of medicine for him when he was down.

After a moment she straightened. "Fine, then. We'll deal with it."

An almost-tangible silence hung in the room as they stared at each other.

Then Kurt asked, "Zoe, how are you?"

Abruptly she stood and gave him a weak smile. "I'm doing well, Kurt. Really well." She scanned the room. "I don't want your coming here...the clinic...to interfere with that."

"Neither do I. I'll try my best to make this easy for you."

She nodded. She seemed about to say more, but didn't. Instead, she inclined her head regally—he'd watched her stem numerous teenage rebellions with just that gesture—and met his gaze. "I'll be seeing you around, then, I guess."

"I'm sorry, Zoe."

"About the clinic?"

"That, too."

She shook her head, turned, walked to the door and

opened it. Holding her head high, she left him. He followed her to the doorway.

In the outer office, Kurt saw a few students talking to the financial secretary. Everybody was trying to ignore the drama that was playing itself out. Seth stood when Zoe came out, approached her, whispered something in her ear, then walked into his office. Alex Ransom rose, too, slid an arm around Zoe's shoulders and guided her out.

For a moment Kurt stared after her, the sense of loss so great it immobilized him. The feeling was akin to losing a patient after months of treatment. Turning, he stepped back into Seth's office.

"Was it hard?" Seth asked

"Yeah." Kurt stuck his hands in his pockets. "It was hard." He picked up his briefcase. "Nothing I don't deserve, though."

Seth's face softened. "I'm sorry things didn't work out for you, Kurt."

"I'm sorry I hurt her," Kurt said roughly, and strode to the door. "See you tomorrow." He exited the office before he embarrassed himself big time. He almost couldn't contain what was inside him.

AFTER ASSURING ALEX she was fine, Zoe hurried to the safety of her classroom, barely acknowledging the greetings and good wishes from her colleagues in the hall. Once she was safely behind a closed—and locked—door, she stumbled to her desk, dropped into her chair and gulped for air. When her breath came in pants, she bent over and put her head between her knees. At last the emotion subsided, and she straightened.

Then reality set in.

Oh, God, she was going to have to work with him. See him. Frequently. She slapped her palm on her desk. "Damn it. Why?" She kicked the drawer. "*Why?* I was doing so well without—"

"Zoe?" Cassie stood in their connecting doorway. Their eyes met.

Cassie's were full of concern. "You know, don't you." Her friend came into the room and pulled up a chair. Grabbing Zoe's ice-cold hands, she said, "I'm sorry I didn't get to tell you first."

"How long have you known?"

"Kurt came over last night to tell Mitch. I wanted to call you right away, but Mitch said it was too late. Then this morning things were so rushed I thought lunch would be the best time to break the news. How'd you find out?"

"Kurt's here. Meeting with Seth. I walked into the office—" she held up her hands "—and bumped into him." Quickly she related the details.

"Son of a bitch." Cassie's face flamed. "I'm so sorry, Zoe."

"Oh, Cass, I'd like to say it doesn't matter that he'll be in town, but I can't kid myself."

A reluctant grin tugged at Cassie's mouth. "You never kid yourself about anything."

"It'll be hell."

"I know. And he's staying with us until we move to the new house, then he's buying the condo."

"*What?*"

Cassie stood and paced the front of the classroom. Dressed in baggy jeans and an oversize top, she looked like one of the kids. "I'm furious with Mitch for offering. We had a terrible fight about it last night. Neither of us slept much."

"Cass, don't let my problems with Kurt come between you and your husband. We managed to avoid that through the whole breakup."

Still Cassie paced. "I'm just so mad."

"We'll all deal with it." Though she tried not to ask, Zoe lost the internal struggle. "Did Mitch tell you what happened with Elizabeth?"

"He didn't have to tell me. It's been obvious all along. She's a cast-iron bitch. She treated him like dirt for years and just showed her true colors again. Only this time Kurt wouldn't put up with it."

Sadness, deep and murky, swirled inside Zoe. "It's such a waste."

"I know."

"Well, no use crying over it." She wasn't ever going to cry over Kurt Lansing again. "I'll learn to live with it." She stood. "Come on, let's go to lunch."

"You still want to?"

Zoe crossed to Cassie and hugged her. "Of course. I haven't seen my best friend in months. I'm dying to hear all about Camille, and about the Taylor twins. Is Lacey coping?"

"A lot better than I am. Camille's giving her big sister competition for the number-one monster in our house."

"Oh, no!" Zoe laughed. "I can't wait to hear about it." She headed for the door.

Cassie lagged behind.

Zoe turned. "Cass?"

"I really admire you, Zoe. You're so strong, so mature. I'd be dying inside about this."

Zoe swallowed hard. "I am, Cass. But I can't let it

throw me like the last time. *I won't,*" she said vehemently. "Now let's go. I want to get caught up."

Coming toward her, Cassie linked their arms. "I'm so glad you're back."

Zoe lied baldly. "Yeah, me, too."

CHAPTER TWO

"ERICA, YOUR DAD won't miss this lovely brew?" Rachel Thompson asked, clinking Baccarat crystal flutes with four of her best friends, then slurping lustily from her champagne.

"Nah." Erica Case lounged on the futon that occupied a corner of her spacious bedroom; the room was long and wide with several tall windows and two skylights. She flipped back a lock of the dark hair that hung in heavy waves past her shoulders. "Good old Jackson knows immediately if there's a possibility that my grade-point average is going to drop a tenth of a point, but he'll never miss a few bottles of this stuff." Erica was currently class valedictorian and it was important her grades remain high the rest of the year. But her father's vigilance about her schoolwork drove her crazy. Defiantly she poured more champagne into her glass and sipped. It was tart and the bubbles tickled her nose. "To our senior year, which starts tomorrow."

Blue eyes twinkled behind glasses that cheerleader Ashley Emerson only wore when she was with her friends. "To our senior year."

Rachel added, "Hear hear..." Her pink hat was pulled down over her long dark hair. Rachel and Ashley were very close, more like sisters, and tended to dress in preppie fashionable clothes and spent all their time together.

"Let the games begin." This from Julia Starr, who was, in Erica's opinion, an all-around interesting person. Julia was into a lot of things, but her passion was theatre, and she was Bayview's best actress. Erica really believed Julia would make it to Broadway.

"Too bad Shondra couldn't be here." Shelley Marco sat at Erica's huge triangular desk with the top-of-the-line computer and other high-tech equipment. Her trim build contorted into a pretzel on the padded chair. "Then we'd all be together."

Shondra Jacobs was the sixth member of the group of close friends who'd been together since ninth grade. Her parents were mega-protective and way too controlling. Erica thought it had something to do with Shondra being black and having to prove herself.

"The guys aren't here, either," Ashley put in. "I wonder how Evan's doing without me the night before school starts."

"He and Robby are having a pity party," Rachel told her. "I talked to Rob just before I came here."

Erica experienced a twinge of envy. A steady boyfriend, especially a nice one like Evan Michaels or Rob Mason, was just another thing she'd missed in her quest to be Bayview Heights's top student. Ms. Caufield had a saying she'd posted on the wall: You can get all A's and still flunk life. It was true, in Erica's case.

"Rob told us you looked great at practice, Shel," Rachel put in. Rob and Evan played soccer. Shelley was captain of the girls' team. "What time's your game tomorrow?"

"It starts at four." Shelley toyed with the braid that hung over her shoulder, probably thinking about the big match with Penbrooke. She took the sport very seriously. She also hoped it was her ticket to college.

Erica noticed that Julia wasn't paying attention to the conversation anymore. Sprawled out on her belly on Erica's queen-size bed, clothed in typical Julia garb—even her pajamas were theatrical, with their flaming-red background and big dragons snarling out across her chest—she had her head down and was reading something. "Earth to Jules. Where are you?"

Julia put her finger in the book and lithely rolled to a sitting position. Cross-legged, she faced the others. "I found it."

"What?"

"The spell I was looking for." In addition to being *the* school actress, she was also one of Bayview Heights's few Wiccans.

"Who's getting zapped this time?" Shelley asked. Practical Shelley often couldn't get into Julia's New Age interests. Still, she attended Julia's performances, and Julia cheered loudly at Shelley's games.

"Bite your tongue, girl, or I'll put a curse on you."

"Wiccans don't do curses." Shelley accepted a refill of champagne when Erica held up the bottle. "You told me yourself it's a peaceful religion."

"I wish we could." Julia pouted like Sister Sarah from *Guys and Dolls,* her last big role. This year she'd be Dolly in *Hello, Dolly.* "I got somebody I'd like to zap."

All ears perked up.

"Who?" Rachel asked.

Julia took a big dramatic pause. Brushing back her short white-blond hair, she scanned her audience with perfect timing. "The Big K is back."

Shelley's mouth fell open. Ashley and Rachel leaned

forward, and Erica dropped her almost-empty glass of champagne. She ignored it as it fell and dripped on the white carpet. "What?"

"He's back. I got a peek at him in Mr. Taylor's office when I was doing money stuff for the drama club."

"Oh, no, poor Ms. C." Ashley frowned.

"She was there, too," Julia continued.

Though Ms. Caufield was big on propriety—she wouldn't even let them call her Zoe—and tried to keep her private life private, the girls had made a point to find out what was happening with her and the doctor. Mostly through overhearing Ms. Lansing and Mr. Taylor talking when they thought no one was listening, and from what Ms. C let slip, they'd pieced together that Lansing had dropped her to go back to his ex. The jerk!

Shelley let loose a very unladylike curse. "Spill it, Jules. Don't leave anything out."

Erica listened carefully as Julia spun her tale. A master storyteller, she didn't miss a detail—how great Ms. C looked in her French jeans and chic haircut, how Rad Ransom was fawning over her as usual, how upset Mr. Taylor was. But she concentrated on that bastard Lansing. "He looked like hell," Julia said, gloating.

"Good." This from Ashley.

"Maybe he doesn't even need a spell." Rachel was frowning.

"The spell is for Ms. C." Julia's tone was wise. "To give her fortitude."

"The son of a bitch has his nerve showing his face in Bayview after what he did to her." Rachel's indictment was diluted by an attack of hiccups.

Julia shook her head. "It gets worse. He's here to stay."

That propelled Erica out of her seat. "No, he can't do that to Ms. Caufield."

"He can, and he is. I followed Ms. C and Rad Ransom down the hall and listened to them talk. The creep's opening that clinic he was trying to get started last year, and he's moving here."

"What happened with him and his wife?" Shelley wanted to know.

"They split. Again."

Erica started to pace. "Damn it all. This is going to be hard on Ms. Caufield. I can't believe it."

Ms. C was so-o-o important to her. Erica thought back to how much the teacher had been a part of her life. She'd taken Erica under her wing when Erica was just a freshman...

"It must be hard growing up without your mother, Erica." Ms. C had walked her to the door after a health class where Erica had talked about her mother's death five years ago.

Erica had just nodded, embarrassed but entranced by the kind and sophisticated teacher.

"Well, honey, if you ever need to talk, I'm here..."

So, for four years Erica had talked. She'd gotten advice on everything from prom dresses to how to cook spaghetti to why high-school boys were such dorks. Now she loved the woman like a mother.

Julia was still talking. "Then Ms. Lansing took her out to lunch. Ms. C looked okay by the time they left."

"You...waited?" Rachel asked. Hiccups punctuated her question.

"Uh-huh. Skulking in corners like an Agatha Christie character. I thought I might have to call out the team to come to our fearless leader's aid."

"Oh, sure." This from Ashley. "She doesn't even know we know what happened."

"Yes, she does." Erica faced her friends. "She figured we knew because we were so mean to Lansing when we bumped into him and his brother at the pizza parlor that night."

"He's lucky we didn't burn down his New York clinic when he left her," Julia said. "'Course we could do it to this new one."

"Or you could shoot out all the windows, Erica."

"Now there's an idea." Erica's father had insisted she learn how to use the arsenal he housed in a cabinet in the den, and the girls were always ribbing her about it. Truth be told, the guns scared her silly.

"Or Julia could make a voodoo doll of him."

"Stop. Voodoo's crank stuff. Wiccan's *real*."

"Whatever we do, we should keep our contempt from Ms. C," Ashley said. "You know how she hates us prying."

Shelley stood and stretched. "Isn't it stupid how teachers think they can keep their personal lives a secret? Kids know everything."

"Speaking of which...Evan got some dope on Mr. Cramer." Ashley let the teaser hang.

"Creepy Cramer? What?" Julia's cat eyes shone with interest.

But Erica tuned out the gossip about the phys ed teacher's suspicious behavior with a female student. Instead, she recalled Ms. Caufield's caring attitude, not only for Caufield's Chicks, but all the kids she taught. She'd been there for all of them.

Pouring herself another glass of champagne, Erica hoped the doctor *was* suffering. Big time. He deserved it.

ZOE TURNED HER BACK to the scene across the room because it was too painful to watch Kurt, nestled in one of the Taylors' big stuffed chairs, holding Alexandra on his lap and reading her one of her favorite Tommy de Paolo books. The little girl cuddled into him, grasping a fistful of his green thermal shirt as she sucked a finger. It brought to the surface shared longings that Zoe had forced herself to suppress.

I wanted more kids, he'd told her as they'd lounged on her couch once night, watching the waves break along the bay.

Really?

Elizabeth wouldn't ruin her figure again.

How foolish.

He hadn't said any more, just caressed Zoe's stomach gently, kissed it and proceeded to make tender love to her right there on her glassed-in back porch.

The following week, he'd gone back to his wife.

Heaping hors d'oeuvres she didn't want onto a plate, Zoe saw Seth approach. "Getting enough to eat?"

"Yes." She sniffed the blend of Mexican and Italian aromas appreciatively. "Lacey outdid herself."

Seth's eyes literally glowed at the mention of his wife. It made something inside of Zoe shift. He glanced over to where Lacey sat with Cassie, each holding one of the twin birthday boys on her lap. "She amazes me. We have help during the day, but she still manages to give the little guys a bath and put them all to bed every night."

"She's not working full-time, is she?" Lacey was the editor of the *Herald,* Bayview's newspaper. She and Seth had met when she'd taken over the position from her grandfather and written some inflammatory articles about the high school.

"No, Philip has been a big help." He nodded at Lacey's grandfather. "And she's hired some new people, too."

Seth beamed at the good fortune in his life.

Zoe returned the smile.

"How about you?" he asked. "How are *you?* I came down to see you this week a couple of times, but you were busy."

"First week of school is always hectic."

"Zoe?" Seth's earnest blue eyes and the years of friendship they'd shared made her thaw a little.

"I'm coping, Seth. That's the most that can be expected with Kurt in my life again."

"I'm sorry about how this shook out."

She watched Kurt throw back his head and laugh at something Alexandra said.

You've got the nicest laugh.

He'd chuckled against her breasts. *Not exactly what a man wants to hear in bed.*

Her hand had slid beneath the covers. *Hmm, that's pretty impressive, too.*

"Lacey didn't want me to invite him today," Seth told her.

"Oh, please, don't let this cause trouble between you and your wife. I'm already worried about Cassie and Mitch fighting over my situation."

"Cassie and Mitch can work through their differences. And Lacey and I never fight. God, I love that woman."

Zoe felt the sting of loss. She scanned the room to dilute it and saw Philip stand and move toward them. Though over eighty, there was a spring in his step and a glint in his eyes. "Nice birthday party for my boys, son," he said, clasping Seth on the shoulder. No one would ever guess Philip had been vehemently opposed to Seth's relationship with his granddaughter a few years ago; Philip's objection had almost kept Lacey and Seth apart. "Thanks, Philip."

"Can we talk shop a minute?"

Zoe said, "I'll go keep the girls company."

"No, Zoe, stay." Philip's gaze flicked to Seth. "We got a problem with the board."

The happiness in Seth's eyes dimmed. "No kidding. And his name is Jerry Bosco."

It was still hard to believe that the worst teacher in the school, whom Seth had coerced into retirement, had run for and won a seat on the school board.

Philip continued, "Leonard says Bosco's making a big stink about Zoe's courses." Formerly a strong opponent of Seth's policies, board member Leonard Small had done a complete turnaround and had happily become a member of Philip's Gray Posse, a group that had evolved out of the Good Deeds activities at the high school. It consisted of more than twenty senior citizens who were now an active force in town politics and school-related issues.

"My *health* electives?" Zoe asked.

"Yes. They're a little too liberal for Bosco's taste— not back-to-basics enough. And he's going after them on numbers."

"Numbers? I have a full enrollment."

"That's the problem. He thinks the cutoff is too low. Either more kids should take the courses, or they should be abolished. Preferably the latter." Philip scowled. "The jackass says they're not cost-effective."

"With all my other classes, I can't supervise more than fifteen students per semester in an intensive program like this."

Seth said, "Jerry's out to get the high school."

"Damn." She faced Philip. "What can we do about this?"

"I suggest you attend the board meeting Tuesday night. There's an open forum for the community and staff, and Leonard's sure this will come up." Philip angled his head across the room. "And have Lansing come, too. His clinic will play a vital role in this program."

Zoe swallowed hard and locked gazes with Seth.

Seth said, "I'll go talk to him."

Philip nodded. "I'll go with you."

Both men headed toward Kurt.

Zoe made a beeline for the kitchen; unnoticed in the doorway, she watched her two best friends at the counter refilling trays. Zoe smiled at how different they were. Lacey was slender and small, with delicate features, amber eyes and soft blond hair. Cassie was tall and big-boned, with wild auburn hair always escaping its braid and large blue-gray eyes. She hadn't yet lost all the weight from having a baby six months ago.

"...we didn't have much choice, Cass," Lacey was saying.

Attacking a cucumber, Cassie scowled. "Damn it, it's bad enough he's living with us."

"All right you two," Zoe said firmly. "Time for some girl talk."

Both women looked up with startled gazes. Even Cassie blushed. "Zoe, we—"

"You guys have to stop this." Zoe crossed to the island counter, snagged a carrot stick and popped it into her mouth. It was cold and crunchy.

Cassie sniffed. "Stop what?"

"This vendetta against Kurt."

"It isn't a vendetta," Cassie said. "We're just really pissed off at him."

Lacey asked, "Aren't you, Zoe? Still mad?"

Retrieving a bottle of wine from the fridge, she poured herself a glass and topped up her friends'.

"Zoe?"

"I never was mad at him, Lace. I was hurt, but not angry. He made what he thought was the right choice. That it turned out to be wrong only makes me feel bad for him."

Zoe and Cassie exchanged worried looks.

"You aren't thinking of…" Cassie frowned. "Zoe, you wouldn't take him back, would you?"

"No, of course not. I could never trust him again. I couldn't live with that kind of uncertainty." She perched on a stool as did the other two. "The first time Drew and I split, I succumbed to pressure from my parents to give him another chance and it was the blackest period in my life." Both women knew Zoe's marriage had ended because of Drew's infidelity.

"Oh, Zoe." Lacey's eyes were compassionate.

"I was never sure if he was seeing her again, if he regretted coming back to me. I knew he'd gotten pressure from his parents, too. Finally I decided it wasn't worth the grief. I'd never give Kurt the chance to hurt me like that."

Just then Mitch came to the doorway; he leaned against the jamb, hands in the pockets of his slacks, eyeing his wife. "If I come in, am I going to get something thrown at me?"

"Of course not," Lacey said.

"Don't bet on it, big guy." Cassie flicked back her braid and shot him a full-of-temper glare.

Mitch gave an amused grin. "Then I won't take any

chances. I wanted to know if I should put Camille to bed.''

"Yeah. You can probably handle that.''

"Want to come with me and neck in the upstairs bedroom?''

That wrung a reluctant grin from Cassie.

"Tell you what,'' Zoe said, heading for the door. "I'll put Camille to bed, and you two can make up out here.''

"Good idea,'' Lacey said, following her out.

Mitch grasped Zoe's arm as she passed him. The teasing disappeared. "You okay, kid?''

"I'm just great.'' She glanced back at Cassie, who was studying the vegetables as if they were newly discovered Shakespearean plays. "Go cuddle with your wife.''

Mitch smiled and strode toward the counter as Zoe and Lacey left.

Out of sight but not earshot, Zoe heard an ornery groan, then a giggle, then a deep, satisfying sigh come from the kitchen.

KURT WAS DRAWN upstairs by some invisible force; he wasn't surprised—Zoe had always been a magnet to him, right from the first day he'd seen her. He was still powerless against it. And so, when he'd watched her take Camille from Celia, Philip's wife, and head toward one of the bedrooms, he'd waited ten minutes, then followed her.

At the doorway to one of the rooms Seth and Lacey had added on to their house, Kurt halted. Zoe sat in a rocker with Camille cradled to her chest. The baby burrowed into the woman, creating a Madonna-like image. The room smelled like baby powder. Zoe sang a lullaby in French. It cut him off at the knees. Of all the things he'd given up in the past year, having another child ranked right up there as one of the most painful. He sucked in a breath against the hurt.

His gesture drew her attention. He expected to see resentment. Maybe revulsion. Instead, she bestowed a warm smile on him and kissed Camille's head. "Our godchild's gotten big."

"Yes."

Would you like to have a baby someday?

She'd looked at him candidly. *With the right man, I would.*

Think I could be him?

Yes.

The lovemaking afterward had been cataclysmic.

"Come in and sit, Kurt. It might do us good to get comfortable with each other again."

Once, he'd been more at ease with Zoe Caufield than his own brother. From the doorway, he asked, "Are you always this generous, or is it just with me?"

She shook her head. "What good does sniping do? Or bitterness? We were both hurt by what happened. I'd like the pain to stop." Clearing her throat, she finished, "I'd like the healing to start."

Slowly he eased into the room and sat at a desk chair, wondering if the still-open wounds of his betrayal would ever heal. "You look wonderful, Zoe."

She smiled. "Thanks. Paris was great for me."

I met Pierre when I was twenty-one. He was so sensitive. So considerate. American men should take lessons...

Kurt had tickled her until she'd begged—in French—for respite. But he'd made a resolution to be more sensitive and considerate on future dates.

"I'm glad you enjoyed your summer."

"You don't look good, Kurt."

He scrubbed a weary hand over his face. "It's been a rough year."

She continued rocking Camille. Finally she said quietly, "What happened?"

He didn't ask what she meant. He faced her squarely. She deserved to hear the truth. "It was a nightmare. Elizabeth hadn't changed, but I had. She was her normal demanding superficial self. I don't know exactly what I expected, but I realized quickly I'd made a mistake." There was more, about what he'd discovered regarding his feelings for Zoe, but he knew she didn't want to hear that now.

"You stayed with her a year. Why didn't you leave sooner?"

"Because of Lauren." His daughter had blossomed while he lived with them again. "You know she'd been having troubles in school. When I came home, she got right back on track for the school year and was accepted into Hartwick."

"Well, some good came out of it, anyway."

He shook his head. "Before she left for school, she told me she felt bad for me."

"Why?"

"Because it was obvious I was unhappy a few weeks after I'd come home. And she suspected I'd stayed for her." He shook his head again. "She's a great kid. She also told me that she'd make sure I hadn't made the sacrifice for nothing."

"What did you tell her?"

"That none of it was her fault. I'd made my bed, so to speak…"

Zoe winced. He immediately regretted his poor analogy.

Finally she said, "That was the worst part for me, you know." Her voice was hoarse. Camille chose that moment to begin fussing, so Zoe got up and placed her in the portable crib. Soothing the child's back, she didn't say any more until she turned around.

What he saw in her face he'd hoped never to see again as long as he lived. It was the same look he'd seen that day in his office when he told her he'd slept with Elizabeth. "It leveled me to know you were making love with her. I couldn't bear it."

He didn't tell her that *making love* was not the correct term at all. He and Elizabeth had sex. And it wasn't even very good. Still, the thought of it made his stomach turn, so he could imagine what it did to Zoe's. "I'm sorry."

She wrapped her arms around her waist. "Me, too." She crossed to the door, but pivoted when she got there. "In case you have any ideas or any hope..." She trailed off. Then began again. "Don't. I wouldn't be able to risk letting myself feel anything for you again, Kurt. Please, don't ever try to convince me, in any way, to get back together."

"I won't. I promise."

"Promise me something else?"

"Anything."

"Take better care of yourself."

It was the last thing he expected.

Emotion clogged his throat. He nodded, and then she left the room.

"IT'S TIME for the open forum." School superintendent Joe Finn, a dark-haired bear of a man with a bushy beard and intelligent eyes, smiled tightly at Jerry Bosco and tried to be civil. But it was obvious to Zoe that the superintendent didn't like the influence the retired teacher had had this year on the formerly smooth-running board. Bosco's contingent, the Taxpayers' Common Sense Group, had supported him and gotten him elected by a narrow margin.

Sitting between Philip and Zoe, Seth stiffened. She reached over and squeezed his arm in support. He patted her hand. Though she was glad to be here for her principal, she dreaded Kurt's arrival. He'd told Seth he'd be late, and by nine, he still hadn't arrived. She hoped that when he got here, he'd sit in the back of the spacious meeting room at the Administration Building, which was set up with tables in the front and several rows of straight chairs facing them.

"Mr. Bosco, would you like to state your concerns?"

Almost completely bald by now, Jerry Bosco dragged his microphone closer. His jowly face wore its usual scowl. Zoe thought idly that the collar of his white shirt looked tight enough to choke him. "Be glad to," he said.

Kurt came into Zoe's line of vision as he approached their row and slid in next to her. Giving her a weak smile, he focused on Jerry. Zoe tried to ignore him and listen to Bosco, but she felt an immediate physical reaction when Kurt sat down; it was hard not to react when his wide shoulders brushed hers and his scent—something woodsy and male—filled her nostrils.

"As many of you know, I've asked the board to examine some of the programs at Bayview Heights High for several reasons."

Shifting slightly, Kurt settled back into the straight

chair and crossed his arms over his chest. His legs were stretched out in front of him, and she noticed the suit he wore. Heather-brown, it was one she'd helped him pick out when they'd spent a day shopping in the city.

You look sexy as hell in that, Dr. Lansing, she'd said.

I'll take it, he'd told the clerk.

"What exactly is your concern, Mr. Bosco?" Finn asked.

"It's threefold. First, I have grave misgivings about the school's increasing role as a social-service agency." He picked up a blue book. "I read the curriculum for these health electives, for example, and there're all sorts of sensitivity exercises to put the students in touch with their *feelings*. There are also lessons to get them to share their personal problems. This is *not* our role." He lifted his double chin. "Second, we should be concentrating on basics, instead. It's the same point I made as a teacher when I opposed the social-studies electives." Not that anyone had listened. Both the English Department and the Social Studies Department had a wide range of excellent courses in place. "We need to study the Civil War, not psychology," he stated pompously.

"God forbid the kids understand how the human mind works," Seth whispered under his breath.

"And last, the budget concerns me. I ran for this board seat on a platform that promised to cut costs. There are many, many places we can reduce our spending." He knuckled the curriculum. "This is one."

Joe Finn took in a deep breath. "I'd like Seth Taylor to address these concerns and then open the discussion up to the community." He smiled encouragingly at the principal.

Seth stood. Zoe could see a muscle leap in his jaw

but he kept his shoulders relaxed. "First, though we don't like having to be social workers for the kids, the fact remains that there are times we have to be. We need all the staff psychologists, school counselors and innovative programs we've amassed just to keep kids out of gangs and curb the violence erupting all over the country." Seth warmed to the topic. "A study done on school shootings just this year indicates that students connecting with teachers and staff about their problems is the most significant factor in stopping student violence. It's *disconnecting* that leads kids to bring guns to school." Zoe knew this concern was vital to all educators.

Seth continued, "Second, the numbers for our health electives had to be limited to make this an effective program. Ms. Caufield can't supervise more than fifteen students per course per semester, given the rest of her class load. And there's a long waiting list for these courses, so you can see they're popular. And valued."

Next to her Kurt moved restlessly.

"And last, the board has been very pleased with our college attendance rate—it continues to rise. I'd like to remind you that colleges insist on community service as part of an applicant's résumé. This course helps fill that need."

Bosco's face reddened. "They can volunteer on their own."

Zoe raised her hand. "May I speak to that?"

"Of course, Zoe." Joe gave her an encouraging nod.

She stood. "The kids do continue their volunteer work after the course ends. Seventy-five percent of them stay at the workplace for the following semester and into subsequent years."

"Speaking of the placements..." Bosco began, cutting her off. Zoe had no choice but to reseat herself. She had more to say, but she'd vowed not to antagonize Jerry. "I'm distressed to see that so many of our students will be working at the teen clinic that's scheduled to open in a few weeks."

"Why is that, Jerry?" Leonard Small asked.

"It's no secret I opposed the approval of that establishment." Bosco had been a busy beaver sabotaging all the programs needed in Bayview Heights to help out kids. "This clinic has the potential for giving our young people wrong ideas."

"How so?" Leonard's voice held traces of impatience.

"God only knows what'll go on there. Birth control without parental consent. Free counseling. Hell, they'll probably do abortions at the drop of a hat."

Kurt straightened. Zoe stole a quick look at him. His jaw was set and his eyes narrowed on the front of the room. He raised his hand, too. "I'd like to address that."

"All—"

Bosco leaned over to his mike and cut off the superintendent. "He can't. He's neither a staff member nor a resident."

"But I am a resident of Bayview Heights. I've moved to this community and am in the process of buying a home here."

"And your relation to this issue?" Marian Smith, a pretty single mother sitting on the other side of Bosco, asked.

"I'm running the clinic, Mrs. Smith. I'm Kurt Lansing." His smile could charm a snake out of its skin. It certainly worked on Marian.

"Go ahead, then," the woman said sweetly.

Jerry Bosco leaned back with a *hrrmph.*

Kurt rose with calm assurance. "My clinic will be run like the others I have in New York."

"This isn't the big city, Lansing," Jerry said.

"No, but you have the same problems here. The difference is, you have a better chance of curtailing them, dealing with them, because you're small. As we all know, frustrated upset teens do dangerous things. Already, the innovative programs, like the health electives and the At Risk courses, and the general Resiliency program Seth started at the high school, have contributed to helping your teenagers cope with their lives. My clinic will support and augment all that."

"Will you hand out contraceptives without parental consent?" Jerry asked pointedly.

"Each case will be dealt with individually," Kurt replied smoothly. "And we'll abide by the law." He stuck his hands in his pockets and smiled at the rest of the board. "I want to be part of the good work you're doing with kids here. I can assure you, I only want to help."

When Kurt sat down, Seth leaned over Zoe. "Thanks, buddy," he whispered.

Kurt nodded. Zoe gave him a weak smile. She appreciated his support, but damn it, one of the things she always found irresistible about the man was his dedication to his work, and his concern for kids. In that, they were perfectly matched.

The thought scared her.

She barely listened to Bosco's rant about how vigilant he intended to be, both on the school board about her classes and on the council about the clinic. Her heart was thumping in her chest.

It would be hard to resist getting drawn in by the

man beside her. She'd have to be very careful to protect herself from him.

At eleven, after heated discussion with the community—including praise by Philip Cartwright's group for both the school and the clinic—the meeting broke up. Seth faced her and Kurt.

"This could be a mess. We're all going to have to work closely to keep Jerry Bosco out of our programs. And we need to avoid any negative publicity."

Her gaze locked with Kurt's. His was apologetic. She imagined hers was fearful.

God, she hoped she was up to this. She simply couldn't let him break her heart again. She didn't think she'd survive it a second time.

CHAPTER THREE

JUST AS JULIA was about to ask her friends whether anyone was up for shopping after school, Ms. Caufield headed toward them. She reached the group with stage-worthy flourish. "Okay, ladies, disperse and find your partners."

Julia sighed dramatically. She wore an electric-blue shirt, which topped a black wraparound skirt she'd gotten for a song in the city. "Just one second, Ms. C. I wanted to—"

"No excuses, Sarah Bernhardt. Find your partner." She gave Julia The Look—which everybody knew meant business. "Now."

It took a few minutes, but soon Caufield's Chicks split up. Julia found herself seated once again with Dan Caruso. The only thing she'd known about him before this week was that he was in the At Risk classes and he dressed mostly in black. Now she'd discovered that his family called him Danny, he was two years older than she was, and he never removed the expensive-looking diamond stud from his ear. Today they'd get into heavy stuff. "Ready to bare all, Danny boy?" she asked.

Looking bored, Dan shrugged. "It's cool. Doesn't matter what you think of me."

"So," she said, opening her notebook and ignoring his comment. From the things he'd told her, she sensed his surliness was a cover for deep feelings. "Where do we begin?"

"Probably with the questions we hammered out in class yesterday." He shook his head. "You in never-never land again or what?"

Julia's chin came up. True, she vagued out some-times, imagining her Broadway debut or her Tony award. But she didn't think it was that obvious. "I was here, Caruso. Every single day this week." She gave him a condescending look that she'd copied from Liz Taylor's old movies. "Which is more than I can say for you." He stared at her. "You know," she said, getting more irritated, "if we're going to do this, you've got to be here."

Something fluttered in his chocolate-colored eyes. A sadness. Now she felt bad. Problem was, Julia played so many roles, on and off the stage, she often got car-ried away. She hadn't meant to hurt him. She tried a Drew Barrymore smile. He opened his notebook and didn't respond.

"You wanna go first or should I?" he asked, staring down.

"Let's do each question together. Since they go from easy to hard."

Ten minutes later, they got to hard. "So Ms. Actress, what's your greatest fear?"

Julia bit her lip. Ms. Caufield had said they shouldn't agree to do this assignment unless they planned to be honest. They'd have a chance to edit out anything too private, but part of the purpose of interviewing each other and presenting your partner to the class was to reveal things about yourself that others didn't know.

"Jules?" Her head came up at the nickname only her closest friends used. "A tough one?"

She nodded. "You?"

"Nah, it's easy for me." His long hair fell onto his forehead. It was squeaky clean and looked soft as silk. "I'm afraid they're gonna take my little brother away from me and my ma."

"Why would they do that?"

"She leaves us alone. A lot."

"I'm sorry."

He shrugged. "Your turn."

Watching closely for his reaction, she said softly, "I'm afraid for people to see the real me."

"That why you assume so many roles?"

"In the plays, you mean?"

"In real life."

His comment hit a nerve because she knew it was true.

"Who *is* the real you?" he asked gently.

"You got it on paper." Her reply was flippant, accompanied by a toss of her bangs off her face.

"Nope. This is surface stuff."

After a very long pause she sighed. "I guess I don't know who the real me is." She peered up at him from under thick lashes. "And if I did, maybe I wouldn't like her."

Just then Ashley walked by on her way back from the washroom and slapped Julia on the back. Julia was glad for the interruption and turned to say something to her friend, effectively cutting off Dan's reply to her revelation.

Ashley spoke briefly to Julia, then sat back down, tugging at the short denim dress she wore. She covered her stomach with both hands.

"All right, we're on number twelve," Ashley's partner, Teresa Lanahan, said. "What are your secret goals in life?'' she asked. ''Even though they might not come true.''

My only goal right now is not to be pregnant, Ashley thought. *Please, God, don't let that be.* ''None of what I want's secret.''

''Let me guess. You want to marry Evan, have a dozen kids and live in Pleasantville, U.S.A.''

Teresa's tone irritated Ashley. ''Why would you say it like that?''

Teresa shrugged. ''Like what?''

''So disapproving. What if I do want that?'' She indicated the drab sweats Teresa wore every day like a uniform. ''Not everybody wants to play for the WBA.''

Teresa's face tensed. ''I'd be satisfied with a basketball scholarship so I can play in college.''

For a moment Ashley was intrigued. What would it be like to have aspirations that had nothing to do with guys? Her mother and three sisters never had any dreams of their own, and Ashley had inherited the Emerson homemaking gene. ''Won't you get a scholarship?''

''I should.''

''Where do you want to go?''

''University of Connecticut. They got a great women's basketball program.''

Ashley smiled thinly. Would she even be going to college? Her gaze strayed to Ms. Caufield, who was interviewing with Madison Kendrick—or Mad Maddie as the kids called her because of her tall, wild-eyed appearance and odd behavior. Would Ms. C be disappointed in Ashley if she got married and never went to college? Hell, if she was pregnant, she wouldn't even graduate high school with her class.

Scanning the room to keep back the tears, Ashley caught Shondra's eye. Her friend grinned, then turned back to her own partner.

Shondra yawned and Mary Kay Sorensen frowned. "Sorry," Shondra said. "I was up late finishing college applications."

Mary Kay gave her a meek smile back. "Where are you applying?"

Harvard. Yale. Radcliffe, Shondra thought. "Oh, just some nearby schools." She fussed with the white blouse she wore with a midcalf beige skirt. "How about you?"

"State schools." Mary Kay's thin shoulders sagged, her drab blue dress way too big for her. "My parents can't afford more."

"What about scholarships?"

"I'm not smart enough. Not like you. You do everything."

"You're editor of the yearbook, Mary Kay."

"Only because you couldn't be that *and* the literary-magazine editor."

"You're good," Shondra said kindly. "I'm glad you got it." She glanced down at her notes. "We're on number fourteen...which parent are you most like?"

Mary Kay's lips curved in a pretty smile. "That's easy. My mom. We do everything together."

Shondra stared at the freckle-faced redhead. Did she have any idea how lucky she was to have a mother for a best friend? Shondra's mother was the policeman of her life, and the jailer.

You have a reputation to uphold. You have to be the best. Because of your heritage. Be proud of it.

Ironically what the Jacobs' ethnic pride had done to

their oldest child was to make her wish she was anything but African-American.

"If I could have your attention please."

All eyes turned toward Ms. Caufield. She looked pretty today in a hot-pink tunic and slinky black pants with high sandals. They made her an almost average height. Chunky gold adorned her ears, wrists and throat.

"You've done very well for the past—" she glanced at the clock "—hour."

There were murmurs around the room; they all knew the true test of a good class was how fast the time flew.

"Let me remind you that what you've shared is private. Keep it to yourselves until your partner decides if she or he wants it written up in the interview."

The kids stared at her in silence.

"I'd like to see nods of agreement, verbal promises." That wrung a smile out of them. And some noise.

"All right." Ms. Caufield held up a typed sheet. "This is the schedule for the volunteer placements."

"Representatives from all four organizations will be here Monday during class to talk about what positions are available. We have enough study buddies and elementary-school helpers, but the day care, and the teen clinic—" she almost stumbled over that and Shondra knew why "—have several positions open."

"I hope I didn't get the clinic," Shondra heard from behind her. It was Erica. Shondra gave her a sympathetic look.

The teacher finished, "I tried to honor your requests, but if there's a problem with your placement, I'll see what I can do."

Sighing, Shondra waited for the papers. She'd asked

to work at a medical facility, so she'd most likely get the clinic. Where that creep who dumped Ms. Caufield worked. Damn, that was all Shondra needed. It was going to be a long semester.

KURT HADN'T BEEN in Hotshots in more than a year. Before the breakup, he'd come to the bar often with Zoe and filled in on the teachers' team in the weekly volleyball games when staff members had meetings or were away on vacations. The drone of the TV monitors broadcasting a football game, the smell of popcorn and beer and the rumble of voices around the courts in the back were soothingly familiar; at the same time he found the memories painful. Would he ever become immune to all he'd given up?

"You okay, buddy?" Mitch asked from beside him. His brother had taken off his sweats and was stretching his leg muscles. Nearing fifty, Mitch was still in great shape.

"Just fine." Kurt had tried to hide his depression from Mitch. Knowing his presence in their house was causing problems between the couple, he'd forced himself to put on a front.

"Bullshit. You don't fool me. You're dying inside."

So much for fronts. Kurt removed the fleece jacket that he'd thrown over khaki gym shorts and a forest-green T-shirt.

Do you have any idea what that color does to your eyes? Zoe had asked him once.

He'd tugged her close and peered down at her. *You like?*

I like.

Show me.

He willed the memories away. It was bad enough

they haunted him at night and drove him from his bedroom to prowl the house like some ghost searching for solace. Four times now, because he was already up, he'd gotten to Camille before Cassie awoke, given the baby a bottle and rocked her back to sleep.

"I'm fine, big brother." He glanced around the huge converted warehouse with its long mahogany bar, seating area and volleyball courts in the back. "I'm just not sure this is a good idea."

Mitch's direct gaze zeroed in on him. "I wasn't leaving you by yourself tonight."

"I could have watched the girls."

"That's what baby-sitters are for." Mitch settled on a stool. "A little exercise will do you good. Zoe and Cassie are meeting with Seth and Alex and the superintendent about the At Risk program, so they won't be here. And we need players."

"It's just that I'm trying to stay out of her life."

"Do you really think it's possible?"

"I don't know. I—"

"Hey, handsome, watch out."

Reflexively Kurt turned to see a ball flying his way. He caught it and smiled at the woman who called out to him. She jogged over. "Hi, Kurt."

"Have we met?" he asked, tossing back the ball. The woman was pretty—long blond hair, long limbs and wide eyes. She resembled Elizabeth.

"Yes, last year. I'm Barbara Sherman, school psychologist."

They exchanged pleasantries and then were summoned to the court.

It was fun, and Kurt lost himself in the play. He let go of his worries and regrets and allowed the sport to absorb him. His team won the first game by two, and as he headed to the bar with Mitch and Barbara for a beer break, he was smiling.

His smile died faster than a flash of lightning when he caught sight of Cassie, Seth, Alex and Zoe approaching the bar.

Damn it!

Cassie spotted him first. Her head whipped around to her husband and she gave him a what-the-hell-is-he-doing-here look. Mitch drew in a deep breath. His eyes narrowed on his wife.

"What are you doing here?" Mitch directed his question to Cassie.

"I could ask him the same thing." Her tone was frigid as she nodded to Kurt.

Mitch set his beer down carefully and straightened, ready to do battle. "You had a meeting with the superintendent. We obviously didn't expect you to show up here."

"It was canceled," Seth said easily. He stepped in front of Cassie. "Finn's son is sick, and he had to go home as soon as we got there." Seth extended his hand to shake with Kurt, who was trying unsuccessfully to fade into the background. "Hi, Kurt."

Kurt smiled at Seth. "Hi, everybody. Looks like you don't need me to fill in anymore. I'll just take off." He placed his beer on the bar and turned to leave.

Cassie's gaze leveled on him.

Seth shot a look at Mitch.

Alex placed his hands on Zoe's shoulders.

And Zoe said, "No, don't leave, Kurt. We need all the players we can get."

"Zoe..." Cassie said.

"Cass..." Mitch said.

"New game," someone yelled.

"Come on, Zoe, let's warm up." Alex tugged on her hand.

She smiled at Kurt. "Stay. I'll be upset if you leave just because I showed up to play."

He nodded.

Cassie stood rooted to the spot as Zoe and Alex headed for the court. "Excuse me," she said, and with a glare at her husband, she strode toward the door. Mitch was a few steps behind her. Kurt watched as his brother caught up to his wife. Cassie's face was flaming as she turned to him. Gently encircling her neck, Mitch drew her off to the side.

They were arguing. Over him. God, he never meant to cause trouble.

Seth touched his arm. "Come on, Kurt. Let's play."

Torn, Kurt pushed away from the bar and followed the principal out to the court.

Cassie would have been happy to know that he was suffering for showing up here. He had to watch Zoe in her navy nylon gym shorts and Teachers Have Class T-shirt stretch and move that compact curvy body as she volleyed and reached for a ball. He also had to watch Alex Ransom's inability to keep his hands off her.

As a ball came to Kurt and he hit it gently to Seth, who spiked it over the net, Kurt recalled a conversation he and Zoe had had about the young vice principal...

"He's hot for you."

"He's a boy."

"How old?"

"Around thirty-two."

"Eight years' difference. You and I are five years apart."

"Kurt, he was my student. True, he's grown up. Linebacker shoulders. Great hair. I—"

Playfully Kurt had tackled her onto the bed and made her confess that younger men had no appeal for her...

Well, things changed, he guessed. Though she wasn't flirting outright with the guy, Kurt could tell they'd gotten close. He tried to keep his eyes off them.

Which was why he didn't see her go down.

"Hold the ball," Seth shouted, as Zoe felt her ankle give way and she hit the floor flat smack on her rump. Pain shot from her foot to her extremities. "Ohh..."

Alex got to her first. "Are you all right?"

She struggled for air, and her skin got clammy from the pain. She heard shouting. People gathered around, then parted.

To make way for the doctor.

In a moment Kurt was squatting in front of her. "Zoe?" He grasped her wrist and placed his fingers on it. "You all right?"

The breath drained out of her. He hadn't touched her in almost a year. The feel of his hands on her skin startled her. His head was bent, and she stared at the thick dark hair that she'd run her fingers through countless times. It smelled like the woods.

"Zoe?" he said more firmly when he looked up. His green eyes were wide with concern.

"I'm fine." She shook her head. "I twisted my ankle." She glanced around her. "Let me get off the court so you guys can play."

"Not yet." His hands slid down to her leg. With trained nimble fingers, he untied her sneaker and removed her sock. His touch was light as he felt her ankle, wiggled her toes and just for good measure gently prodded her calf. Tears formed in her eyes. He must have seen them.

His dark brows knitted. "Hurt?"

She nodded. Their gazes met in silent communication. His were apologetic. "But it's eased a little."

"Seems like a minor sprain." He took her pulse again. "Let's get you onto a chair. We'll elevate the foot and ice it down." He glanced up. "Seth, could you get my bag out of Mitch's car?"

"Sure," Seth answered as Kurt stood and started to reach for her hand. "Can you stand?"

"No need." Big arms slid under her, and she was caught in Alex Ransom's strong grasp.

"Alex," she said with a soft cry, "what are you doing?"

"It's called seizing the moment." He grinned boyishly. "Don't think I'm gonna pass up this opportunity, do you?"

In spite of the tension, she smiled.

Until she caught Kurt's expression. It was purely male and primal. With a trace of pain.

Well, that couldn't be helped, she thought, hardening herself against him. She looped her hands around Alex's neck and let him carry her off.

In no time she was seated, her leg elevated under a cushion as they waited for the ice. "Go play," she told the group. "I'm fine."

Kurt handed her a glass of water and sat beside her. Cassie approached them. "What happened?"

"While you were off fighting with your husband, Zoe took a tumble," Alex told her, smiling down at Zoe.

Cassie straightened. "We weren't fighting."

Mitch came up behind her and placed his hands on

her shoulders. She leaned into him, and he kissed her hair. Seth was right—Cassie and Mitch could work this out.

Seth returned and handed Kurt his bag. "Want us to stay with you?" he asked.

"I want everybody to go play volleyball." She took a bead on Alex. "You, too, young man."

"Ah, I love it when you get tough."

Abruptly Kurt stood. "Where the hell is that ice?"

A waitress finally brought it. His movements were efficient as he encased the ice bag in cloth from his kit, placed it around her ankle and then wrapped it in large ace bandages, which he called cravats. His hands were gentle, and Zoe was reminded of his skill as a doctor.

And in bed.

He rummaged through his bag again as Cassie, Mitch, Seth and even Alex went back to the court. For all intents and purposes, they were alone. He handed her some tablets. "Ibuprofen," he said simply. "It'll help the pain and reduce the swelling. Be sure to take two every four hours."

"Thanks." She swallowed the pills with water.

Staring out over the court, Kurt linked his hands between his legs. He appeared a little more rested tonight, or maybe it was the exercise. His face had a healthy glow and his cheeks weren't so gaunt. She was glad he was on the mend. "I'm sorry," she heard him say.

"It's not your fault that I fell."

He shook his head, raked back his hair impatiently. "I'm sorry that I'm here. I should have known better."

"I wasn't supposed to play tonight, Kurt. You're entitled to go out for an evening with your brother."

"We just never imagined your meeting would be canceled."

"I know." She watched Cassie's spike fly past an orderly from the hospital, and then Seth served again.

"If I could change this...being in Bayview..."

"Look," she said firmly, "some things can't be changed. We just have to deal with them." She gave him a hard stare. "I'm over the worst of it, Kurt."

Was that sadness in his eyes?

"I can handle your being here." She hoped she could.

His look was grave. Torn.

"Can *you?*" she asked.

"I have no choice," he whispered raggedly.

"Yeah, well, like I tell the kids, it's the tough things in life that make you strong."

He nodded. And adjusted the ice on her leg. She returned her gaze to the court, trying to concentrate on the play and wondering just when she'd get strong.

ON THE LAST MONDAY AFTERNOON in September when Kurt came to Zoe's class to talk to the clinic volunteers, he recognized what was happening right away—and why. He thought about putting an end to the hostile behavior; the clinic work was too important to allow personal feelings to endanger it.

But given that six of his new workers who seemed bent on using him for target practice were Zoe's girls, he held back. His only ally appeared to be a dark-haired boy dressed in black named Dan.

The fact that Zoe's classroom was decorated with streamers and balloons and a big *Happy Birthday, Ms. Caufield* sign, didn't help. It was a visual reminder of what had happened exactly a year ago today.

At the beginning of class Zoe had explained who was working where, then divided the students into four groups, each headed by the supervisor of the particular area—an elementary-school principal was in charge of the students who would be helping with the lower grades; Carolyn Spearman, another vice principal was overseeing the Study Buddies for reluctant learners at the high school; one of Seth's former students, Mary Jarrett, was in charge of day-care placements; and, of course, Kurt got the group for the clinic.

Seated in a circle, he smiled at the kids. Only one smiled back. "Let's start with why you volunteered for the clinic."

A pretty, dark-haired girl Kurt recognized as Erica, one of Zoe's favorites, scowled and gave a slight shake of her head. All the others caught it and averted their gazes from him. Nobody spoke.

Ah, a teenage girl's biggest weapon. Freeze out the adult. Kurt had experienced it numerous times with his daughter, Lauren.

Finally Dan said, "I did my junior research paper in Ms. Lansing's class on how towns need teen health centers. I think they're a cool idea."

A girl Kurt had seen in a play here at school with Zoe, kicked the boy who spoke, without trying to hide the censure.

Enough, Kurt thought. The kids needed to see who was in charge. He waited, then said, "Since no one else will volunteer, we'll go around the circle." He zeroed in on the leader. "Erica, is it?"

She nodded haughtily.

"Why did you ask for this placement?"

"I asked to be out of the school system, and I didn't want the day care," She shrugged slender shoulders. "Process of elimination, I guess."

"All right." He turned to a striking black girl and read her name tag. "Shondra, what about you?"

"I'm thinking of med school. Working at the clinic is a logical choice, though *now* not such an appealing one."

Bingo. Girls had gotten better with their barbs than in his day. And feistier.

"Rachel?" He smiled again, though it was getting harder.

She stared at him blankly, then flicked a gaze at a blond girl.

"Why did you choose the clinic, Rachel?"

Rachel shrugged. "Dunno. It's a place."

Kurt zeroed in on the blonde. "Ashley?"

"Same here."

Erica sighed dramatically. It must have been a signal that the cold war was over and the offensive was to begin. "To tell the truth, Dr. Lansing, we didn't exactly ask to work at *your* clinic. Most of us said we wanted a place that helped teenagers. We thought we'd get the rec center or maybe a branch of Planned Parenthood."

A girl named Shelley, who wore a BVH Soccer T-shirt, jumped in. "We didn't know Planned Parenthood would be part of your clinic."

He straightened and scanned the rebels with a forthrightness that seemed to surprise them. "Would you like me to ask your teacher to switch your placements?"

Caufield's Chicks all scowled. Zoe would never tolerate their rudeness, and they knew it.

"No?" he pushed.

The girls shook their heads weakly.

"Okay, then I'd like some cooperation. And enthusiasm."

From the looks on their faces, he knew they got the point.

Just then Zoe approached the group. "Everything okay here?" She was dressed in a classic white-silk pantsuit that fit her perfectly and contrasted with her dark eyes and hair.

"Just fine," Kurt said dryly.

"The necklace looks good, Ms. C," Julia told her.

Zoe's hand went to a single jet-black stone at her throat. Kurt cocked his head.

Before Zoe could tell him what the reference was, the actress added, "We got Ms. C a special gift for her birthday, Dr. Lansing. It's an Apache Tear."

Again, as if by silent signal, Erica picked up on the comment. "Stones have mystical properties, you know. We got this one especially for Ms. C at Hecate's Palace."

"Hecate's Palace?"

"A store Julia works at." This from Rachel of the *Dunno*. "It's a witch shop."

"Wiccan," Zoe corrected.

Shondra said, "The stones have otherworldly powers." She grinned. "Powers we wanted Ms. Caufield to have."

Now he got it. Another zing. Well, he'd dealt effectively with thugs in his New York City clinic. He guessed he could take on a few suburban girls who hated his guts.

Ashley finished up. "The Apache Tear protects you from the evil of others. Like when they do rotten things to you."

Zoe frowned as she finally caught on. Her gaze flicked to Kurt's. It startled him a minute. He expected to see amusement, perhaps sympathy, even a little anger.

Instead, he saw, *You poor bastard.*

Hmm, Kurt thought, maybe the thugs in the city weren't so bad, after all.

When the bell rang, Zoe said simply, "I'd like to see every single member of this group after school. No excuses. Be here at three sharp."

CHAPTER FOUR

THE MAYOR OF Bayview Heights stood proudly before the crowd gathered around the doors of the Bayview Heights Clinic for young adults. No one would ever guess the wiry little man in the expensive suit had thwarted this venture at every opportunity; eventually he'd buckled under pressure from the community.

Zoe rubbed her hands up and down her arms, trying to stay warm in the lightweight coat she'd purchased on the Champs-Elysées.

"Neat coat, Ms. C." Rachel Thompson smiled from beneath her ever-present hat. Today it was army-green to match her cargo pants and jacket. Close behind her, Rob Mason had donned a matching hat and similar clothing.

"Thanks." She grinned at Rob. "Playing the Bobsey Twins again?"

"Huh?" Rachel said.

Zoe groaned, feeling old. "Never mind." She glanced around, noticing Erica, Julia, Shondra and Shelley near the wall of the hospital. Because the building in which the clinic was housed had formerly been doctors' offices, minimal structural renovation had been needed. The clinic had been ready to open in record time after garnering the town's approval.

Lucky me, Zoe thought. She could have used another year to get over Kurt Lansing. Another ten years!

"Where's Ashley?" she asked Rachel as the mayor introduced the members of the school board. Absently she noted no one cheered for Jerry Bosco, but there was warm applause for Philip Cartwright, who looked younger every day.

"Dunno." Rachel bit her lip.

Zoe had a fleeting feeling that something was wrong; she frequently got these kinds of blips about her kids. But she was distracted from analyzing it or questioning Rachel when she heard the mayor announce, "And now I'd like to introduce the head of the clinic, who will in turn introduce the staff. Dr. Kurt Lansing."

Zoe's heart seemed to stop for a moment as Kurt stepped out of the shadows into the early-October mid-afternoon sunlight. Dressed in a gray pin-striped suit and an impeccable white shirt and striped tie, he slipped his hands in his pockets and smiled. His hair, ruffled by the wind, was appealingly disheveled. It had gotten a little long.

Give me a haircut.

Hmm...okay.

Naked.

What?

You heard me, woman.

Stop it! she chided herself. But it was hard not to think of the past when she was confronted by him in the present. He was still too thin, but his face seemed a little fuller and he looked as if he'd put on some weight at least. She knew that Cassie, even though she wasn't happy that he was living with them, would make sure her brother-in-law ate well.

"Thank you all for coming." Kurt smiled, and Zoe had to glance away from his warm green eyes.

Her wandering gaze landed on her students; she saw

Erica stick her hands into the pockets of her short canvas jacket and frown. Shelley adjusted the hooded BVH sweatshirt she wore with a long fleece skirt, then straightened. Julia, decked out today in a yellow slicker and pants to match, whispered something to Shondra, who was wrapped in a tailored black raincoat.

"Excuse me," Zoe said to Rachel and Rob. She threaded her way through the crowd to the girls. Guilt suffused their faces when she reached them. She'd already made it clear she'd tolerate none of their shenanigans.

Last week, she'd confronted the prospective clinic volunteers after their rude behavior to Kurt. "What's going on?" she'd asked bluntly

Dead silence.

"Got me," Dan Caruso had finally put in. "The chicks were playin' Dump on the Doctor, big time."

"Chicks?" Julia had affected an outraged glare. "Join the twenty-first century, Caruso."

Dan had rolled his eyes. "It's what you guys call yourselves, Starr. You're just pi—" he glanced at Zoe "—mad that I wouldn't go along. Lansing's an okay guy. Give him a break."

Getting the gist, Zoe smiled at the boy. "Dan, you can leave. It's obvious you're not a part of this."

When he was gone, Zoe slid onto one of the desks and nodded for the girls to sit down. "Spit it out, ladies," she said after they circled around her.

Rachel played with her hair. Ashley studied her science notebook. Julia wouldn't meet her gaze. Only Erica faced her. Zoe wasn't surprised. The girl loved her like a mother and was probably the ringleader in this little game.

"He's pond scum!" Erica blurted out. "We don't want to work with him."

Zoe gentled her voice. "Please don't call him that, Erica. He's a brilliant doctor with a heart of gold. He wants to help people more than anyone I know. And this clinic is a big asset to the community and the school."

Erica scowled. "He hurt you." For all their sophistication, these girls were still young in so many ways.

Swallowing hard, Zoe counted to ten. "Yes, he did, though I don't think it's really any of your concern."

"Why not?" Ashley said. "We talk about boys with you. You've helped me a lot with Evan."

"I'm a teacher. That's my job."

Julia rolled her eyes in a theatrical gesture. "You're more than our teacher. We love you. And we hate him for hurting you."

Spontaneously Zoe reached out and squeezed Julia's hand. "Jules, he didn't hurt me intentionally. I guess you know the story. But just to set the record straight, he went back to his wife—that's all he did. Men and women have problems like this, where it's nobody's fault."

"What happened?" Erica asked candidly. "Why's he here, then?"

Zoe shifted uneasily. "It didn't work out between them."

"You're not getting back with him, are you?" she asked, clearly horrified.

"Girls, I really don't want to get into a discussion of my personal life."

"All right," Julia said. "But just tell us that."

Zoe knew when to give in with kids. They did love her, and they were worried. "No, I'm not getting back with him. And I am a bit uncomfortable having to work with him now. But remember how I told you I thought Hemingway was right—anybody can handle things well when life is good. It's when things get rough that you have to come through. It's called—''

''Grace under pressure.'' Erica's tone had been impatient.

''Yes, honey, it is. And we all need to behave well during this difficult time.''

Obviously Erica hadn't agreed. She'd walked out then, and Zoe hadn't had a chance to talk to her since...

Zoe was brought back to the present by Kurt's announcement.

''First I'd like to introduce the counselors.''

''Hi, everyone.'' Seth came to stand beside Zoe as he scanned the crowd. ''Lacey here?'' he asked.

''Right up front,'' Zoe answered. She watched Seth smile at his petite wife.

''She's writing a feature for the paper,'' he said proudly.

''Good.''

Seth's eyes narrowed. ''I forgot *he'd* be here.''

''Who?''

''Linc McKenna.'' Zoe saw the handsome high-school counselor standing next to Lacey lean over, say something to her and make her smile. Zoe remembered that Lacey had dated McKenna briefly before she and Seth had gotten together.

''Most of you know Linc McKenna,'' Kurt continued as if addressing Seth's statement. ''He's a school counselor and will be the clinic's liaison with the high school. He'll help us with all aspects of educational coordination. We're lucky to get him. He has a masters from Cornell and has worked with…''

"Hrrmph," Seth grumbled, sticking his hands in the pockets of his suitcoat.

"Back off, buddy," Zoe whispered. The Taylors had a marriage made in heaven, and certainly Seth had nothing to worry about there.

"Next is our drug-and-alcohol counselor, Mark Grayson."

Zoe watched a tall reed-thin man wave to the crowd. He looked impossibly young with his poet's face, longish hair and earring winking from underneath.

"Mark's got three years' experience at City Hospital and has had a number of internships in New York. He's a certified alcohol counselor and we're lucky to get him, too."

Zoe watched Kurt smile warmly at the man. Then he introduced Louise Sheffield, a PhD from Columbia, retired for ten years to raise her kids. An old friend of Kurt's, she'd agreed to come back at his urging. He'd told Zoe stories of the miracles the woman had worked with hard-core kids.

Next he introduced Diane Diaz, a nurse. She was a petite woman who lived in town and had two children in high school.

"As you probably know, Dr. Max Johnson runs the Planned Parenthood program, which operates out of South Avenue, but he'll be moving the division in with us." A big black man with steel-gray hair and a friendly smile stepped out to be seen. Zoe knew him well, and she liked and respected the hardworking, often beleaguered counselor.

"On the medical side, I'll be handling the checkups, pediatric care and minor medical mishaps, along with

Dr. Abraham Frank, who will be joining us in November. We're also fortunate to have a premed student from Columbia—John Battaglia.''

''Yummy,'' she heard Shondra say.

''De-licious,'' Shelley added.

All the girls but Erica giggled over Johnny. Dressed in a black T-shirt and black denims under his battered black leather jacket, he saluted the crowd and stepped back next to Mitch, whom she hadn't noticed before.

A former At Risk student, Johnny had practically been adopted by the Lansings when Mitch had broken up the gang to which the boy had belonged. In those five years he'd become a vital part of the Lansing family. And for three years he'd worked at Kurt's clinic—Mitch had gotten him the job when he was in high school and he'd continued during his first two years at Columbia. When the clinic in Bayview Heights got the go-ahead, he'd gleefully switched to this one and freed himself up on Thursdays through Saturdays. He planned to live with Mitch and Cassie in the new house for that part of the week. The Lansings were elated to have him back even part-time, and had added a suite of rooms at one end of their new house for him. They'd all move in next week.

''That's it.'' Kurt smiled again and thanked everyone for coming.

The mayor handed Kurt scissors to cut the big red ribbon. They'd all go inside now, have a short reception, then Kurt would meet with Zoe's volunteers, who'd start work tomorrow.

Taking a deep breath, she watched the girls file in ahead of her, and with Seth behind her, she inched slowly forward, repeating the mantra in her head.

Grace under pressure. Grace under pressure. Grace under pressure.

Damn, she never did like Hemingway.

IT WAS LIKE facing a teenage firing squad. They sat stiffly in the conference room, itching to take shots at him, but instead, they'd been ordered to hold their fire. He expected nothing less after Zoe got through with them yesterday.

Zoe sat cool and collected in the midst of them. She'd taken off her raincoat and wore a tailored navy suit with a red blouse. Her hair was a fluffy mass and fell onto her forehead in sexy bangs. The overhead lights in the small conference room winked off of her dangling red-jeweled earrings. Though he wasn't close enough, he swore he could smell her perfume.

"Good afternoon," he said simply.

"Afternoon," the lone boy, Dan, returned cheerfully. He sat close to Julia, a little away from the other girls. Dressed in all black, he reminded Kurt of a young Johnny Battaglia.

Little by little the kids acknowledged him.

"Hello."

"Hi."

"Good afternoon."

Holding up a sheet of paper, he said, "I have several jobs available here, but I thought I'd give you my opinion first on where you might be the most helpful and the most effective."

Zoe's eyes shone with approval. He might be a personal failure with her, but he knew his job, and he knew volunteers.

"I've studied your résumés carefully and made notes during our discussion last week. I tried to match your interests, your talents and particularly your goals in life with the positions we have open. In some ways I've mimicked the shadowing program you have at school." The shadowing program was a project where students paired up with adults who worked in a profession the teenagers thought they might want to pursue; it had been implemented by Zoe and Linc McKenna.

A slight smile breached Zoe's lips at the reference.

"Let's start alphabetically. By the way, if you disagree with your placement, I'll change it." Tongue-incheek, he added, "We wouldn't want any unhappy workers here." He sat on the desk, and made eye contact with each girl. All of them, except Erica, shifted uncomfortably.

"Dan Caruso. I've put you in the nursery. You expressed an interest in working with little kids, and since we've got an area set up for patients' children and pediatric patients who are waiting to be seen, I thought you might like that."

"Yeah, I would," Dan said casually, but the shine in the boy's eyes told Kurt he'd made the right choice.

One down.

"Ashley Emerson." He smiled at the girl and she smiled back weakly. Kurt had noticed she'd come late and looked rather pale, despite her cheerful pink sweater and slacks. "Planned Parenthood. With Max Johnson. You indicated a desire to work with teens on life choices."

Ashley went paler, nodded, then shared a worried glance with Rachel.

"Shondra and Erica, you'll work in the medical facility. Shondra, as you expressed an interest in studying medicine, you'll work with the new doctor, Abraham Frank, when he comes. Erica, you'll be with me in administration.'' He smiled. ''Both of you will help out John Battaglia.''

Erica's face flushed. ''I don't want that.''

''You don't want to work with John?''

''I don't want to work with you.''

Shondra kicked her under the table.

''All right, Erica. Stay after everyone leaves. We'll discuss this.''

He read the other placements by rote, his mind whirling. He hoped he hadn't made a mistake with the Case girl. He didn't think he had; he trusted his professional instincts. It was his personal instincts that weren't worth a whole lot these days.

He finished with the students. Julia would work with Louise and Linc, the psychologists; Rachel Thompson, who wanted to be a nurse, and Shelley Marco, who was going into sports training, would help out Diane.

''Of course time frames and hours will vary—I'm leaving you to schedule that with your respective 'bosses.''' He glanced at the clock. ''Why don't you go find them and see what they have in mind for what you'll do and when you'll start.'' He smiled warmly at Erica. ''Stay with me, Erica. Shondra, you can meet with John in my office.''

Slowly everyone but Zoe and Erica filed out.

Zoe stood. ''I'd like to talk to Erica first.''

Kurt shook his head. ''You've already talked to Erica. I think it's time she and I had a little chat.'' He took in the girl's stony features, tight lips. ''Alone.''

One of the Zoe's eyebrows shot up. ''I don't think—''

''I want to talk to him alone.''

Zoe shifted her gaze. ''Erica, we discussed this.''

''I'll be polite. But you taught us to express our

opinions. I want to do that.'' She raked Kurt with an adult glare. ''Alone.''

Glancing from Kurt to Erica, Zoe shrugged, squeezed the girl's arm and left with, ''I'll be right outside.''

Kurt studied Erica as she scrutinized him. In an arena they'd be circling each other, figuring out how to go for the jugular. But he'd taken an oath to heal, not hurt, and he'd already planned this encounter. He began without preamble. ''I assigned you to work with me primarily because it will help you in the college-application process. Clinic-administration experience will look good on your résumé.''

The girl swallowed hard. She wore a simple white ribbed shirt and beige skirt. Tall and lanky, she would have been nondescript if it wasn't for her penetrating dark blue eyes. With typical teenage bravado, she flipped her hair back off her shoulder. ''I won't have any trouble getting into college.''

''Every bit helps. You've applied to Georgetown.''

She nodded.

''I went there.''

Her face fell. He was sorry to hit below the belt, but a lot was at stake here. And sometimes the cure was worse, initially, than the disease.

''I also picked you to work with me because I can tell you don't like me and I thought it would help if you got to know me.''

''I don't want to get to know you.''

He glanced out the window. His daughter had interned him well in teenage girlhood. He faced Erica squarely with his best doctor gaze. ''I hurt someone you love, Erica, and I regret it more than I can say. If I could change that, I'd do so in a second. But since I can't, I'd like to keep Ms. Caufield from getting hurt further.'' He waved his hand around the clinic. ''This is a terrible situation to put her in. I want to be able to count on you to make it as easy as possible for her.''

Bingo! The teenage bravado faded. The child surfaced.

And the love. Did Zoe have any idea how much these kids loved her?

How much he did?

I have some things to say to you, Zoe. Important things. Your fortieth birthday is the perfect time.

He'd been ready to tell her he loved her, had loved her for a long time. And wanted to marry her. God, how had he gone so wrong?

Erica sank back into the chair and flipped the pages of her notebook. Then she raised troubled eyes to his. ''You think I can help her with this?''

''Absolutely.''

''I won't ever like you.''

He was surprised at the little zing of pain that caused. ''I don't expect you to. But if you stay here, you'll have to work at getting along with me.''

''For Ms. Caufield.''

''Yes.''

She stood. ''I'll try.''

He held out his hand. ''Truce?''

The girl stared at it with a faint flash of disgust on her face. ''Sure.'' She shook his hand. ''Let's go find Ms. Caufield.'' But she didn't move. ''If you ever...do anything to her, hurt her again, you'll have to deal with me.''

Kurt should have felt like laughing; he outweighed the girl by at least fifty pounds. He was older, wiser, had dealt with junkies and hoodlums for years in his city clinic.

But he wasn't amused. Instead, he was very sad.

"I won't hurt her, Erica. I promise."

She snorted.

Rightly so. His promises weren't worth much these days.

Sighing, he followed her out; later he'd bury himself in work.

DR. LOUISE SHEFFIELD was a motherly looking woman with a perky smile and animated eyes. Julia liked her on sight. And Mr. McKenna, hunk track coach, was cool—he'd come to see all her plays. She was damn lucky to have them and not Dr. Lansing.

He seems sad.

The thought came out of nowhere. Julia, who read faces like they were maps to the soul, had recognized the suffering on his.

Good, Erica would say. She was probably right.

"Here's a list of duties you'll perform, Julia. Of course, we need to be careful about what you do and have access to for confidentiality reasons, but Ms. Caufield assures us you're reliable and discreet."

Julia scanned the list. Help the secretary/receptionist answer phones, tidy the outer office and patient waiting area, make coffee, clean up, maybe do some filing and scheduling. "This is easy."

Mr. McKenna leaned forward, his blue eyes kind. "At school, you'll be helping me run some groups. The one I'm planning now, Teen Choices, will include role-playing, which I was hoping you could organize."

I'm an expert at role-playing. "Sounds terrific. Have people signed up?"

"Yes."

Dr. Sheffield continued, "We're happy to have you working with us, Julia, and we hope this experience will benefit you in making decisions about your future."

"Oh, I've already decided. I'm going to be an actress."

"Well, maybe a minor in something else might help. Just in case..."

...*you don't make it.* The woman was too tactful to finish the thought, the one that scared Julia to death. She didn't want to think about living in the world as herself. She planned to be other people most of the time. It was easier.

That why you assume roles, Jules?

She wondered how Dan was doing. And the others. Erica was probably dying. Shondra would be okay. Julia was a little worried about Ashley.

ASHLEY SAT before Dr. Max Johnson and pasted on a brave smile.

"Are you all right, young lady? You look a little pale."

Oh God, with his experience, could he tell she was pregnant? She grasped her purse, which held the pregnancy testing kit she and her boyfriend, Evan, had stopped to buy before he'd dropped her off. He wouldn't take it home with him. They were going to do the test tonight, together.

"I'm fine." She gave him her cheerleader grin. "I'm really glad to be working here."

"What do you plan to do with your life, Ashley?"

The question of the day. "I'm not sure. Maybe some area of health—community health or education." *Or maybe just be a mother. It's probably what I'd be best at, anyway.*

She tried not to think about Evan's reaction. But his stunned face and angry flush haunted her...

You're on the pill, damn it. How could you be pregnant?

I, um, went off it because it made me gain weight.

When were you going to tell me?

I figured the first half of the month was safe...

For a smart girl, that was pretty stupid.

Only when she'd begun to cry had he softened up. That ploy always worked with him, but it made her mad sometimes to have to resort to it.

She tried to focus on what Dr. Johnson was saying. She'd do office work, stock supplies, make coffee, and maybe eventually she could get a little more involved with patients, if it was all right with them. Ashley didn't much care. All she wanted was to be done here, go home and find out what her future was *really* going to be.

She hoped Shondra would finish on time. She was catching a ride with her; Ashley wasn't sure how much longer she could wait.

JOHN BATTAGLIA had the most beautiful eyes Shondra had ever seen. So brown they were almost black, with lashes a girl would kill for. And they sparkled like onyx when he talked about medicine. He was a dedicated man, she could tell.

"I worked for Kurt when I was your age," he told Shondra.

"In New York?"

"Uh-huh." Buttoning his white lab coat, he sat

down behind a desk. "You'll be doing the stuff I did. Very similar to orderly work."

"I've volunteered at the hospital for years."

"So I see from your résumé." He smiled, and Shondra's heart, which had never been pledged to a boy, tightened in her chest. "You wanna be a doctor."

"Yes. You're in premed, right?"

"Columbia. I've taken extra courses each semester and gone summers, so I'll be through a year early. I'll start medical school in September."

"There?"

"Yep. I've already been accepted." He looked past her to the exit. She followed his gaze.

Dr. Lansing stood in the doorway with Erica. "Oh, sorry, I thought you'd be done by now."

"We are. I'm going to take Shondra on a tour of the facilities. Erica, wanna come with us?"

"Not now." Dr. Lansing smiled and answered for her. "We need to get some things outlined before she leaves."

Erica's expression was sulky, but okay. Shondra wished her friend could chill about this assignment. She wasn't helping Ms. C at all.

"Need a ride home?" Shondra asked Erica as she and John headed to the door. "I'm taking Ashley."

"No, my car's out of the shop. Thanks."

"See you later."

John nodded to Erica, then squeezed Dr. Lansing's arm. His knowing look didn't escape Shondra.

Erica's anger was obvious to everybody.

She should just get over it and get on with things.

EMOTIONS SWIRLED in Erica like the paint on a Van Gogh canvas. Torn between doing what was right and her dislike of the man behind the desk, she sat stiffly in the chair and tried to be civil.

"Can you type?" he asked without preliminaries.

"Of course."

"Good. Then you can type some of the weekly and monthly reports I have to do for the city and state."

"I didn't know I'd be a secretary." She winced at her tone. She really was going to try harder.

Lansing either didn't catch it or ignored it. "I thought it might help you understand the workings of the clinic."

"Oh."

"And you can sort through my mail. Separate junk from what needs my attention."

"So I can see how the place runs."

He smiled as if she'd said something smart. Like her father did—*only* when she said something smart. "Exactly." Leaning back, he crossed his arms over his chest. "And I thought you might do crossover checks for supplies. All of this will give you valuable business experience."

"Sounds okay." She fidgeted with the strap of the purse her aunt had bought her for Christmas. Erica knew she was going into business like her father, had known since she was little, but she also wanted to help people. Big business sometimes took advantage of the public.

She and Ms. C had talked about that a lot. Once while they were shopping for shoes and stopped at Starbuck's for coffee, Ms. C had gone on about how much she loved teaching...

It's so rewarding, Erica. I hope you get into a profession that gives you as much satisfaction.

CEOs probably don't feel like you, Ms. C.

So, you don't have to be a CEO.

Tell that to Jackson Case, Erica had said…

"Do you like running clinics like this?" she asked Lansing.

"I love it." He studied the half-empty bookshelves, the bare walls and the boxes stacked in the corner. "It gives meaning to my life."

"You like it better than practicing medicine?"

"I still practice, though not as much as before. But, yes, I like starting programs that help people. I like the excitement of running a clinic." He cocked his head. "Is that what you want, Erica? To run a business?"

"I guess. The money's there."

"Is money important to you?"

It's important to my father. It's the only measure of success to him.

"Yeah, but…" She trailed off.

"But?"

She scowled. What was she doing sharing personal stuff with this guy? "Look, can we talk about my schedule? I have to rearrange some things to work here."

He scanned her résumé. "I can tell. Is there any club you're not in?"

She smiled in spite of herself. "I think I missed the chess club." She sobered. "Extracurricular activities are important to get into college." He looked like he was going to object, so she cut him off at the pass. "The schedule?"

He glanced back down. "Fine. Let's hammer it out."

It took a half hour. When they were done, he nodded at it. "Looks good to me."

She stood. "Okay."

His shoulders sagged as he rose, too. And his face was lined with fatigue. She glanced around—his office was still a mess. Yet he'd spent a lot of his time accommodating her. ''Um, thanks for taking the time to do this.''

''You're welcome. I'm sure you'll be a real help here, Erica.''

Pleasure shot through her. Her dad never said things like that. ''I will be.''

She turned and headed for the door. He followed her. She was feeling okay about him—until she found Ms. Caufield in the waiting area.

DÉJÀ VU. ALMOST A YEAR AGO today, Zoe had sat in Kurt's New York waiting room, blissfully happy—and totally unaware that her world was about to fall apart. This place even smelled the same—coffee brewing in the corner, the faint scent of cleaning fluids and antiseptic. Well, that was the past. She was done with it and she refused to fall victim to the pain again. Dropping the magazine she held, she stood and smiled pleasantly when Kurt's door opened and he and Erica came out.

''Things okay?'' The issue of Erica's dislike of Kurt needed to be addressed openly.

''Just fine,'' Kurt said. ''Right, Erica?''

She saw Erica struggle. Her chin came up and her hand closed around the strap of her purse. But finally she smiled. ''Yep, just fine. Dr. Lansing and I have a schedule all worked out.''

Unexpectedly she walked over and hugged Zoe. ''Don't worry, Ms. C,'' she whispered. ''I won't let you down.''

Touched by the sentiment, Zoe hugged back. "I know you won't."

Erica left with a lukewarm, "Goodbye Dr. Lansing," and suddenly Zoe and Kurt were alone.

The late-day sun shone through the windows and glanced off Kurt, accenting his high cheekbones, kissing the cleft of his chin. He looked tired—and alone. A wave of sadness swept through her, but she ignored it. "I'm glad things went well with her."

He leaned against the doorjamb, looking at Erica's receding back. "She'll do anything for you. They all will."

"Years of building their trust," Zoe said simply.

"Mmm. Trust. That's the key, right?"

"Absolutely."

"They ever abuse it? Your trust?"

"Of course they do. They're kids."

"And you forgive them."

"Yes." Pique arose in her. "Where are you going with this, Kurt?"

"Nowhere. I'm sorry." He straightened. "Do we need to meet?"

She glanced at her watch. "Yes. If you have time, I'd like to do it now." She didn't want to schedule another meeting and spend days dreading it.

"I've got nothing but time." He sighed.

"May I use your phone first? I left mine in the car."

"Sure." He stepped aside so she could enter his office; tactfully he waited in the outer area.

His office was bigger than the one in the city, but just as jammed. Unpacked boxes, walls bare of photos and certificates told her he hadn't settled in yet. She crossed to the oak desk and picked up the phone. Dialing quickly, she waited. The call went unanswered.

She dug into her purse, looking for the cell-phone number she had in her pocket directory. After several rings, he finally answered. "Ransom."

"Hi, Alex, it's me. I'm running late."

"That's fine. I'm caught up in something here, anyway."

She smiled into the phone. "You work too hard. Is six-thirty good?"

"Great. We can still have dinner and make it to the football game." He pitched his voice low. "Don't dress in heavy clothes. I'll keep you warm."

"Stop. I'm going home to change."

His laugh was happy and uncomplicated. "I'll pick you up at your condo."

"See you then."

"Zoe?" he asked, concern in his voice. "How'd it go today?"

"Just fine. See you soon." She hung up and pivoted; Kurt stood in the doorway watching. Listening.

There was an unmistakably possessive look on his face. His whole body was tense as he came toward her. "I thought you wouldn't date him because he was too young."

He is. "I'm not dating him."

"Sounds to me like you are."

"Look, this really isn't any of your business."

Raking a hand through his hair, he circled around her and sat behind his desk. He looked like a student who was so full of emotions he didn't know if he could contain them. "I knew it was going on." He swallowed hard.

"You have no right to say anything about what I do, Kurt."

"I realize that. It doesn't change the facts. I've been imagining you with him for the past year—"

She held up a hand. "Stop right there. I won't listen to this. We're history. Dredging up the past and how you felt when you went back to your wife is not of any interest to me."

He blew out a heavy breath. "Fine. Let's talk about the kids, then. What do you need from me?"

She cleared her throat. "We'll have to meet weekly. Though the students are working with other people, you'll be their direct supervisor."

"Yes, I know that." His voice was cold.

"Let's set a regular time, if we can." *So I can prepare myself.*

"How about Friday afternoons? Johnny's going to work that day, and I'll be able to get away."

"Fine for me." She drew her day planner out of her purse. Opened it. "How about four?"

"I'll come to the school."

"You don't have to do that."

"I want to. I'll need to get out of here."

She was going to make some comment about controlling his tendency to overwork, but she refrained. "All right."

He looked up. "What else?"

Her sigh was resigned. "There's an annual weekend thing for all the Life Issues kids and their supervisors. The program's called Down to Earth. We go to a cabin in the woods and do activities designed to test strength and stamina and to build self-esteem and confidence. Everything's geared to teach team-building and cooperation." Her eyes narrowed on him. "Under the circumstances, I'd ask you not to go. But the girls need to get to know and trust you. I think you should participate this year.''

''Fine. What's the date?''

''The third weekend in October,'' she told him and he wrote it down on his desk calendar.

''Anything else?'' he asked.

''No. Not now.'' God, she just wanted to get out of here. ''You?''

''Nothing about the volunteering.''

''What, then?''

''I'm helping Cassie and Mitch move at the end of next week.''

Her throat clogged. ''So am I.''

''I know.''

She stood. ''It doesn't matter.''

''Doesn't it?'' he said tightly.

Looking down at his strained features, her temper flared. ''You seem angry at me. I don't understand why.''

He threw the chair back and stood, too. ''I'm angry at myself, Zoe. Every time I see you, I realize what I've lost, and it eats away inside me.'' He shot a quick glance at the phone. ''When I hear you chatting cozily with another man, I want to tear something apart.''

Turning her back on him, she blocked out the sight of his face. ''I don't want to hear this.''

She felt him come up behind her. ''I know. I'm sorry.''

Fearful he'd touch her, she straightened and moved away. ''Maybe you need to get some help if you can't control your emotions around me. I don't want to deal with them.''

Without looking back, she left the office and Kurt behind.

CHAPTER FIVE

"IT'S GORGEOUS." Zoe stood in front of the Lansings' new house and marveled at the wood-and-stone exterior. The three-story structure nestled on a two-acre lot next door to the Taylors' home just outside of town.

"We like it." Cassie's comment was restrained, though Zoe could see her friend's eyes glow with excitement. Mitch had been the one to push for a new house, and Cassie hadn't paid much attention to the details; but once it was under way, she'd become fully involved. Zoe had helped her pick out colors, wallpaper and flooring.

"Come on, girl, let's go inside and start unpacking those boxes." Zoe slid her arm through Cassie's and they went into the house. The movers had come during the week and delivered the furniture and crates to the appropriate rooms, but there was the huge task of unpacking and settling in to be done on this beautiful Saturday morning. Zoe had dressed for the job—baggy jeans, sneakers and a denim shirt over a red Bayview Heights T-shirt that teachers and kids wore every Friday.

Pulling open one of the double front doors, they stepped directly into the two-story foyer. The scent of new carpet and wood permeated the house.

Cassie frowned at the long winding staircase. "Oh,

God, every time I see this, I panic. I can just picture the two little devils sliding down that banister.''

''Not until they're older. For now, the gates Mitch built will prevent that.'' Zoe looked around in admiration.

The foyer was beautiful, with its polished wood and skylights, inviting the Columbus Day-weekend sun to pour in. Off to the left sprawled a huge great room with a fieldstone fireplace. The ceiling was vaulted with three more skylights. To the right was an oversize den with desks and floor-to-ceiling bookshelves.

Voices filtered out from the rear of the house. As she headed there with Cassie, Zoe braced herself. *I can handle this.* She'd had the meeting with Kurt about the Down to Earth program yesterday, and it had gone without a hitch. She could do this, too.

The back of the house was even more spectacular. The kitchen sparkled with gleaming white appliances, white-oak cupboards and hardwood floors, windows and skylights everywhere. Mitch and Cassie's bedroom suite took up a whole wing, and down a few steps were Johnny Battaglia's rooms. The girls' rooms were upstairs, as was the spacious guest area.

Around a big butcher-block table sat the rest of the crew. Seth, in an old track sweatshirt and jeans, looked tired. Mitch, wearing a golf shirt and jeans, brimmed with suppressed energy.

And Kurt stole her breath away. He'd donned indecently fitting worn-to-white denims and a navy polo shirt. Arms corded with muscle reminded her of things she'd rather forget. Sipping coffee, he was staring out the window to the wooded backyard in thoughtful silence.

''Here you are.'' Mitch crossed to Cassie and

hugged her. "Thought maybe you'd chickened out on me, love."

"Never, big guy." She kissed his cheek. "The house is beautiful. You were right."

"Well, record that," Seth said mischievously. "It's rare to hear Cassie Lansing admit she was wrong."

Cassie socked his arm. "I've mellowed in my old age. Where's Lace?"

"Still next door. Josh is cranky this morning." Seth yawned. "He was up during the night, too."

"Josh, the angel child? That's rare. It's usually the twins who keep her up."

Seth scowled. "I know. Philip's trying to shoo her out." Philip and some of his friends had volunteered to watch the four Taylor children today, along with the two Lansing girls.

Zoe chuckled. "No easy feat."

At her comment Kurt pivoted. Every time she saw him, he looked a little healthier. Today he appeared rested and relaxed. She was glad.

"Morning," he said over his cup.

She smiled. "Hi, Kurt."

Cassie nodded. Then her eyes zeroed in on his coffee cup and Mitch's. "You guys eat anything?"

"Doughnuts. They were great," Mitch quipped.

"You need good breakfast food."

"We need to start unpacking." Mitch exchanged a meaningful look with his wife. "I thought the guys could arrange the furniture the way we want it and set up the beds and do the other heavy stuff, and you ladies could start with the boxes."

"Fine with me," Cassie said easily.

They're trying to keep us apart.

Which was good.

A half hour later, the "ladies" were knee-deep in Shakespeare and John Grisham, shelving books in the den, when Lacey hurried in. Her long plaid shirt and tan jeans were wrinkled, her blond hair tied back in a ponytail. Her pretty blue eyes were worried. "Sorry I'm late. What can I do?"

From her position on the floor, Cassie scowled. "Are you all right?"

"Yes. Josh is coming down with something, though." She blew her bangs out of her face. "I'm worried the rest of them will get it." She gave Cassie a frown. "Including yours, though Grandpa's keeping Josh in his room."

Cassie shrugged. "He and Alexandra had a tea party yesterday and drank from the same cup. If he's got something, she already has his germs."

Lacey smiled weakly. "I guess."

"Lace, if you want to stay with him, go ahead. This stuff can wait."

"Are you kidding? And risk a senior citizens' revolt? They hustled me out of there so they could have the kids all to themselves."

Cassie pushed hair that had escaped her braid out of her face. "What could they be thinking of?"

Unexpectedly Zoe felt a fist squeeze her heart. She turned away from the two mothers and their loving concerns to focus on the books. "Lots of neat stuff here, Cass. I can't believe you've replaced most of what you lost."

A few years ago the gang Johnny had belonged to had broken into Cassie's house and destroyed a lot of her possessions.

Cassie's face shone with an intensity that took Zoe's breath away. "Mitch did it. He systematically found almost every single book I lost, or something similar. I still can't believe he did that for me."

Lacey and Zoe exchanged a smile. Sometimes their friend was in awe of her husband's devotion. "He'd do anything for you, Cass," Zoe said.

"He's even trying to hunt down the yearbooks I lost. He'll do it, too, with his cop's skills."

They worked and chatted for two hours about school, the newspaper and the kids; Lacey called home before noon to check on Josh. Philip reported that he was sleeping.

"He must be sick. He never naps in the morning," she told Zoe and Cass.

"Why don't you go home?" Cassie suggested again.

"No, Grandpa threatened to turn Seth on me. They conspire constantly to get me away from the kids."

By noon the house was taking shape. The Lansings ordered subs for lunch and set them out in the dining room. Zoe had been touring Johnny's rooms, so she was the last to help herself to the food.

Kurt was still there, again staring somberly out the window, a plate in his hand. He looked over his shoulder when she entered. Green eyes glowed at seeing her, and he gave her a half smile. "Nice house, isn't it?"

"Yes." She searched the contents of the table.

"Yours is right there," he said pointing to the meatball sub in front of him.

She glanced up at him, surprised.

He shrugged. "I haven't forgotten anything, Zoe."

Placing a piece of the sandwich on her plate, she scooped up a handful of chips. "I know." She shook her head as she found a napkin. "Me, neither. I thought I had, until you came back."

He sighed.

She sank onto a chair, aware of the buzz of the others who'd gone into the kitchen to eat. Kurt leaned against the wall and munched on his ham-and-cheese.

"Are you all settled at the clinic?" she asked.

"Pretty much. Your little vigilante, Erica, is a nurturer at heart. She unpacked all my books one afternoon and put my degrees up on the wall."

"Sounds like her."

"I guess she doesn't hate me so much anymore, though she's far from friendly."

"Give her time." Zoe frowned. "I worry about her choice of careers, given that nurturing streak. Her father's set on her going into business."

A frown knitted his brow. "I'm a little worried about her, too."

"Because of that?"

"Because she does too much. Have you talked to her about it?"

"Yes, and Barb Sherman, the school psychologist, has seen her, too, at my request. It's fairly common among the bright kids to be overachievers, though I have to say Erica and Shondra are right up there as the worst—or best—I've ever had."

"They're a lot like you were, aren't they?"

She smiled and bit into her sub. "Yes. And like you were, too." It was just one of the zillion things they had in common. "Are you still working long hours?" she asked after a quiet moment.

"Not much else to do with my time."

His time was something Zoe had begun to covet again, particularly when she was alone with him like this. She stood abruptly. "I'm going to find the others."

His bleak look told her he understood. She strode

out into the kitchen to see Seth and Lacey coming in through the glass sliding doors. Mitch and Cassie sat adjacent to each other, sharing a beer, their shoulders touching.

"How is he?" Mitch asked Lacey.

"Listless. He says his tummy hurts."

From behind Zoe, Kurt asked, "What did he eat today, Lace?"

"Not much. Celia got him to take some juice and crackers." She scowled. "Yesterday he had apples, though. They never agree with him, but he sneaked them when I wasn't looking."

"That's probably it." Kurt circled around Zoe and crossed to the door. "I can go over, if you like."

"Let's wait a bit. Philip insists I'm being overprotective." She leaned into Seth. "But Josh is so little."

"He's six, honey. We got three littler ones."

She shrugged.

"Let's tackle hooking up the washer and dryer, then," Mitch suggested to Kurt. "Seth, you want to help?"

"No. I'm not good with machines. I'll set up the crib in Camille's room. I'm an expert at that!" He laughed.

Zoe headed back to the den, struggling to stay cheerful. She was happy that the Lansings and Taylors had settled into ordinary family life. Both couples had endured hardships and deserved some joy in simple things like home and kids.

So did she.

As she watched Kurt disappear through the doorway, she wished...

But stopped herself. It was time to move on.

AT ONE O'CLOCK the dryer was working. Kurt dropped the wrench into a toolbox and stood. "I'm going next door."

"Why?" Mitch asked.

"Just a feeling. I want to check on Josh."

"You gonna tell Lacey?"

"No, let me see him first. No need to worry her further."

Forgoing a jacket, Kurt left by the side entrance and jogged across the lawn from the Lansings' new house to the Taylors. The sun beat down on his head, refreshing him. He knocked at the garage door and Celia opened it.

"Hi, Kurt. Lacey send you to check on Josh?"

"No, I just had a minute and came over. Where is he?"

"Upstairs with Philip. We've taken turns sitting with him. He's not sleeping well."

Alarm tingled along Kurt's spine. "I know the way." Hurrying down the hall to the stairs, he mounted the steps two at a time and found Josh's room. "Philip?"

Philip turned. A look of relief washed over his weathered face. He shook his head. "I was just going to call Mitch's. Josh isn't any better. Maybe worse. Celia said I should have called sooner. I'm sorry."

Kurt stared down at the bed. Josh was in a fetal position, hugging his knees. "How long has he had his legs up like that?"

"About fifteen minutes. And he's hot now."

Quickly Kurt crossed to Josh. Felt his forehead. It was sweaty. He soothed the boy's blond hair. Though not her natural child, Josh looked amazingly like Lacey. Sitting on the edge of the mattress, Kurt gently turned Josh from his side. He moaned and opened his eyes. When Kurt tried to pull down his legs, he stiffened. "Got a tummyache, Josh?" Kurt asked.

Big blue eyes rounded on him. "I want my daddy."

"Call Seth and Lacey," Kurt said to Philip. "Tell them to come over."

Philip swallowed hard and left the room.

Insinuating his hand between the boy's torso and knees, Kurt prodded his stomach. Josh cried out. Kurt checked Josh's pulse and examined his eyes.

When Philip came back, Kurt asked, "Has he vomited?"

"No." Philip looked worriedly at Josh.

"Get me a damp cloth, would you? Lukewarm water."

Philip returned with the wet washcloth just as Lacey and Seth appeared at the doorway. The Lansings and Zoe were lined up behind them. By this time, Josh was moaning loudly.

"What is it?" Lacey asked, rushing into the room, her face white.

Kurt mopped Josh's brow and said calmly, "He has symptoms of appendicitis, Lace."

"What?"

"Just symptoms. I won't know for sure until I see blood tests, but his lower right quadrant is extremely tender." Kurt glanced up. "Mitch, go get the Bronco. You and Seth can ride in front." He began to wrap Josh in the light quilt. "Lacey, you ride in back with me and Josh."

"Shouldn't we call an ambulance?" Seth asked

"This'll be quicker." He pulled his keys out of his pocket. "Somebody get my bag out of my car."

"I will," Zoe said. "And I'll drive Cassie into town, too."

"And me," Philip said.

Kurt was all business now. "Philip, have Celia call the hospital emergency room and alert them we're coming." He bent to scoop the little boy into his arms and headed downstairs.

Within minutes the caravan was on its way to the Bayview Heights hospital. Josh lay curled up in the back seat of the car with his head on his mother's lap, in real pain now. Kurt checked his blood pressure. It was low. And his fever was 104.

Lacey said, "I took his temperature at noon. It was ninety-nine. And he wasn't in this kind of pain."

"It happens fast in cases like this, Lace."

Seth turned around. "Honey, it's not your fault."

"Of course it's not," Kurt said, soothing Josh's forehead. "You can't run to the hospital for every tummyache."

Lacey bit her lip and nodded.

In ten minutes—thanks to Mitch's police light—they reached the emergency room. Kurt carried Josh in; the boy moaned pitifully at the jostling. As gently as he could, Kurt laid Josh on the gurney and followed it down the hall.

The pediatric surgeon on duty introduced himself as Tom Ryan. "What's going on with the boy here?"

Kurt filled him in on the details as they wheeled Josh to an examining room.

"You can come in with us if you like," Dr. Ryan said.

"Go, please, Kurt," Lacey said.

He turned. "Of course." Squeezing her arm, he told her, "I'll be back with news as soon as I can."

FROM HER PLACE by the window, Zoe watched Seth stroke Lacey's hair as he kept her close to him on the orange vinyl chairs.

"I'm so scared," Lacey whispered.

Seth mumbled something Zoe couldn't hear.

Zoe was scared, too. The only thing that kept her together was Kurt's calm demeanor and assurances. She prayed he'd come out soon. It had been twenty-five minutes.

Cassie waited by the emergency-room door. Mitch paced in front of her. Philip, looking a little gray, sat stiffly in a straight chair at a small table. Zoe crossed to him. "Can I get you something, Philip?"

"No. Sit with me, though."

She sank into a chair next to him and took his hand. "It wasn't your fault, Grandpa."

"My head knows that. I just wonder if I was wrong to shoo Lacey out this morning. She might have realized Josh was so sick."

"Hindsight's twenty-twenty."

He smiled weakly. "Same thing Kurt said."

"He'll be—"

The door swung open and Kurt strode out. He headed for the Taylors and knelt down in front of them. Tenderly he took Lacey's hands in his. "He has acute appendicitis, Lacey. Fortunately the appendix hasn't ruptured, but it's inflamed. He's being prepped for surgery right now."

Tears formed in Lacey's eyes. "Surgery?"

"We have no choice, honey. It has to be done. But the procedure's relatively simple. He'll be given a general anesthetic, hydrated with intravenous fluids and dosed with preoperative antibiotics. We have to move quickly because we need to get the appendix out right away. They're coming out now with papers to sign.''

"Oh, my God, if you hadn't gone over…if we hadn't gotten him here, it might have ruptured.'' Lacey's tone was a little wild.

"Well, it didn't,'' Kurt said, adopting his calm doctor voice. "And it won't. We're on top of this.''

"Will you be in there with him?'' she asked.

"I'm going to scrub and watch, but I won't assist.''

Lacey gripped his arm. "But you'll be there.''

He smiled. "Yes.''

"What does the procedure entail?'' Seth wanted to know. He, too, had gone pale.

"There'll be a small incision in his lower belly, then they'll tie the appendix off and cut it out. There shouldn't be any complications.''

"What about infection?''

"In any operation, infection can set in.'' Kurt stood. "But there's no reason to expect anything to go wrong. The surgery shouldn't take more than a half hour.'' He glanced over his shoulder. "Here's Dr. Ryan to talk to you about it.'' Kurt stepped back as the pediatric surgeon approached them. "Mr. and Mrs. Taylor? I'm Tom Ryan…''

Zoe watched Kurt head to the doors of the emergency room. Without thinking, she darted over before he disappeared through them. "Kurt?''

He turned.

She squeezed his arm. "Thanks.''

Spontaneously he covered her hand with his. "Stay close to them,'' he said indicating the Taylors.

"Things *are* okay, aren't they?''

"Of course, I'd never lie about something like this. Even to the people I love.''

She understood his integrity, had always admired it. Not until she sat down next to the Taylors did she realize the irony of the thought. Men with integrity didn't sleep with their ex-wives.

When Kurt came back out thirty minutes later, everybody stood. He pulled off the mask, which matched his green scrubs. "Josh is fine. The surgery went without a hitch, and he's gonna have a scar to show to his brothers and the girls." Kurt gave them a few more details; his calm demeanor allowed everybody to relax.

Lacey started to cry and buried her face in Seth's chest. Cassie's eyes watered, too, and Mitch pulled her close.

Zoe turned her back to them all and crossed to the window, saying a silent prayer of thanks. Against her will, tears of relief slipped from her eyes. She swiped at them impatiently.

She felt Kurt come up behind her.

Trying to be strong, she didn't face him.

His hands went to her shoulders and squeezed gently.

She was assaulted by her senses—the feel of his big frame behind her, his unique scent surrounding her. Against her will, she leaned back into him. Just for a moment she let herself revel in his touch, his smell, his *presence*.

Slowly he circled her around. Without looking up, she let him pull her to him. His chin rested on her head, then he kissed her hair. "It's all right, sweetheart. He's fine."

"I know," she mumbled against his chest. "I was just so worried."

"Me, too."

"You were wonderful. They'll never forget it."

"I'm just glad everything turned out all right." He hugged her closer.

And she didn't have the strength to pull away. For just a few minutes she let herself be held by the man she'd never stopped loving.

ERICA STARED at the math test as if it was written in an alien language. She'd never seen an eighty-anything on one of her papers. AP calculus was hard, but that had never mattered before. What could have happened? She held back the panic rising in her.

"This must have been an unusually hard test," Mr. Hanson said. "The highest grade was eighty-nine."

The kids called out, "Erica didn't get a hundred? Not even a ninety? We need a curve..."

She caught Shondra's eye. Shondra shrugged and showed her the eighty-eight marked in blood-red numerals on her paper. "My mother will kill me," she mouthed.

"I know," Erica said back. Quickly she computed her average. Even with this grade, it came to a ninety-eight. That was only one point down from last time.

But her father would have a fit. She remembered when Ms. Caufield spoke with her dad at Parents' Night about her grades...

Ms. C had pulled herself up straight but had still only reached Jackson Case's shoulder. *I think Erica's under a great deal of pressure, Mr. Case. Not all good.*

Her father's tanned face had reddened. Though only forty-five, he looked older, with lines around his mouth and his hair graying. *I know my daughter, Ms. Caufield. She's got potential and she's going to use it. Now, if you'll excuse us...*

Ms. C had called her father several times for private

appointments, but he'd refused to go. If he knew how much time Erica spent with Ms. C he'd object. But he wasn't home long enough to know how Erica spent her days. He was only interested in her marks.

As Mr. Hanson talked about the most-missed questions, Erica realized her mind had wandered—and that was the problem. Her focus was off. She'd been too caught up with other people's issues. Ashley's. This thing with Ms. Caufield. Working at the clinic. She needed to center herself.

And she needed to feel better.

Her gaze strayed to one of the boys two rows away. Carl Pike. Big-time dealer. She knew Shondra had gotten some uppers from him a while back when the pressure from her mother had been too much. At the time Erica had warned her against dabbling in drugs, and she was glad when Shondra stopped using altogether.

But the pills had worked. Shondra had been like a different person, able to concentrate and focus for long periods of time without sleep.

For a few weeks, how harmful could they be?

Fishing in her purse, pretending to search for a tissue, Erica checked her wallet. She found a fifty-dollar bill stashed behind her license in case of emergency.

Hmm. She thought about it the rest of class.

When the bell rang, she hurried out the door.

Just behind Carl Pike.

When they were away from the others, she tapped him on the shoulder.

"YOU CAN'T ATTEND Down to Earth. Ms. Caufield will just have to excuse you."

"What?" Shondra looked at her mother incredulously.

"You received a low grade on this test. You have to study. I'll call Mr. Hanson to see if you can do extra credit." Joanna Jacobs wore her dark hair tightly cropped, and was dressed, even late at night, in tailored pants and a blouse. She'd come home from her law office and changed from her suit into the outfit. Shondra knew from the past that she even left her panty hose on.

"Ma, that's ridiculous."

"Do you have the highest average in the class?"

"No, Erica does."

"You won't get the math award at graduation."

"I can't get *every* award."

Joanna's black eyes widened. "You need to aim for every award."

"That's unrealistic."

"Not for you."

Shondra swallowed hard. They'd been through this before. "I need some downtime, Ma. I can't study every minute."

"Your downtime is that volunteer work you're doing. The only reason I agreed to it was for college acceptance. And you have time with your family."

Time with family. Watching National Geographic specials and the History Channel. Attending lectures on cultural diversity. Participating in book discussion groups. All four Jacobs children were so indoctrinated they squeaked with their responsibility to their culture.

It was too much. She faced her mother mutinously. "I'm going."

"What?"

"I said I'm going to Down to Earth, with or without your permission."

"Well, we'll see about that, young lady."

"Yes," Shondra said in a steely voice. "We will."

THE LITTLE MAN looked like Bob Fosse, with his goatee and lean build. "Next," he called out. "Julia Starr."

Julia rose from her seat in one of Juillard's many theaters, mounted the stairs and crossed to center stage as if her stomach wasn't leaping like a garden full of grasshoppers. She stopped in the middle, poised and ready.

"What scene have you chosen, Ms. Starr?"

"Act V Scene 1 from *Macbeth*. I'll be Lady Macbeth."

"Proceed, then. Our assistant will read the other parts."

Julia tilted her chin and threw back her head. She stared off into space, imagining Lady Macbeth walking in nightclothes carrying a taper. Julia had even worn a long white flowing dress to look the part. Gracefully she held out her hand. "'Yet, there's the spot.'" She swallowed hard as the assistant read the other lines; in her mind, she watched the blood materialize on her fingers. Her eyes widened, moistened with fright, as she neared the famous soliloquy. "'Out—'" she hesitated "'—*out* damned spot, out I say! One, two, why then...'"

Losing conscious awareness of the auditorium, Julia felt the stickiness of the blood, smelled its sweetness and experienced the terror of a murderer. "'Who would have thought the old man to have had so much *blood* in him...'"

Her voice trembled, but held an undercurrent of menace. Of excitement. By the time Lady Macbeth was led away by the servants, she'd shrunken into a ball.

It was a minute before Julia was aware of the applause. Strong. Sure. Even the director clapped.

"Well-done," he said, then glanced down. "Next."

Julia crept back to her seat. She was always exhausted after a performance, but she had to get up for her dance/music number, anyway. She plunked down next to a guy wearing a sweat suit and hair that brushed his collar. She noticed a Celtic Cross around his neck. "Great job," he said softly.

"Thanks."

"What are you singing?"

"'What I Did for Love,' from *Chorus Line*. How about you?"

"This year I'm doing 'Music of the Night' from *Phantom*."

Julia frowned. "This year?"

He gave her a beleaguered grin. "Yeah, it's my second tryout. I didn't get in last year."

"Oh, I'm sorry."

He shrugged. "I knew it was tough when I applied. I hope I don't have to wait another year. Three times, you know..."

Unkindly she thought he must not be very good.

Which was why she was stunned when he gave one of the best performances of Stanley screaming "Stella," from *Streetcar Named Desire* she'd ever seen, or when he belted out the part of the phantom better than Michael Crawford.

An hour later Julia left Juillard's auditorium shaking. Not from the residue of her role as Lady Macbeth.

But because, for the first time, she realized that despite her incredible talent and her stellar grades, she might not get into the school of her choice.

"I CAN'T GO to Down to Earth," Ashley told Evan when he presented her with the permission form given out in class today. She'd been too nauseated to go to school. The pregnancy test had been positive.

"Why not?"

"You've seen the videotape of that weekend, Evan. It's climbing trees and crossing logs and limbs and high wires. I could—" she laid a hand over her stomach "—hurt the baby."

He gave her the standard jock shrug. Insolent and insulting. "So what?"

Ashley dropped the glass she was holding and it shattered to the floor. "What did you say?"

"You're not gonna have it, anyway. Goddamn it. Haven't you heard what I've been saying all week? We're not gonna have a baby. We're too young. It'll ruin our lives."

"But I'm pregnant."

He watched her coldly. "That's what abortions are for."

"Evan, I told you—that's a sin."

He rolled his eyes. No longer was he the sweet wooing boy she'd taken off her clothes for. He was a man today, dark and dangerous. "So is premarital sex, according to you. Grow up, Ash."

Battling the ever-queasy feeling in her stomach, she stared at him. "You don't mean this."

"Not only do I mean it, but I want you to talk to those Planned Parenthood people you volunteer for and find out how to go about it. Sammy's girlfriend had one last year, but I'd just as soon the whole soccer team didn't know you're in trouble."

"Jenny did?"

Disgusted, he dropped into a chair. "You're so naive. Most of the guys on the team have been through this.''

She bit her lip. She was just another girl who got knocked up. A terrible thought hit her. ''Did this...has this ever happened to you before, Evan?''

''No, of course not.''

''I wasn't your first, like you were mine.''

''So what? I've never been careless in my life.''

Left unspoken was, *like you.*

She didn't say anything else.

He glanced at his watch. ''Look, I gotta get to work.'' Standing, he shoved the paper into her hands. ''Sign this and find out how to take care of the other problem.''

Still she didn't answer. Tilting her chin up with a finger, he raised her face to him, then bent over and kissed her. Gently. Tenderly. Like the old Evan, not the Mr. Hyde he'd turned into for a few minutes. ''It'll be okay, Ashley. After you fix this, we can go back to like it was.''

He turned then and sauntered out the door.

She scanned the kitchen. Everything looked normal. *Like it was.* But her whole world had changed. And in her seventeen-year-old heart, she knew no matter what she did, nothing would ever be the same again.

CHAPTER SIX

"DOWN TO EARTH is all about cooperation, self-confidence and trust building." The manager of the site, Franz Hoffman, spoke in a deep bass that matched his burly appearance—longish hair, slightly graying beard, sturdy build covered in denim and flannel. Kurt had heard the kids label him Paul Bunyan.

Having inspected the sleeping and eating areas and toured the grounds, the Bayview Heights contingent had gathered in the open grassy area in front of the lodge for instructions about the weekend to come. The sun had just set and the wind blew gently around them, turning the warm late-October afternoon into a cool evening.

"I'll conduct the physical activities tomorrow," Hoffman continued. "And Ms. Caufield will handle the psychological part."

Along with the school counselor, Kurt knew, who would be here tomorrow morning. The one who looked like Elizabeth. He wondered if Zoe had noticed.

The director smiled. "Get a good night's sleep. You'll need all your energy in the morning." The kids grumbled at his words. "Meanwhile, the fixings for dinner are ready. Your first lesson in cooperation is to cook together." Zoe, who stood next to him, held up an envelope. Hoffman continued, "These are the chores. Everybody take one and head to the kitchen."

More grumbling. Just as they'd complained when they'd seen the rustic sleeping accommodations.

Kurt's gaze strayed to Zoe, who was passing out the jobs. Dressed in jeans and a red BVH sweatshirt, with sneakers on her feet and a smile on her face, she bounced from person to person offering a pleasant comment to each of them.

He'd sleep on a dirt floor if he could share it with her. He smiled, remembering how she'd cuddled into him at night, and how he'd awaken with her wrapped around him. They'd manage just fine on one of the cots—or anywhere else.

Zoe approached Alex Ransom. Kurt scowled, as he had when the young vice principal had shown up at the front of the school to leave on the bus with everybody else...

What's he doing here? Kurt had asked.

Turning, Zoe had followed his gaze. *Alex oversees the health program. Besides, it's good to have an administrator along. It helps him bond with the kids.*

Did you ask him to come?

She'd given Kurt a scathing look and hadn't answered, which had been confirmation enough. Damn.

Now he watched the big guy lean over and whisper something in her ear. She giggled girlishly.

It was going to be a long weekend.

When she reached Kurt, she raised her brows and said lightly, "One job left." She smelled fresh and clean, like soap and the outdoors.

Giving her a phony smile, he drew it out of the envelope. "What'd you get?" he asked.

"Dishwasher." Her gaze dropped to his paper. "You?"

He looked down. Well, the god of the woods must be watching out for him. "Dish dryer."

She shrugged, as if it didn't mean anything to her. "I'll see you then."

The group trekked back into the big lodge. The place resembled a ski chalet, with a big stone fireplace and stuffed couches and chairs. To the right were the three bedrooms that had been assigned to the girls. Above was a loft where the guys would sleep. The kitchen was in the back. The cooks—Ashley, Erica, Shondra, Alex Ransom and two guys from the class Kurt didn't know—started back there.

Julia, lounging at the huge trestle table that would seat the twenty of them, watched the kitchen helpers go. "The blind leading the blind," she called after them. "Only Ashley knows her way around a kitchen."

Ransom, having heard her comment, turned to the girl. "I resent that, young lady. My mama raised me good. *I* can cook."

Kurt mumbled under his breath, "Anybody can do spaghetti sauce."

Zoe froze on her way past him to the bedrooms. He cursed his tongue.

They'd been making dinner at his place...

Here, taste this. He'd held out the wooden spoon. She'd leaned over the counter and licked it. He'd gotten hard, watching her.

Hmm. Needs more salt.

He'd lifted the spoon to his mouth and closed it over the spot where her lips had been. *It's perfect.* Holding her gaze, he'd ditched the spoon and circled the counter. Fast and furious, he'd picked her up and set her on the table, knocking off papers and assorted paraphernalia; he'd had her horizontal in no time. *So are you,* he'd told her before he claimed her…

It had been cataclysmic. Neither had been able to mention spaghetti sauce again without conjuring up the memory. Swearing to himself, he sought out his bunk.

Dinner was a lively affair. The food was a bit heavy on the garlic and missing the hot pepper Kurt liked, but Zoe praised each and every bite. When most of them were done, she said, "All right, take your plates to the kitchen and then give us a half hour to clean up. We'll meet back here at eight for the first exercise."

"Anybody want to shoot some hoops?" Ransom asked, bounding off the bench.

"I do." Dan Caruso got to his feet.

Julia frowned. "When did he turn into Mr. Jock?" she asked when Dan left.

Shondra and Erica exchanged a look.

"What's with you and that guy?" Erica asked, tapping her fork on the table in a nervous staccato. "You've been picking on him for weeks."

"I keep getting paired up with him." Julia stood. "Can't you do something about it, Ms. Caufield?"

"Can't do much about the pairings, Jules. Just like in class, they're either assigned according to your volunteer groups or they're random. The point of this weekend is to work well with everybody." She was careful not to glance at Kurt.

Once the dishes were under way, he thought she'd relax. But she didn't. At the sink, her posture was stiff. She'd taken off her sweatshirt, beneath which was a plain white T-shirt. He could see the lacy outline of her bra beneath it.

"Switch some music on, will you?" Her hands delved into the water, chasing soap up her arm.

"Why? So we don't have to talk?"

She shot him a sideways glance. "I'm not sure we have a lot to say to each other."

He stared at her. "This is hard for me," he finally confessed.

"What is?"

"Being around you."

"Then stay away."

"As you said, we can't pick our partners." He lifted plates and began to dry them. "Maybe it wasn't such a good idea for me to come."

Her shoulders sagged, but she didn't look at him. "No, it was a good idea. All the other supervisors came."

"They don't have the history with you that I do." He set a plate down on the shelf a little too hard; it clattered into the others. "Except maybe Ransom."

"Jealousy doesn't become you, Kurt."

"Well, excuse me if I hate seeing another man touch you."

She stiffened even more and said cuttingly, "If we're going to cast stones in that area…"

He swore. After a tense silence, he flipped on the boom box. The most godawful heavy metal blared from the speakers.

But it precluded any more conversation.

"ALL RIGHT, who'd like to explain to our adult participants what 'reaction sheets' are? You've all done them in class with me."

Shelley raised her hand. Zoe nodded to her. "They're open-ended statements where you fill in the blanks. Their purpose is to get a discussion going about what's on your mind."

"Thank you, Shelley," Zoe said. "Tonight, we'll start out with small-group discussion. We'll work first in our volunteer groups. Day-care people together, elementary-school people together, et cetera."

"Where'll you and Mr. Ransom be?" Erica asked.

"Mr. R will work with the peer helpers, since Rob and Evan aren't coming up until tomorrow." The boys had a soccer game tonight and were driving to the site with Barb Sherman in the morning. "I'll drop in and out of groups this first time to see how you're doing."

Zoe distributed the sheets to group leaders. "All right, ten minutes to fill these out. Remember, you have to be honest or it won't work. And don't worry, if you write something that you don't want to share, you don't have to."

Everyone smiled at that.

"But at least half of your answers should be shareable."

After the kids got to work, Zoe sank onto a pillow in the corner as far away from Kurt as possible. He'd taken a seat at the picnic table and was hunched over his reaction sheet, his face a study in intensity. Left-handed, he scribbled on the paper. His forest-green thermal shirt stretched across his broad shoulders, and she tried not to notice the muscles in his forearms and chest.

She forced herself to concentrate on her reaction sheet.

The five most important people in your life are...

Zoe swallowed hard, heard herself admonish the kids to be honest. She wrote Cassie, Lacey, Seth. Who else was she really close to? Erica.

Be honest. She wrote, *Kurt.*

Next question. *One professional goal you have is...*

That was easy. Keep the electives going, despite the Jerry Boscos of the world. He'd made an appointment to observe some of her classes next week, and she groaned inwardly at the thought.

One thing I'd change in my life is... Unfortunately that was easy, too. *Forget Kurt. Get on with my life.* Damn, she'd been doing a good job with that until he'd come back to Bayview Heights.

Ten minutes later after everyone had filled out their sheets individually, Zoe directed them to form groups. When assembled, she wandered around as they talked about who was important to them.

"...my mother."

"...Evan, of course."

"...my little brother."

The kids' most important people echoed through the room.

"Mitch," she heard when she passed Kurt's table. In spite of her resolve, she wondered who else he'd put down. His daughter, Lauren? Was Elizabeth on his list? Was *she?*

Finally Zoe joined a group. She smiled at Alex when he asked, "What's one thing you think is a waste of time, Ms. Caufield?"

She glanced down at her paper. "Regrets."

"We should live life for today," one of the students said.

"Yes," she said glancing in Kurt's direction. "We should."

BLINDFOLDED, KURT STUMBLED on something in the yard. A surprisingly strong hand gripped his arm.

"Don't like this, do you, Doctor." Erica sounded amused.

She glanced over his shoulder at Zoe. "Maybe," she said, and accepted the blindfold.

"THIS IS THE OBSTACLE COURSE that each group member will navigate. The teams are *not* in competition." The Down to Earth director eyed the kids and adults assembled at nine o'clock Saturday morning. "Your team of four has several activities to complete. Each person must do each activity. If someone has difficulty with one, it's the rest of the group's job to help them."

Barb Sherman, who'd arrived an hour ago with Evan and Rob, said brightly, "That's the objective of this morning, kiddos. Cooperation, problem-solving as a group and trust-building."

Good-naturedly the kids moaned. Already they were tired of hearing why they were here. Zoe knew that, but it was important to reiterate that they weren't just out for fun.

"Which group would like to go first?"

Kurt stepped right up. He looked rested today and sexy in a Georgetown sweatshirt, worn jeans and boots. "We do."

Julia, Shondra and Dan rolled their eyes. "Why do the adults always volunteer to go first?" Julia asked.

"Who knows?" Shondra answered. "God, I'm going to be so embarrassed."

Kurt faced them. "It's best to go first. Get it over with." When they frowned at him, he said, "Where's your sense of adventure?"

The three kids smiled and crowded around the director for instructions on the first activity. Hoffman held on to a ten-foot rope that was suspended from a sturdy tree limb far above their heads. "This is called the 'swing obstacle.' Grab on to the rope like this—"

he clasped his hands as high on the rope as he could reach "—take a running leap, or have your peers push you off, and swing over the grass past that marker on the ground. You have to get on the other side of it. Once there, stay and catch your partners."

After the explanation, he demonstrated the task.

Then Dan said, "I'll go first." Grabbing the rope, he stepped back several feet. "Me Tarzan!" he yelled as he took the leap and crossed the grassy area, easily clearing it.

Julia rolled her eyes. "How cute."

Shondra went next. She missed on her first try. And her second. "I'm a klutz," she told the others.

"All right, let's help her." Kurt grinned as he showed her how to grab the rope; then he and Julia swung her back and forth three times and gave her a final shove; she made it over. Dan grabbed her on the other side and hugged her.

"Help me," Julia said to Kurt.

Again he grinned. "Be glad to."

With Kurt's assistance, she made it to the other side. His turn now, Kurt grasped the rope, stepped back several feet and took some running steps; he flew over the grass, well past the marker. With so much momentum behind him, when the kids tried to catch him, the four of them toppled over in a heap.

Giggles and masculine chuckles emanated from the ground as they gathered themselves up; Dan dusted dirt off the back of Kurt's clothes and Shondra picked leaves out of Julia's hair. Zoe smiled.

An hour later they got to the next activity. The kids crowded around as the director indicated a log suspended horizontally about ten feet above the ground by a chain on either end. "Each person has to crawl up onto the log, sit on it, then come down on the other side.''

"Nobody can reach it," Shelley said. "It's too high." Her group, along with Zoe and Rob and Barb Sherman went first this time. Ashley, who'd gotten dizzy on the swing obstacle, had been excused from this one.

"Right," Hoffman said. "The group has to boost each person up, and then get them down on other side. It's called cooperation."

Rob mumbled, "No fair. Some groups got the short stuffs."

Zoe marched up to Rob and poked him in the chest as she looked up at him. "No short jokes, buddy. I can hold my own." Her height didn't matter on the Tarzan thing, Zoe thought five minutes later, but it clearly was a drawback on the "log mount." Her diminutive stature necessitated several more tries than the other participants. Twice, her group fell to the ground, laughing. But finally Zoe was perched on top of the log. "Hey," she said, raising her arms. "I made it."

They completed two other obstacles—a mechanism called the "traverse," where, ten feet above the ground, they crossed a tightrope holding on to another horizontal rope, which was chest high. For the second, they had to crawl on their bellies or hands and knees through big pipes and square boxlike objects. Finally came the last and most complicated obstacle. It involved pulleys, safety harnesses and tightrope lines, all of which they'd used in other exercises, but this thing was higher than the others, and more precarious.

Kurt's group went first again.

"Okay, Dr. Lansing," Julia said; Zoe noticed the

girl was smiling. "Since you're such a hotshot, you start us off."

Kurt stepped right up.

"I'll walk you through it," the director said after he'd demonstrated the four part obstacle. First—" he held out a rope ladder "—climb this. Your group will anchor it."

"Cooperation," Kurt mumbled under his breath as he whipped off his sweatshirt, revealing a gray cotton T-shirt underneath. Muscles bulging, he ascended the rope ladder. The kids let it sway a bit to tease him, but mostly held on tight. When he reached the first platform—all platforms were attached to huge trees—he punched the air and shouted, "Yes!"

"Now, lock one end of the safety harness to the overhead safety line. Check that the other end is tight at your waist." Kurt followed the directions. "The best way to get over the tire bridge—" the director pointed to the molded-together tires that looked like a rubber cylinder suspended between two platforms "—is to walk. But you're allowed to crawl, too, if you can't get your balance. You can hold on to the horizontal anchor rope over your head."

Zoe swallowed hard, suddenly uncomfortable when Kurt chose to walk. He got his balance easily and stepped over the tires like a Barnum and Bailey pro, lightly hanging on to the stretched overhead line until he reached the other side.

"This is freakin' scary," Julia said, scowling as she watched Kurt.

"I'm not gonna be able to do that," Shondra put in.

"Wow!" Erica's comment came from behind her. "I wanna fly like that."

Erica's was an odd comment, especially for a girl

who'd refused to go on the roller coaster when they'd gone to Six Flags last year.

Zoe's stomach clutched when Kurt reached the last part of the obstacle. Though she'd done this very course before, it was different watching Kurt do it. He seemed inordinately high up. And the final obstacle was the toughest. The object was to cross the last space by stepping on a series of three tiny swings; Zoe herself had had trouble with this part.

"Okay, Kurt, make sure the harness is secure to the overhead line. And don't grab on to the caribiner if you fall," Hoffman said, referring to the harness attachment. "Now grab the ropes of the first swing and step out into it."

Standing on the platform, Kurt grasped the two ropes of the small swing. He stepped out with one foot, then another to stand fully on the first board. The thing swayed back and forth with his weight. "Jeez," she heard him say.

Hoffman told him, "Now grab the other swing, bring it close to you and hold both ropes with one hand."

Following Hoffman's orders, Kurt made it to the next swing. Zoe felt her breathing pick up.

She was about to turn away so she didn't have to watch him finish when a bird flew out from the trees; it was a huge crow, followed by two others. The flapping of their large wings seemed as loud as a small plane.

Zoe cupped her hands to warn Kurt, only to hear a collective gasp come from the kids.

It all happened quickly.

Kurt jerked as the birds flew near him and lost his balance.

His foot slipped off the last swing.

His hands slid down the ropes.

And he fell.

Luckily the harness held. But he was suspended a good thirty feet from the ground.

"Everybody quiet!" the director yelled.

The kids went completely still. Hoffman rushed to a ladder lying on the ground and threw it against the tree. "You're not going to fall, Kurt," Hoffman assured as he climbed up.

"If you say so."

"Just stay still." In seconds the director was at the top of the ladder on the platform. He unwound another coiled rope fastened to the tree. His voice was calm. "I'm going to toss this to you, and I want you to grab it."

"Sure."

Kurt missed the first toss. Several kids gasped. He also missed the second. Zoe felt her eyes sting. He caught hold of the rope the third time. Her hands covering her mouth, Zoe watched as he followed the rest of Hoffman's instructions to swing over on the rope and pull himself up to the platform.

His face etched with concentration, Kurt swung toward the platform. When he came up to it, Hoffman, kneeling and secured by his own harness, grabbed Kurt under the armpits. Kurt, in turn, grabbed onto the base of the platform and held tight; he managed some footing against the tree. With Herculean strength and the help of Hoffman, Kurt dragged himself up to safety.

The students let out a raucous cheer. Zoe turned away. There was yelling behind her, comments, shouts of praise.

She stumbled into the trees. Shaking, she made her

way to a log and sank onto it. She buried her face in her hands and ordered herself to calm down. It had all worked out. Kurt was safe.

But her hands wouldn't stop trembling, and her throat worked convulsively. Never had she felt the kind of stark terror she had when she'd watched Kurt dangle thirty feet off the ground.

She didn't know how long she'd sat there when she felt someone drop down beside her. Without even looking, she recognized his scent, the feel of him.

"I'm all right, sweetheart."

They'd been too close for too long to pretend. "I know. It's just that watching you... I've never been so scared in my life."

"I'm glad it didn't happen to one of the kids." His arm came around her. She leaned into him. "Hoffman's canceling the last obstacle. They're too shaken to try it."

Still Zoe said nothing, just turned her face into his shoulder. They stayed close for several seconds. His embrace felt good. He was so solid. So alive, smelling like clean honest sweat and the outdoors.

Finally he kissed the top of her head, drew away and stood. "Zoe?"

She looked up. Backdropped by the sun, he seemed tall and invincible. "I'm sorry you were worried." He smiled. "But then again I'm not that sorry." He turned and left.

For a minute, anger replaced fear. "Well, hell," she said aloud. She hadn't expected him to *use* this. Frowning, she stared after him.

KURT AWAKENED Sunday morning in a bad mood, the source of which he decided not to ponder, though he knew the situation with Zoe was a large part of it. As the boys slept around him, he grabbed sneakers, sweat-pants and a shirt and headed out to the basketball court to work off some of his frustrations.

It was a glorious Indian-summer morning. The birds chipped happily in the sunlight, and the grass and trees had a dew-kissed sheen that made them sparkle like polished jewels.

The paved basketball court—a twenty-foot circle of blacktop and a hoop—was nestled in a copse of maple trees some distance away from the lodge. When he reached it, he heard the familiar thud of the ball against the ground.

"Oh, sorry, I didn't know anybody'd be here." Even to Kurt's own ears his voice was petulant.

Alex Ransom turned toward him, looking healthy and young and supremely confident. "No problem." He bounced the ball, then took a shot. "Wanna play some one-on-one?"

Last night the man had danced with Zoe at the kids' impromptu party, and he'd held her way too close. This morning, male challenge and a trace of primal com-petitiveness shone in Ransom's dark eyes.

"Yeah, sure."

Ransom turned, smiled and whipped off his T-shirt, revealing world-class muscles. So the guy visited a gym. Big deal.

"You take it out." Ransom shot the ball hard at him.

Kurt caught it without flinching, dribbled in from the perimeter and headed straight for the basket. Ransom kept in front of him, edging backward. Five feet from the basket, Kurt went up for a shot. Ransom's hand came down on the ball...and slapped Kurt's arm in the follow-through. It stung like a son of a bitch.

Kurt's answer was to dive for the ball and make a quick and dirty layup. Ransom took the ball out-of-bounds and drilled it down center court. Kurt planted himself in the pathway to the basket. Ransom rammed right into him, knocking him flat.

Surprised, Kurt's eyes narrowed on the other man from the pavement. "I'd call that charging."

"Yeah? Sorry." Ransom jammed the ball to a still-seated Kurt. "Your ball, then."

In minutes Kurt was ahead, three to one.

Ransom grabbed the ball out-of-bounds and went straight for a layup. Kurt charged him from the opposite side—in an effort to block him of course. It had nothing to do with a flash of memory—seeing the young vice principal and Zoe leave for a little moonlit stroll after campfire songs. Barreling forward, Kurt leaped up and missed the block. His elbow caught Ransom's rib cage.

Ransom grunted, but said, "My point. Down by one."

Ten minutes later, Ransom leaped up and came down to block what the last shot of the game—they were tied—and missing the ball, managed to smack Kurt hard across the mouth. Stunned, Kurt dropped the ball and raised his hand to his face. He felt stickiness on his lip.

Ransom stared at him. "Oh. Sorry." He watched the ball roll to the side. "I'd say we're done." Walking to the edge of the court, he picked up his shirt and wiped his face with it. Then he turned to Kurt, who was wiping the blood from his mouth with the end of his T-shirt.

"I'm not going to leave her alone," Ransom said simply.

Kurt's eyebrows raised. "I didn't ask you to."

Ransom rubbed his rib cage, where he'd probably have a king-size bruise. His gaze flicked to Kurt's mouth. "The hell you didn't."

SUNDAY'S ACTIVITIES were to end at three, when they'd all be bussed back to the high school. Barb Sherman began the day with a "trust fall." Kurt watched Madison Kendrick, a quiet unassuming girl struggle with the natural fear she was feeling.

"It's okay, Maddie," Barb said, standing on the ground while Madison perched on a platform about eight feet above. "Stay stiff and fall back."

Six people lined up beneath her gauntlet style, three on either side, forming a human net with their outstretched arms to catch her.

"I don't wanna do this," the girl said.

"If you really don't, you can pass." Barb smiled. "But I think you can do it. These people are your team. They'll catch you."

Cheers of encouragement abounded.

Kurt studied the kids in his group, wondering if they could handle his weight. He rubbed his shoulder. All he needed was to be slam-dunked into the ground again. He was already feeling all kinds of aches and pains from his contest with Ransom. Man, had that been stupid.

Taking in a deep breath and an even deeper gulp of courage, Madison went stiff and fell backward. The gang caught her easily.

Kurt groaned as his name was called. What the hell was he doing out here in the wilderness with all these young bunnies? he thought as he climbed the platform.

The emotional exercises were no easier for him. The

last half of the day was devoted to a "twenty-four hours to live" series of responses.

Kurt stared down at his paper. They'd been told to be honest, but they could keep private anything they put down. Unfortunately Zoe was in Kurt's group—the first time all weekend. Dressed in clingy black leggings and an oversize teal-blue sweatshirt, she looked young and healthy. The sun had kissed her face all weekend and her skin glowed.

As group leader, Dan Caruso said, "All right, everybody done?" When they nodded, he zeroed in on Zoe. "Ms. C, if you had only twenty-four hours to live, what are some of the activities you'd do, and what wouldn't you do?"

Zoe rolled her eyes. "I *wouldn't* do administrative paperwork," she said, smiling. She glanced down. "I *would* go for a walk at midnight. I *would* spend some of the day on the water." She smiled at them. "And I'd take a nap."

"What?" Erica's voice was stunned. Her color high, she was full of restless energy today. "You'd sleep part of your last day on earth. Why?"

"Because I couldn't enjoy the hours I had on no sleep."

For some reason Erica and Shondra exchanged a long look.

The kids argued vehemently about that with her, then Dan asked, "Dr. Lansing, what about you?"

I'd spend every second with Zoe.

He named the things on his list he could share. "I'd want to see my daughter. I'd go out on my boat. I'd spend a few hours making sure things were intact at the clinic."

Barb Sherman interrupted. "I want you all to compare the list of what you'd like to do with how you actually spend your days and nights.''

There was stark silence. Adults, like him, knew and accepted that most people did what they should do, not what they wanted to. Kids always found it a surprise.

''All right,'' Caruso said. ''Who would you miss most and least if you died? Share one of the five on each list.'' He glanced at his own paper. ''I'll start. I'd miss my little brother most. My mother least.''

''I'd miss my mother the least, too,'' Shondra said.

''My father the least,'' Erica put in.

Kurt battled back a groan. What would Lauren put here? Which list of his daughter's would *he* be on?

When Barb admonished them to think about who they spent most of their time with now in comparison with the list, the kids were again astonished to see how much time they spent with people not on the ''miss most'' list but those on the ''miss least'' one.

The counselor said, ''This is the last activity of the weekend. Write a letter to one person in your life telling them how you feel about them and what they mean to you. You might want to clear up some old baggage between you, if there is any. I'd pick a person from list number one,'' she said, smiling.

The kids nodded wisely.

''These will be private. You won't be sharing them with the group. But we're going to collect them and return them at the end of the course. At that point, if the person you wrote to is still as important to you, we'll urge you to give the letter to him or her.''

They stayed in their groups to write.

Hunkering over his paper, Kurt forced himself not

to look at Zoe. Every bone in his body yearned to know who she was writing to. Cassie? Ransom? Him?

He began his own letter, which he had no intention of turning in: *Dear Zoe...*

CHAPTER SEVEN

JERRY BOSCO had squeezed himself into a student desk in the back of Zoe's room and was watching her like Big Brother. He'd shown up Monday afternoon unannounced, no doubt to catch her either unprepared or perhaps doing something unacceptable; he'd completely ignored her suggestion that today might not be the best day to observe the curriculum.

Typical of the Monday after their Down to Earth weekend, the kids were buzzing excitedly. They ignored Bosco's presence, which might not be good, as they retold stories and highlighted memorable events.

On the blackboard, Zoe had written, ''Down to Earth,'' with ''Most Valuable'' and ''Least Valuable'' columns underneath. She smiled at the class. ''Hi, guys. Long time no see.''

They laughed and settled into the semicircle of desks or into the beanbag chairs. Some kids even sprawled on the carpeted floor. The casual seating arrangement would clearly be strike one in Bosco's playbook.

''Who'd like to write?'' she asked.

''I will.'' Madison Kendrick surprised Zoe. It was the first time the shy girl had volunteered for anything in class.

Score one for the good guys, Zoe thought. Here was tangible proof that her course was helping kids.

Dressed in clingy black slacks and a black tank top,

her hair pulled severely off her face, Maddie picked up the chalk and faced the class. The kids knew the drill. Zoe would elicit responses, and the volunteer would record them.

"Let's start with the positive. What was the most valuable thing to you about the weekend?"

"Seeing you take five tries to get do the log mount," Rob teased her from his desk, where he lazed in typical teenage-boy fashion, half in, half out.

"Five?" She feigned indignation. "It was only three. Four at the most."

From the corner of her eye she saw Bosco frown and write furiously on his yellow pad. When he'd taught at Bayview High, his classes were a series of formal lectures during which the kids claimed they often fell asleep. She didn't think he'd know anything about establishing a positive atmosphere with students.

"I thought it was cool when Dr. Lansing got chocolate all over his face." This from Erica, who giggled loudly. She'd been unusually talkative lately.

Zoe tried hard not to remember how "cool" Dr. Lansing had looked and what a good sport he'd been. She'd thought about him all night after they'd gotten back yesterday and a lot today, though she struggled against it. For the first time since he'd dumped her for Elizabeth, she was truly angry. Watching his success with the kids this past weekend, she couldn't help thinking that the two of them should have been together, doing things like Down to Earth as a couple.

She tried to listen with interest as the students threw out other funny or embarrassing incidents: Evan losing his sneaker in the "crawl-through" and the kids playing keep-away with the big jock; Vivian getting doused with cold water in the shower before they realized it wasn't working properly; Shondra's general klutziness, which she acknowledged with good humor.

Madison wrote nothing and just rolled her eyes.

Bosco checked his watch. No doubt he thought she was wasting time. The guy just didn't have a clue.

"All right," she said easily, "let's get serious. The most valuable things—for real."

"The way we helped each other Saturday during the physical activities," Shondra said. "I couldn't've done it without everybody."

"How we mastered things we were sure we couldn't do," Erica put in. "I didn't know I had it in me to do that pulley thing."

"I liked the written exercises best," Dan said. "They made me articulate what I was feeling."

"Hey, Caruso, where'd you learn that fifty-dollar word?" Vivian teased. Yet there was something underneath—some genuine sarcasm. Zoe made a mental note to watch her.

"I thought having Dr. Lansing and the rest of the supervisors along was the best." This from Rachel.

The others shouted a chorus of agreement. Zoe turned away, ostensibly to check the board, hoping they wouldn't extend this line of thinking.

"Wow, Maddie, I didn't know you could do that," Zoe told the girl. Madison had scripted the list in calligraphy. "It's lovely."

She gave Zoe a pained look that clearly said, *There's a lot about me nobody knows.*

"That's another thing," Rachel added. "We never knew Maddie could write like that before she took notes for our group this weekend. We all let other people see things about us that we kept to ourselves before."

"I got a 'least valuable,'" Shelley Marco said. "Seeing Dr. Lansing dangle from the safety harness. I thought I was gonna sh—" the girl blushed "—die when he fell."

Bosco sat up straighter. Here was something concrete he could grasp on to. No doubt he was scrawling "physical risk" in big letters on his pad.

"Dr. Lansing was perfectly fine, wasn't he?" Zoe asked. Feeling like the worst hypocrite—she'd never forget how she'd panicked when Kurt fell—she needed to clarify this point. She stared right back at Bosco. "These kinds of glitches happen. No one was hurt."

"Yeah, and he was so cool," Rachel added. "He never yelled or swore or anything."

"Grace under pressure," Julia called out. "Right, Ms. Caufield?"

"Right," she said. "Now let's finish debriefing. We've got a writing assignment to go along with this."

The kids groaned and Bosco's eyes narrowed on them. It was going to be a long afternoon.

"DAN?" VIVIAN STARED UP at him from eyes laden with heavy liner. "You coming?"

Julia and Dan stood in the hall outside Ms. Caufield's classroom after school when Vivian approached them.

"Yeah, Viv," he said. "In a sec."

"Ms. Lansing won't like it if you're late for our meeting. You know she usually leaves at noon. She stayed just for this."

"The room's right there," he said, pointing to the door connecting Caufield's and Lansing's rooms. "I won't be late."

Julia frowned. "What's that all about?" she asked as the other girl stomped away.

"Dunno." Dan shrugged. "What'd you wanna talk about?"

Suddenly Julia felt shy. They'd gotten close this weekend, or so she thought. Now he was treating her as if they were Jets and Sharks. "Um, I was just wondering... You were worried about your brother all weekend, and I..."

He smiled and Julia blushed furiously. He *knew*. He knew this was just an excuse to talk to him, to be with him for a few minutes before she went to work.

So she found a role she could play. Haughty sophisticate, like Katherine Hepburn putting Spencer Tracy in his place. "Never mind. Sorry I was concerned." Shoulders back, head up, she started to walk away.

Dan grabbed her from behind and pulled her around to face him. His chocolate-colored eyes warmed to the color of hot fudge. "Look, if you wanna be with me, you don't need an excuse."

An arched eyebrow. A curl of the lip. "Who says I want to be with you, Caruso?"

He straightened. He was usually slouched over in his seat or against the wall like a reincarnation of James Dean, so she was always surprised he was so tall. "*I* say," he told her, tightening his grip. "*This* says," he added, stepping closer. And then he took her mouth in a deep sexy kiss.

"Oh, for heaven's sake, Ms. Caufield. Can't you get these kids to control their hormones?"

Julia sprang back from Dan. The remark came from Bosco, and Julia saw Ms. C's gaze narrow on the man.

"Sorry, Ms. C," Dan said quickly, though he shot

Julia a look that said he was anything but sorry. "We know not to do this here."

Ms. C smiled at Dan gratefully. The message to Bosco—that their teacher had taught them decorum—was clear. Julia, actress extraordinaire, was tongue-tied and couldn't get a word of defense out.

Well, damn, she thought as Dan walked away and the two adults left. What the hell had happened here?

ERICA STROLLED into the clinic at four o'clock, whistling. She'd completed her physics homework before she left school, so after she finished volunteering, she could spend all night on her English paper. She felt like a million bucks, and it had only taken one Bennie to give her the energy she needed. So far she'd kept her usage to a minimum, having researched on the Net the negative effects. She only had a few minor ones—dry mouth, an itchy scalp, some dizziness. And she hadn't been sleeping well. Long-term effects could be severe—she could do without increased blood pressure, hallucinations and fidgetiness. But she had things under control. Any more side effects and she'd stop.

Mostly she was concerned about getting the damn pills.

Thoughtful, she headed to Dr. Lansing's office. There was a little problem with that...

I'm uppin' the price, Carl Pike had told her.

Why? They're exorbitant as it is.

Your daddy can afford it, he'd said.

Squelching the sinking feeling in her stomach, she knocked on the open door to Lansing's office.

He glanced up from his desk, and the genuine smile he gave her made her heart hurt. Dr. Lansing's daughter was a lucky girl. Erica wished her father would look at her like that just once—as if he was glad to see her, as if she didn't have to do anything to earn his love.

"Have a good day?" Dr. Lansing asked, eying her carefully.

"Yep."

He stared at her a long time, as if assessing her mood. "I'm surprised. Sometimes reentry's hard."

"Reentry?"

"Coming back from a weekend of intense camaraderie can be difficult."

She smiled. "It was, sort of. I liked the debriefing in Life Issues class today, though."

His smile slipped. Damn, she didn't want to remind him about Ms. C. "Did the debriefing go well?" His voice had all the casualness of a bulldozer.

"It was fun, except for Bosco being there."

Dr. Lansing tossed his pen to the desk and leaned back in his chair. It had been a kick seeing him in jeans and sweats all weekend when he was usually dressed like this, in pressed suits and starched shirts. "Oh, no, was this the day he came to observe?"

"Yep."

"Poor Zoe."

"She was cool. She always is."

He sighed. "Good."

Actually she wasn't always cool. Erica remembered the time Ms. C had found out that Caufield's Chicks had been to a bar in the city...

"Well, this makes me feel terrific." There'd been sarcasm in Ms. Caufield's voice, which was a rarity.

"What do you mean?" Erica had asked.

"What good have all my drug-and-alcohol-use lessons done if my best kids go out and do this?" She'd shaken her head. "I feel like a failure."

"It isn't your fault."

"And, anyway, you're underage. Think of what might happen if you were caught."

"We weren't driving," Shondra had said defensively.

"It's still illegal. All those fancy schools you ladies applied to would love something like this on your record."

They'd said nothing. Ms. C had stormed out of the room then, saying, "I'm very disappointed in all of you…"

The Chicks still drank, but not as much, and mostly at Erica's house.

"Erica? Are you all right?"

"Huh?"

He was leaning over his desk. "You zoned out." Again his gaze narrowed. Jeez, he was a doctor. Could he tell she'd been taking Bennies? She usually tried to take them when he and Ms. C weren't around, but today she'd needed one, and she didn't think there were any visible symptoms of her use, anyway. *Distract him,* she told herself. "I was thinking about Ms. C and how neat she is, that's all."

Her answer seemed to satisfy him. He cleared his throat and fished some papers out of his in-box. "Here's the drug order for last week. They came in this morning and Diane Diaz is going to unpack them today. I'd like you to help her check them against the order forms."

She could hear the thump-thump of her heart pounding in her chest. "I get to handle drugs?"

"Ah, no, we're not quite that liberal here. The drugs are Diane's responsibility, but you can help her inventory them."

"Oh."

"It's nothing personal, Erica. Bosco's on the town council, too. He'd love to see us allow students to handle drugs. Then he'd have a reason to close us down."

"So why do I even do this?"

"You should have some experience with ordering controlled substances." He smiled. "Besides, it's a tedious job that has to be done."

"And I'm a peon."

Apparently he caught her teasing tone. "You got it, girl." She never would have joked with him before the weekend. Nor he with her. It made her heart swell and scared her at the same time. She didn't want to like him.

"Then I'll go don my serf's dress and get to work."

Lansing laughed. She was halfway out the door when he said, "Erica?"

She pivoted. "Uh-huh?"

"I enjoyed getting to know you better this weekend."

Her throat tight, she said, "Me, too."

He looked as if she'd given him a gift. "Thanks." He coughed nervously again. "Now go make sure my drugs are in order."

When she got out to the hall, she glanced down at the sheet. Her heart stopped.

At the top of the list, under A, was amphetamines.

SHONDRA SIGHED HEAVILY Tuesday night as she cleaned the coffeepot in the waiting area of the clinic.

"Crummy job, huh?" she heard from behind her. Turning, she found John Battaglia in the entryway. He'd just come from outside, and his jet-black hair was wind-whipped, his dark eyes smiling. Damned if he didn't look like a tall Andy Garcia.

"No, it's not that." She smiled back. "What are you doing here? You don't work tonight."

"I came to Bayview to see Alexandra's preschool play, and while I was in town, I thought I'd pick up a book I left here."

Reaching into a cupboard, she drew out a heavy text. "Endocrinology." She rolled her eyes. "Even the books in med school are weighty."

He took it from her. "You'll know soon enough. Heard from Harvard yet?"

"December fifteenth is early-decision notification."

"You don't look happy about that." He cocked his head. "What's wrong? You were sighing like an old lady when I came in."

"Parent problems. Immature stuff to you, probably."

His face sobered. "No way. My life was on a fast track to nowhere because of my 'rents." He smiled, but it was not a happy look. "If it hadn't been for Cassie, I'd be lying in a gutter somewhere now."

"What happened with your parents?"

John dropped onto a vinyl chair and stretched his long legs out in front of him. As always he wore black jeans, tonight with a gray T-shirt under his battered bomber jacket. "My dad died when I was ten. He was a Vietnam vet and was...not a good father. My mother was ineffective, to say the least." His face darkened. God, he was cute, even when he was sad. "If it hadn't been for Cassie, then Mitch—" here he smiled brilliantly "—I'd never be where I am today." He shuddered. "Sometimes I still have nightmares about it."

"That's a nice story about Ms. Lansing and her husband."

"So, you neglected, too?"

She rolled her eyes. "Just the opposite. My mother's on my back all the time about my grades, how I act...*everything*." She shook her head. "She says I have to set an example...you know, because I'm black."

"No kidding?"

She laughed at his reaction; most people shied away from talk about race. "And she won't let me do anything that interferes with schoolwork. She told me I couldn't go to Down to Earth this weekend, but I went anyway."

"She get pissed off?"

"Big time." Shondra scowled. "You know, I never defied her before. It was like she didn't know what to do when I said I was going—so she ended up signing the permission form in a state of shock. Now she's not talking to me, though."

"Was it worth it?"

"Yep. We had a blast."

"I heard Kurt almost fell. Cassie got really upset when she was telling me about it."

"He was so cool...so blasé about it."

"I'll bet Zoe almost freaked when she saw it."

Shondra scowled. "They're not dating anymore."

Johnny stood. "Yeah, I know. Well, I gotta split. I still need to do a couple of hours of studying tonight." He watched her. "Want some advice?"

"Uh-huh?"

"Work it out with your ma. Mine's in Florida now, living with her sister. She drove me nuts in high school, but I miss her."

"Thanks. I'll try."

"Oh, and Shondra?"

"Yeah?"

He nodded to Kurt's office. "Go easy on the doctor. He's a great guy. Relationships, you know, between men and women—they're funny. Full of ups and downs. People hurt each other all the time, and it's nobody's fault."

"You speaking from experience, Romeo?"

"Me? Nah. I'm too busy with school." He winked at her and headed out the door.

She sighed heavily again, staring after him. Only this time, it had nothing to do with her mother.

ASHLEY GRABBED the colorful brochure from the stacks in Dr. Johnson's office reception area and ducked into the hallway. She'd waited until almost everyone was gone. Leaning up against the wall, she put on her glasses and read the front of the leaflet—"All about Abortion." She hadn't been able to do what Evan wanted, and last night he'd literally screamed at her to get her ass in gear.

Swallowing the bile in her throat, she promised herself again, as she had in the middle of the night, to deal with this pregnancy thing first, then to make a decision about her relationship with Evan.

He wasn't the man she thought he was.

Slowly she opened the brochure. Her eyes devoured the print until she came upon what she wanted. "NY State law requires no parental notification/approval of abortion for minors."

She could do it, and no one would be the wiser.

Except God. And yourself.

For a moment she leaned her forehead against the

wall and moaned. It was cool against her cheek. Oh, Lord, how had she gotten into this?

"Ashley? Is that you?"

She stuffed the brochure into her pocketbook and looked up into Dr. Lansing's face. "Um, yeah."

"What are you doing here? It's late." He came closer. "Are you all right?"

Suddenly it was all too much. The secrecy. The shame. The fact that she hated what she was going to do. She opened her mouth to speak when her stomach lurched. Oh, no, not again.

She dropped her purse and bolted for the bathroom. The door slammed shut and she made it to the toilet just in time.

She was violently ill.

Wishing Dr. Lansing would just disappear, she washed out her mouth, threw water on her face and headed out to find her purse.

He was holding it in one hand. In the other hand was the brochure. His eyes were kind as he asked, "How far along are you, Ashley?"

KURT PULLED some tissues out of the box on the low table in front of his couch and handed them to the girl next to him. Her emotional distress was heart-wrenching.

"Cry it out, Ashley," he'd said as he helped her to his office. So far she'd done nothing but; it wasn't easy to watch, but he knew such a catharsis was the best antidote to her despair.

"I'm sorry. It's just that nobody else…I don't have anybody…just Rachel, and she's so mad at Evan…"

Sympathetically Kurt nodded.

When Ashley quieted she told him, "I'm two months pregnant."

He glanced at her purse. "And you're considering an abortion."

"Evan says I have no choice."

Ah, the plot thickens. "And what do you think?"

"Ms. Caufield says there's always a choice."

"You probably know that's true."

The girl slapped her hands on her pink jeans. She looked ludicrously young in them and the matching blouse she wore. "I'm so confused. I don't know what to do."

"Then you should take your time in deciding."

"Evan says I gotta do it soon, before it's too late."

Be neutral. "An early abortion is safer than one in the second trimester."

"I just never expected him to be so *mad,* you know, like it's my fault. Like *I* did something wrong."

"That should tell you something about him, Ashley."

"I don't like to think about that."

"Denial won't make it any different."

"You don't understand."

"Then tell me."

"Evan's the first real boyfriend I've ever had. He's the only..." She broke off, flushing furiously.

"The only boy you've ever been with." *The bastard.* Though he'd learned long ago to remain objective, Kurt allowed himself to feel anger at the irresponsible boy.

"I'll deal with our relationship afterward. First I gotta deal with *this.*"

"Aren't they related?"

"How?"

"If you decide to have the baby, you should consider the state of your relationship with its father."

The phone rang and Kurt ignored it. Elizabeth had called earlier and sounded as if she'd been drinking, so he didn't want to talk to her, especially in front of Ashley.

"You can answer that."

"No, it's my private line. I'll get it later." He glanced at the clock behind her as he heard a woman's voice on the machine.

Ashley lay her head back against the couch and said, "Do you think it's a sin?"

"What?"

"Abortion."

"As a doctor, I think it's a right all women should have. As a man, I think I might feel differently if it was my child…" He gave her a small smile. "How about you? Why don't you tell me your beliefs, and we'll see if that helps you figure this all out."

"Okay." She checked the clock. "I was supposed to call Evan for a ride."

"We won't worry about Evan now."

"Why are you being so nice to me?" she asked. "I've been rotten to you."

Again he smiled. The child in all these kids peeped out regularly. "I like you, Ashley, and I'm here to help. Let's put the past behind us."

And so the girl talked, about her values, about her beliefs, about her hopes and plans. Where appropriate, he made comments and answered direct questions, but he tried just to let her articulate her thoughts.

An hour later he stood in front of Zoe's condominium door, Ashley by his side.

"She'll be disappointed in me." In the dim light of the porch, he could see Ashley's eyes tear up.

"No, she'll help you sort this out." As he smiled down at the girl, he said, "You need adult guidance in your life now, Ashley. We're here to give it to you." During their talk, he'd advised her more than once to tell her parents, but she absolutely refused.

The door opened.

Zoe stood before them in jeans and a plain white cotton top. Over which she'd thrown a flannel shirt he recognized. It was one of his that he must have left here last year. Seeing it on her stunned him for a minute. Finally, he found his voice.

"Sorry to bother you so late, but I think this is something you'll want to deal with tonight."

Zoe transferred her gaze to Ashley. "Are you all right, honey?"

The young girl threw herself in Zoe's arms, sobbing. "No."

Zoe stared at Kurt over Ashley's head with questions in her eyes.

"She needs to talk to you." He reached out and squeezed Ashley's shoulder. "Take care," he said.

The girl turned. Still holding on to Zoe, she grabbed Kurt's hand. "Thanks, Dr. Lansing."

"We're here for you, Ashley. Don't ever forget it."

He heard the door close as he hustled down the sidewalk. He tried to ignore the fact that he never thought he'd be at Zoe's place again, never thought his life would entwine with hers like this.

Being at her house was hard, though, harder than he thought.

He stopped at his car and turned to face the condo

on the bay. What the hell had she been doing, wearing his shirt?

AT MIDNIGHT Zoe rang Kurt's doorbell. She'd just dropped Ashley off at home, and the Lansings' old condo was only a few blocks from the Emersons, so she'd driven here.

Poor excuse, girl.

Damn it, she was tired. And upset. Right now she wanted to shake Ashley for being so stupid. And she wanted to wring Evan Michaels's neck. Since she could do neither, she gave in to the urge to see Kurt, to talk to him, to let him help her deal with this, just as he'd helped her sort out so many problems in the past.

She rang again. The lights were on, so...

The door opened and Zoe's mouth went dry. Kurt stood before her in his glasses, forest-green sweatpants and nothing else. He looked so sexy, so male, she told herself to turn and run for her life.

But she had few emotional reserves left. She looked around at the porch. "I'm upset. I need to talk. Since you know about Ashley..." She shrugged. "Can I come in?"

"Of course." He stepped aside. "I was just reading in bed. Come on into the den." He led the way to the back of the house. Zoe had spent countless hours here with the Lansings, and the familiar surroundings made her feel safe. Comfortable.

The fact that Mitch and Cassie had left their leather couch and chair put her even more at ease. "Cassie didn't want this furniture?" she asked inanely.

"No, not yet. They're going to take it once they've finished their basement."

"Did you bring any of your own things?"

His eyebrow arched at her query. She'd avoided any personal talk for weeks. "Yeah, sure. My living-room furniture and kitchen set." He cleared his throat. "My bed."

Zoe nodded.

He sank onto one end of the couch. "You didn't come here to talk about decorating, Zoe. Sit."

She gave him a once-over. "Could you put on a shirt?"

Looking surprised, he stood and shrugged into the flannel shirt he'd thrown on the couch. "That better?"

She nodded, thinking of the shirt she'd had on when he came to the door. After her workout and shower, in a moment of weakness, she'd donned it. She'd also been looking at the photo album he'd given her of the trip they'd taken to the Bahamas. She didn't often allow herself to wallow in her self-pity over what she'd lost, but she'd been weepy tonight, about him. Her only hope was that he hadn't noticed the shirt.

"I wanted to thank you for helping Ashley."

"Is that why you came?"

"Partly. The other part is I'm furious about this whole thing, and I need to talk about it. Nobody else knows, and I can't betray a confidence, so…"

"You came to me." He smiled. "It's okay. I'm glad you're here." She stared at him. The darkness outside was broken by a sliver of moon, which sneaked in through the blinds. The room itself was dimly lit by two sconces in the corners. "How is she?"

"Better, now that she cried it out. She said you were wonderful."

"I did what I could for her. What will she do, do you think?"

"I don't know." Zoe sighed heavily, toed off her

shoes and curled her legs under her. "I don't know how to advise her."

He stared off out the window. "I don't know what I'd want Lauren to do if she was in this situation."

"How is Lauren?"

"Good. I saw her last week for dinner. I drove up to Binghamton." When Zoe didn't comment, he added, "She asked about you."

"She's a nice kid." Zoe felt her insides tighten. When she was dating Kurt, she and the girl had shared some fun shopping trips.

"Evan Michaels is not pulling his weight here, is he?" Kurt said.

"No. I'd like to kick his butt for it, too."

"Guys do stupid things, Zoe, especially when they're under pressure." He looked at her sadly. "I should know…"

"Is that how you rationalize what you did to me?" She didn't know why she'd responded this way. The look on his face…the photo album…the shirt…a guy you couldn't count on…

"No, I never rationalized it." His voice was hoarse. "I was simply wrong."

Closing her eyes, she threw her head back for a moment. "I couldn't believe it, you know? I just couldn't believe you'd do that to me."

He said only, "I'm sorry."

"I was in love with you."

A muscle leaped in his jaw. He waited a long time before he said, "I loved you, too."

That drove her from her seat. "Don't tell me that! Don't you *dare* tell me that now. You don't hurt someone you love like you hurt me." She stalked to the window.

He rose and followed her. "I was going to tell you that night," he said achingly. "I was going to ask you to marry me."

A ball of pain formed inside Zoe. She turned and stared at him, allowing the feeling to surface, ignoring the rapid rise and fall of his chest. "How can you say that? If you'd loved me, you wouldn't have torn my life apart. If you'd wanted to marry me, you could never have gone back to Elizabeth."

His eyes darkened with pain. "I made a mistake."

"Stop saying that. It's as if you think that makes it all right."

He grasped her upper arms, and his hands clenched on her as if he was trying to control himself. "No, no sweetheart, it doesn't. I know what I did was unforgivable. So I'm not making excuses for myself."

His candor took the wind out of her sails. She went limp and stepped back. "It doesn't matter."

"Doesn't it?" His hands fisted at his sides. "Then why are you here?"

"To talk about Ashley."

His expression was skeptical. "All right, then why did you almost faint when I was dangling on that harness last weekend? You were terrified for me. You still care about me."

"Stop this. You're fighting dirty."

"You've given me reason to hope."

"No, I haven't."

She saw the temper flare in his eyes. "Yeah? Then why did you have my shirt on tonight?"

Her face flamed. She just looked at him. *Oh, God, was he right? Was she giving him reason to pursue her again? Did she want that?*

They squared off like enemies, staring at each other.
And then he reached for her.

A VOLCANO OF EMOTION, long dormant, erupted out of
Kurt at the first touch of his lips on hers; it had been
so long. Blood pumped like hot lava through his veins,
scorching him from the inside.

He took her mouth, consumed her.

Just as ravenous, she devoured him. He felt her nails
dig into his back. The beast inside had claimed her,
too.

Eyes closed, he covered her mouth with his; reaching
for the hem of her sweater, he dragged it up, then released her long enough to yank it over her head, un-
hook her bra, toss it aside and finally tear off his own
shirt.

Somewhere in the back of his mind, he knew she
wouldn't do this if she was sane, if she gave it any
thought, but he was too desperate to care. So he did
his best to keep her crazy. His hands gripped her bottom, lifted her up and toward him for another full kiss.
Letting her mouth go, he buried his face in her breasts.
She cried out and hung on.

With her, he stumbled to the couch and set her on
her feet. She fumbled at his sweatpants, pushed them
down. He tore at her jeans. When they were finally
naked, he pressed her down to the couch and covered
her. She moaned. His heart beat so fast he thought it
might explode.

Passion clouded her eyes, and Kurt knew it matched
what was in his. *I don't care, I don't care. I just want
her.*

She tasted his jaw, his throat, sucked there, took little
bites. Neither spoke; grunts, groans and long deep

moans created a sexual chorus of accompaniment to their fevered touches. He rose on his elbows, then reached down to part her legs. She opened up to him.

Without thought, he thrust inside her. She was hot and tight and wet for him. Tears burned behind his eyelids with the knowledge that he'd willingly given this up. Because of it, he thrust hard and long and more forcefully than ever before.

It only took seconds for Zoe to spiral, then shatter. Seconds more, and he, too, climaxed. It was earthshaking and tumultuous; she didn't come back to reality for a long time. All she could think of when she did, as he collapsed on her, was that she'd had him again. Finally.

Sanity returned in degrees. He eased her to the inside of the couch and rolled onto his side. She whimpered when he withdrew and she curled into him. When she shivered, he dragged the plaid blanket from the back of the couch and covered them both.

Snuggling under it, she forced her mind to go blank. She didn't want to think about what she'd just done and how cataclysmic it had been. In a few minutes she would. Not yet.

He seemed content to simply lie there with her, brushing his hand up and down her bare back, occasionally kissing her head. Finally he said, "What are we going to do, love?"

His question brought back the ghosts. He'd touched her like a man in love tonight, but he'd done the same thing the weekend before he'd gone to bed with his ex-wife. Suddenly images of him and Elizabeth were superimposed over what she and Kurt had just shared. She tried to banish them, but she couldn't. He must have felt her stiffen.

"Zoe?"

"I can't forget about it."

For a moment he didn't say anything. "Would you be willing to try?"

She drew back. "No, I don't think so." Sitting up, she reached for her shirt. "I'm afraid, Kurt, and I don't trust you."

"I know." He grasped her arm and she looked at him. His hair was deliciously disheveled and his face high with color. "I lo—"

She clapped her hand over his mouth. "Don't say it. I don't want to hear it right now." She stood and finished dressing. "I think we should forget this happened."

"No."

"It's my choice, Kurt. You gave up all rights to make decisions in this relationship when you slept with Elizabeth."

Pain deepened his green eyes. "So you keep reminding me."

Finding her shoes, she said throatily, "I'm going. Let's not talk about this again."

In minutes she was at the door and out of his house. She breathed in the night air and with renewed determination battled back the tears.

CHAPTER EIGHT

Abortion. Gay/lesbian support groups. Condoms. Counseling about safe sex in middle school. Parents, beware. Thanks to a new local establishment, these are the things your children can get without your even knowing about it. It's no secret that I opposed the Bayview Heights Clinic for young adults.

KURT FINISHED READING the neatly typed, single-spaced letter, then looked up at Lacey Taylor, who sat across from him in his office. "When did you get this?"

"Today. We have to run it in the *Herald,* Kurt. I'm sorry. Bosco's on the town council—"

"Damn. It's not only inflammatory, but inaccurate. We don't perform abortions."

"But Planned Parenthood does abortion counseling for minors, right?"

"Yes, of course. All over the country, Lace."

Her pretty blue eyes smiled sympathetically. "Hey, you don't have to convince me. I think kids should have all the help they can get. I wish there'd been more places like your clinic when Kevin was in high school."

Kurt nodded in understanding. Lacey's brother had died in prison three years ago. Kurt didn't have to be

a doctor to know there was no cure for that kind of
loss. "You must miss him."

"Yes. I do. But his memory is one of the things that
makes me support the clinic."

"Thanks." He knuckled the paper in front of him.
"What can I do about this?"

"Write a rebuttal. We'll print it along with the letter."

"Bosco will love that."

"We do it all the time, to be fair." She smiled, her
blue eyes earnest. "The *Herald* wasn't always fair,
Kurt. Making it unbiased was one of my goals when I
took over."

"You're referring to the articles your grandfather
wrote against the high school." Kurt had heard the
story from Mitch. After he became friends with the
Taylors, they'd talked about it openly.

"Yes. Grandpa admits he wasn't being fair to Seth,
and now he supports my editorial position fully."

"Philip's turnaround was amazing, wasn't it?"

"People change." Lacey focused on him. "And they
can forgive each other."

Did Lacey think Zoe could forgive Kurt? He
couldn't ask, couldn't even think about last night.
"*Sometimes* people forgive each other." His gaze
dropped to the letter. "I'll write a response tonight."
Glancing at the clock, he asked, "Want me to drop it
off at your house later?"

"That would be great." She checked the clock, too.
"I'm meeting Zoe and Cassie for pizza in an hour. But
Seth will be home with the boys."

"Then I'll stop by."

"Go inside. Josh asks for you all the time." She
grinned. "You're his hero, after the appendix thing."

"It's nice to be liked."

"What's wrong?" Lacey asked softly. "Is it Zoe?"

He started to deny it. But Lacey was a friend and he cared about her, didn't want to be dishonest with her. "Yes."

"It must be hard working with her."

You don't know the half of it. "It is." He could still see her face when she'd recovered enough from their lovemaking to remember what was between them.

Lacey waited a minute. "Can I ask you a question?"

"Of course."

"Would you get back with her if you could, Kurt?"

"In a heartbeat." He scowled. "I know you and Cass would hate that. I don't blame you."

"No, I wouldn't hate it. But I *am* worried about Zoe. She was overwrought last year when you split up."

He remembered Cassie's indictment. *She cried for days. She missed school. You know what a Pollyanna she's always been. But she was depressed for a long time, and so sad it broke my heart.*

"It's not going to happen, anyway, Lace. She's made that clear."

Lacey stood. Surprising him, she circled the desk, leaned over and gave him big hug. "I'm sorry. I wish I could help."

He let himself take comfort in Zoe's words. "You're helping a lot with the clinic." He indicated the letter. "I'll get right on this."

With a squeeze of his hand, Lacey turned and left. Kurt sat in the shadowy early-evening light and watched her go. She and Seth had had a devil of a time getting together. Just like Mitch and Cassie. He shook his head. Maybe...

Don't think about it.

He didn't, at least while he was writing the rebuttal. But when he finished, inactivity gave way to uncontrolled thoughts. And now he had more recent memories—vivid and in 3-D—with which to torture himself.

Weary, he got up and, on his way to the couch, remembered he should lock his private-entrance door. Security in clinics these days was crucial, especially at night, because of the drugs they housed. Once he was safe and sound, he crossed to the sofa and stretched out. He hadn't been sleeping again. For a while his insomnia had abated. Now, since Down to Earth, he was mired in the vicious cycle of watching the red numbers flip over on the digital clock. He was more exhausted than he'd been in the days of his internship and residency.

He rubbed his eyes tiredly. Had he been wrong to make love to Zoe? His fingers flexed. How could anything so wonderful be wrong? She'd felt like silk and tasted like honey under his hands and mouth. Her scent—sexy and womanly—had lingered with him for hours. Her response had been unbridled. She'd been as frantic, as desperate, as he. If nothing else, those few fleeting moments on his couch had shown him she still cared. She still loved him.

It was the aftermath that haunted his waking hours...

I can't forget about it...I'm afraid...I don't trust you...you gave up all rights to make decisions in this relationship when you slept with Elizabeth...

He sighed and opened his eyes in the dim office. A tree limb beat a soft pat-pat on the building, creating an ominous accompaniment to his thoughts. Frustrated beyond measure at the turn of events, he rolled off the couch.

And as he'd done all week, he went to work.

He might not be able to salvage his relationship with Zoe, but he'd be damned if he'd let anybody sabotage his clinic.

It's all you have, buddy.

"YOU LOOK AS BAD as Kurt," Lacey told Zoe, who sat across from her and Cassie at their favorite place, the Spaghetti Warehouse.

Her mouth full of pizza, Cassie scowled. After she swallowed, she asked, "What's wrong with Kurt? Is he sick?"

Lacey shook her head. "No, he just hasn't been sleeping."

"Problems at the clinic?"

Silently Zoe listened as Lacey told them about Bosco's letter.

"How did Bosco find out about all that?" Cassie asked.

"Kurt's advertising the clinic's services."

"What a jerk!" Cassie's words were vehement.

Lacey reached out and squeezed Cassie's hand. "Cass, Kurt's doing his best. The kids need to know what the clinic's about."

Sheepishly Cassie glanced at Zoe. "I didn't mean Kurt. I meant Bosco."

Zoe took a bite of pizza and chewed, gathering her scattered thoughts. Finally she suggested, "Can we change the subject? What time do you need me next weekend to watch the kids while you and Mitch go on your romantic getaway?"

"In a minute," Cassie said, surprising them. "I wanna say something about Kurt."

Please, God, not another onslaught. Zoe couldn't

handle listening to Cassie's list of grievances against him today. Not after last night.

"I think I was wrong about him." Cassie's face was somber. "I'm not sure you shouldn't give him another chance."

Zoe sputtered soda all over her plate and shirt. *"What?"*

"I've changed my mind about him."

Wiping up, Zoe asked, "What brought this on?"

"When he was living with us, we…talked. A lot. He got up with Camille several times during the night and gave her a bottle so I could sleep. Even when I got to her first, he was usually awake. We ended up sharing some things."

Oh, no, this was the last thing Zoe needed now. "Cass, I know you mean well, but I'm not letting him back into my life."

Hypocrite. He couldn't get more *into* her life than last night.

"He's sorry for what he did. He's changed." She shrugged. "He made a mistake."

Zoe felt anger rise inside her. "Cassie, this wasn't a matter of his not calling one night or forgetting my birthday. He left me for his ex-wife; he *slept* with her while he and I were still together, and he broke my heart. I won't give him a chance to hurt me again." She drew in a breath. "I won't risk it."

Cassie frowned.

"What's life without a little risk, honey?" Lacey asked.

"I can't believe this. Two months ago, I was telling both of you to ease up on him. Now he's a saint." She slid out of the booth. "I don't want to talk about it anymore. I'm going to the ladies' room. Change the

subject, and when I come back, let's enjoy our meal.''
She stomped away.

In the restroom, she threw water on her face and
watched her reflection in the mirror. The feel of Kurt's
muscles bunching under her hands, the image of him
driving into her with a passion she'd never known from
him, made her shiver right there in the small bathroom.

It was hard to regret that time on his couch. Hard to
wish it away. She'd never been happier in the past
fourteen months than she was for those few stolen moments in his arms.

Which didn't change a thing. It just made the whole
situation harder. Because one truth remained. She
couldn't trust Kurt Lansing.

MITCH DRAGGED OPEN his front door, a look of weary
exasperation on his face. His hair was askew and the
sleeve of his dress shirt sported some odd-looking
stain. Against one shoulder cuddled a tiny bundle of
pink, enthusiastically sucking her thumb. Clinging to
his dress-pant leg was a three-foot imp who immediately hurled herself at Kurt.

''Boy, am I glad to see you, buddy.'' Mitch gave
him a baleful look.

''Girls keeping you busy?'' Kurt asked.

''They behave for Cassie, but I don't stand a chance
with them.'' Mitch stepped aside. ''Come in. *Please*,
come in.''

With Alexandra in his arms, Kurt entered the foyer
laughing. ''All right.''

''What are you doing way out here? Not that I'm
complaining.''

''I had to drop something off at the Taylors'.'' He

focused on the baby. "Isn't it past Camille's bed-time?"

"Every time I put her down she screams."

"Mommy says Daddy's a cream puff," Alexandra mumbled into Kurt's shoulder. The little girl rubbed her eyes and yawned; she was ready for bed in her yellow footed pajamas, and she smelled like bubble bath. "She says he picks *her* up too much."

"Harrumph." He ruffled Alexandra's auburn hair, which was now down to her waist. "All those street punks would be shocked to hear that your daddy's such a pushover." They made their way into the great room, which was strewn with toys, blankets and other para-phernalia. Kurt asked Alexandra, "Did a tornado come through here?"

"Yep," Mitch answered, dropping into a rocker. "And its name starts with *A*."

"My name starts with *A*. Johnny taught me."

Kurt knew Alexandra thought Johnny hung the moon; Johnny, in turn, spoiled the little girl shame-lessly.

Mitch's smile was profound. "I know, sweetheart," he said. He looked at Kurt helplessly. "If Camille's up, Alexandra won't go to sleep."

"Camille's not up." He nodded at the now-sleeping infant.

Alexandra studied Mitch and Camille, reminding Kurt of Cassie's intense scrutiny. "But she's not in bed," the toddler said matter-of-factly. Oh, Lord, Mitch had his work cut out for him with this one.

Kurt sank onto the couch, Alexandra on his lap. "But she *is* asleep. Want me to put you to bed, honey?" he asked her.

"Daddy promised me a story." Her blue-gray gaze narrowed on her father. "I want *him*."

"After Camille's bottle," Mitch said tiredly.

"I'll feed Camille," Kurt offered. "Get me her bottle and you take this one upstairs."

"You're a lifesaver, bro."

After a hug from Alexandra, Kurt settled in the rocker with Camille and the bottle. She'd awakened to eat and was staring at him with big eyes the color of Mitch's. And of his.

She sucked vigorously and patted the bottle with chubby little hands. "There you go, darlin'," he crooned softly. He smoothed back the tuft of dark hair curling on her head. "You're gonna be a beauty, you know that?"

She smiled around the nipple and Kurt's heart turned over. He loved these kids. Hell, he loved kids in general. He'd always wanted another child and had hoped he and Zoe—

He froze at the thought.

His heartbeat speeded up.

Baby…baby…*baby!* He stopped rocking. Camille fussed, and he automatically started to rock again. She quieted with the motion.

In sequence Kurt pictured the night before: they'd torn each other's clothes off, stumbled to the couch and made love there—without using any protection. Caught up in the emotional drama of the night, it hadn't once entered his mind that Zoe could have gotten pregnant. Could *be* pregnant.

He was still reeling with the possibility when Mitch came back down fifteen minutes later, but he tried not to show it. After all, it was only one time. Many people tried for years to conceive. What were the chances?

His brother stood in the doorway, watching him. "You know, when you guys had Lauren, I used to envy you so much I couldn't stand it."

"I never knew that."

Mitch crossed to them and smoothed a hand down Camille's hair. "I know. I never told you. Hell, I didn't admit it to myself until I met Cass." He surveyed the mess in the brand-new house and shook his head. "And now I have all this. Sometimes I can't believe it, you know?"

Despite his state of mind, Kurt smiled. "You deserve it." Easing the bottle from Camille's lips, he set it down, then cuddled her to his shoulder and rubbed her back. "You're a lucky guy."

"Don't I know it." Mitch gave the messy floor and the couch another sideways glance, then, as if deciding the litter was too much to handle, sat on the leather recliner and stretched out. "What about my baby brother? How's he doing?"

Holding Camille close, Kurt frowned. "I'm okay."

"You look like hell. I thought you were sleeping better."

"I was."

"It's Zoe, isn't it?"

He nodded. "Things keep throwing us together." *Especially last night.*

"Kismet."

"Think so?" He kissed Camille's head. "You told me to stay away from her."

"I don't like what this is doing to either one of you."

Kurt remembered Zoe's anger and bitter words last night. "She's finally angry at me."

"Well, maybe that's good." Mitch sighed. "You'll never get past this if she buries it."

Silence.

"Something else happen? Besides the Down to Earth weekend and the clinic stuff?"

Kurt shook his head. "No. Nothing I want to talk about, anyway."

"Maybe you should look for somebody new, Kurt." He nodded to Camille. "Have your own little bundle of joy."

Camille stirred and let out a shriek. "Oh, God, what's that?" Kurt rocked again and patted her back.

"It's the 'Banshee wail.' She does it from a sound sleep. Scared the life out of Cassie and me the first few times."

Laughing, Kurt stood up to walk her. Could Zoe possibly be pregnant with his own "little bundle of joy," who'd have her own Banshee wail? As the one in his arms screamed her head off, he wondered if he could ever be so lucky.

AT FOUR O' CLOCK on Friday afternoon, Zoe surreptitiously studied Kurt over the folder she was perusing. His dove-gray suit fit him better, but the signs of fatigue she hadn't seen in a while were back. And he looked sad.

Exactly how she felt. Making love had unearthed too many memories, which kept coming to the surface. "Julia's review is great," she said.

"She's a good kid. Louise says she's very perceptive and would make an excellent therapist."

"She wants to be the next Julia Roberts."

"Plans change." Kurt shrugged. From across the table, his green eyes bored into hers. "People change."

"Yes," Zoe said pointedly. "I'm well aware of that."

"Are we going to talk about it?"

"What?"

"The elephant in the room with us."

That made her smile, albeit reluctantly. "No, we're going to ignore it."

"I can't stop thinking about what happened between us."

"Don't." She picked up another folder. "How about Dan?"

With a sigh Kurt said, "The nursery kids love him. He's the best child-care worker I've ever had."

"I always liked that boy. You know he dropped out for a year. We got him to come back, and he's been our top At Risk student since Johnny." She smiled again. "I think there's something going on between him and Julia."

Kurt shook his head. "How do you keep up with them?"

Zoe said, "It's hard these days. The older you get, the more difficult teaching is."

"Well, you look pretty good for an old lady. Especially in that red Bayview Heights T-shirt." Today she wore it with denims and low-heeled boots.

Zoe focused more intently on the folder, ignoring the jolt of pleasure his words gave her.

"You looked especially good the other night."

Time to change the subject. "Have you noticed anything different about Erica?" she asked.

A pause. "She seems even more driven than she did a month ago. College pressure, you think?"

"I don't know. I'm going to try to spend more time with her." She sighed. "I've asked her if anything's wrong, and she says no. Still, I feel I'm missing some- thing.'' Zoe read the folder again. "Her work's good, this says.''

"It's super. I wish she'd go to Georgetown and then come back to run the clinic here.''

Zoe sighed nostalgically. "I'm going to miss these girls when they graduate.''

"You should have more in your life.''

"I won't talk to you about personal things, Kurt. I mean it.''

He didn't want to spook her—he knew she was run- ning scared, and this new possibility was going to push her into high gear. But it had to be said. "Well, you might just be forced to.''

"Why?''

God, she really hadn't thought about it. Reaching over, he covered her hand with his. Gently he said, "Sweetheart, we didn't use any protection Tuesday night.''

It took a moment for awareness to dawn. And just before the mask slipped into place, he caught a tiny fleck of hope in her expressive eyes. It gave him cour- age.

"That's ridiculous. It was only one time.'' When he just stared at her, she said, "You're making too much of this because you want it to be true.''

"Maybe I'm making so much of it because of what happened with Ashley.''

Her hand slid to her stomach. "No, it won't happen to us. People try for years to conceive.''

He shrugged. "Maybe. What part of your cycle were you in?''

Her face paled. Shakily she said, "The middle. Ex- actly.''

She closed her eyes, trying to block out the ramifications of his words, he guessed. Well, she was entitled. The possibility of her being pregnant, however remote, had had *him* up most of the night.

"Would it be so bad, Zoe?" he finally asked.

She looked at him as if he'd grown two heads. That hurt, especially since by this morning, he was thinking a pregnancy might be their way back together. Maybe fate had intervened.

"I don't believe—"

Her comment was interrupted by a deep male voice from the doorway. "Ah, there you are."

Zoe's head whipped around. Kurt followed her gaze.

In the entry stood a tall slim man whose hair was graying slightly at the temples; he wore what looked like a Saville Row suit and a delighted smile. And he was looking at Zoe as if she was tonight's dessert. Kurt didn't need the confirmation when she said, "Pierre? What— I can't believe you're here."

"I am, ma chère." His voice was low and sexy.

Kurt stiffened. He watched as Zoe stood, a huge smile on her face, and crossed the room—where Pierre enveloped her in an affectionate embrace.

It was in that instant that Kurt made a decision. He'd be damned if he let some slick Frenchman, or some young buck of a vice principal, have the woman he loved without a fight.

This was war!

Zoe glared at Jerry Bosco across the conference table in Seth's office. With him was the superintendent of schools, Joe Finn.

"It's ridiculous what that trip cost the district."

Bosco rapped his chubby knuckles on a pad in front of him. "For a fun weekend at camp?"

Seth had warned her to let him do the talking. "It's not just a fun weekend, Jerry. It's instructive—it teaches cooperation, self-esteem, working as a team and trust. We went over this when you came to see me last week."

"It's also dangerous. Last year a student broke her leg."

"Jerry," Finn said. "Two kids broke their legs in *gym* class last year."

"A man hung suspended from a harness for fifteen minutes." Bosco's eyes narrowed. "And the kids relished it like a scene from the latest horror movie."

They hadn't. Actually they'd been scared witless. Zoe shivered, thinking of Kurt, dangling in the air. She crossed her legs, smoothed her skirt and tried to stay calm.

"Dr. Lansing was perfectly fine." Seth's tone was admiringly patient. "Franz Hoffman says the safety harness functioned exactly as it should."

Bosco's face grew florid. "Well, I object to this field trip. And to these other activities—the outing at Northern Lights Park, the overnighter in the school gym."

"You've always objected to them, Jerry," Zoe finally said. She was tired of his bullying. "You were vocal about it when you were a teacher here." *And wrong!* she wanted to shout, but didn't.

"Yes, but now I can do something about it."

Zoe shook her head and turned to the superintendent for help.

Finn was angry. A muscle leaped in his jaw. "You can bring this up at the next executive session, Jerry, but I have to tell you that I won't let you use the board for a personal vendetta.''

"You should watch how you speak to a board member.''

Finn's eyes were cold. "I am.'' He stood. "Thanks, Zoe, Seth. We'll be in touch.''

When they were gone, Seth sank into the chair behind his desk. "He's an albatross, isn't he?''

"Yes.'' She shrugged. "With power now.''

"It'll work out.''

Nodding her head, she said, "Sure, things always do. You coming to volleyball tonight?''

"Yep. We're short because Mitch and Cassie won't be there. They're getting ready to leave for the weekend.'' He smiled. "Lacey's coming with me. I talked her into leaving the kids on a weeknight. You?''

"Uh-huh.''

Zoe said goodbye and left Seth's office, her mind a muddle. She was exhausted, what with Kurt's little bombshell of a suggestion—*Would it be so bad?*—and then Pierre showing up, and trying to deal with him all weekend.

Now this. She wondered what was next.

ZOE SAW HIM as soon as she and Pierre entered Hotshots. They were late and a game was already in progress. Kurt was on the court, giving a high five to Seth, after which Lacey hugged him. He looked good in his jock clothes, his hair messy, his color high.

"Shall I get you a drink, *ma chère?*''

Smiling up at Pierre, she said, "Just a club soda.''

"Are you—How do you say it?—on the buckboard?''

Zoe scowled. "Buckboard?''

"You have had nothing to drink all weekend."

"Oh, on the wagon." She laughed and kissed his cheek. "No, I'm just not drinking for a while." Though she knew rationally that the chances of conceiving were slim, not drinking was the one concession to the possibility she'd made. "I need to stay sharp for the game."

Giving her a smile, Pierre headed for the bar. As she neared the court, she watched Kurt straighten his arms and, with his hands clasped together, pop the ball into the air, to Alex this time; Alex slammed it over the net. They all cheered—and came off the court.

"Ah, there she is." Alex strode right to her and swooped her into a big hug. "Where's that Frenchman?" He made an exaggerated frown. "It's time to challenge him to a showdown."

"At the bar getting us a drink, cowboy."

Kurt's head came up. Zoe turned away, but not before Barb Sherman handed him a beer. Barb, who looked remarkably like Elizabeth, his ex-wife.

Alex made his way to the bar. Zoe took a seat at one of the tables. Bending over to get a tissue from her bag, she saw sneakered feet first, then muscular hairy legs, then a trim torso. Finally she looked into Kurt's face. "Hi. How are you tonight?" he asked.

"Fine."

Pierre joined them, precluding a response. She'd introduced the two Friday and, contrary to the congenial competition between Alex and Pierre, there was real animosity between Kurt and Pierre.

"Here you go, *ma chère*," Pierre said.

Kurt stiffened visibly. At the endearment?

"Nice to see you again, Lansing." Pierre's tone said it was anything but.

"Same here," Kurt lied.

"What are you doing here, Kurt?" she asked bluntly.

"Subbing for Mitch. He suggested it."

Seth joined them. "Hi, guys." He turned to Zoe. "Did you tell Kurt about Bosco's rant today?"

Zoe sighed and filled him in.

"Next game!" someone yelled. Putting down their drinks, the group headed to the court. Zoe was playing for the teachers.

As she stretched on the sidelines, Kurt came up to her. Nodding to the bar where Pierre sat, Kurt's whole demeanor changed. "Did he stay with you?"

"Kurt, please."

"Did he?"

"He stayed at my condo, yes. Now leave me alone." She was saved from his tenacity by the start of the game.

Zoe played enthusiastically but carefully. It was only sensible…if she was… No she wasn't…but if she was, she'd never forgive herself for acting carelessly.

"Heads up, Zoe!" someone called.

She turned and narrowly missed catching the ball on the chin. Damn that man!

Kurt watched her play from the corner of his eye. She was damn cute in her tan shorts and teacher shirt. He would have taken joy watching her if it hadn't been for Jean-Claude Van Damme sitting at the bar.

Who'd stayed with her this weekend.

Kurt tried to banish the thought during the second game, but it plagued him. What if she'd slept with Pierre? And what if she *was* pregnant? Would she think it was the Frenchman's? Would she even know? Damn it, why hadn't she considered all this? By the time the last point was called, he'd convinced himself he had a real issue. He needed to talk to her now.

When she headed toward the ladies' room, he seized the chance. Following her, he lay in wait outside the door. "I want to talk to you," he said implacably when she came out.

She sighed. "Why?"

"We've got to get something straight." He grasped her arm and dragged her down the aisle of tables to a small alcove that held the telephones and some bench seating. Inside, he faced her squarely. "I want to know if you slept with Pierre."

Zoe's huge brown eyes widened. "Where do you get off asking me that?"

His temper rose. "Though you don't want to consider the possibility, what if there *is* a baby, Zoe? And you sleep with someone else. How will you even know…" He broke off, unable to articulate the heinous words aloud.

She said nothing.

He swallowed hard, dreading the words to come. Finally he asked, "Does your silence mean you slept with him?"

She studied her sneakers.

"Sweetheart, please," he whispered. "I need to know. It's driving me crazy."

She raised her gaze. "Not that it's any of your business—" her eyes glistened "—but no, Kurt, I didn't sleep with Pierre. I haven't been with anybody but you since we split."

His throat tightened and he bent his head to get control of himself. "Thank God."

Her hand went to his hair. Then her lips brushed his head. "I've got to go."

It was a few seconds before he was able to stand. He stepped back and jammed his hands in his pockets to keep from reaching for her.

At the doorway she faced him. "If there's something to deal with, we will—when we know for sure. Not before, Kurt. I haven't changed my mind about us."

"Maybe you will if there's a third person to consider."

She didn't respond. Just turned and walked away.

He plunked down on the bench. The vinyl was slightly warm from her body, the air lightly scented by her perfume. *Well, one step forward,* he thought, trying not to be too hopeful.

But it was hard. Since this was the very first vestige of that emotion he'd felt in more than a year.

CHAPTER NINE

KURT LEANED BACK in his office chair and scrubbed his hands over his face. He felt eighty-six, not forty-six. The week had been tough—and it was only Wednesday; he was also dreading the long Veterans Day weekend to come. He'd forfeit his stock portfolio, his house and even his boat if he could just spend the three days with Zoe.

Julia skidded to a halt in front of his office doorway. Always sassy and pert, today she looked frazzled—her blue eyes wide and frightened, her hair askew. "Dr. Lansing, come quick."

Bounding out of the chair, he hurried to the door. "What's happened?" he asked as he accompanied her down the hall.

"It's Ashley."

"Ashley?" The girl had been overwrought for almost two weeks. He'd spoken with her several times, using her obvious ambivalence to encourage her to talk to her parents about her situation. Again she refused.

"She's…something's happened…" Julia stopped at the ladies' room. "She said to get you."

Kurt pushed open the door and rushed inside. Ashley was slumped in front of a stall. She was doubled over and clutching her stomach.

He dropped to a knee beside her. "Ashley, what's wrong?"

"I didn't want to. I really didn't."

His heartbeat escalated. "Didn't want what?"

"An…an abortion."

His mind whirled. Gently he stretched her out as best he could to diagnose the problem. It was then that he saw the blood staining her tan jeans. "Julia," Kurt said calmly. "Run and get Johnny. Tell him to bring the gurney in here."

Julia flew out the door.

Moaning, Ashley brought her knees to her chest.

"Ashley, did you go somewhere for an abortion?"

She stared at him with glazed eyes. Finally she shook her head.

"Did you do something to yourself?"

Tears formed in her eyes. "I didn't want to, I didn't want to," she repeated.

He steeled himself against the fear that she might have taken things into her own hands. Whipping off his suit jacket, he stuffed it under her head. He crooned soft words to her and waited for the gurney.

Johnny burst through the door in minutes. His face was composed, but his eyes were worried. "What happened?" he asked Kurt as they went into action. Behind him stood Shondra, along with Julia.

"I don't know. She's about two and a half months pregnant. Or at least she was." Kurt filled Johnny in as they lifted Ashley onto the gurney. Behind them, the girls gasped.

Quickly Johnny covered Ashley with a sheet. "Miscarriage?" he asked Kurt.

"I don't know." Placing themselves at each end of the gurney, they headed out. "I hope so."

Luckily the hallway from the clinic connected directly to the hospital's ER. Shondra and Julia held hands and followed.

Curled into a fetal position, Ashley was sobbing by the time they arrived.

"What's her situation?" the attending nurse asked as she came around to the front of the desk to check Ashley.

"Pregnant seventeen-year-old. Miscarriage or induced abortion. We're not sure."

"Abortion?" the admitting receptionist asked. Vaguely Kurt recognized her.

"We don't know. Just get her inside and find an ob-gyn to examine her." He nodded to the girls. "Her two friends can give you the necessary information." As the steel-gray swinging doors opened and Kurt and Johnny pushed the gurney through, he glanced over his shoulder. "Call her parents, would you, Jules?"

Kurt heard the woman at the desk harrumph.

Then the swish of the closing doors shut out the rest of the world.

ZOE SAT IN A CORNER of the emergency-room waiting area clutching Julia's hand, talking softly with her, Shondra, Erica and Rachel. The other two girls had arrived shortly after she did and, amidst the smell of stale coffee and antiseptic, they'd all been waiting about thirty minutes.

"I didn't even know she was pregnant," Julia said tearfully.

"Me, neither." This from Shondra.

Rachel was stone-faced and silent. Zoe was most worried about her, since she and Ashley were like sisters.

Giving them all a brave smile, one Zoe hoped was

convincing, she said, "We have to have faith she'll be all right."

"Did she have an abortion?" Julia asked.

"She was going to." Rachel finally spoke. Her tone was cold, her eyes flat. "Over the long weekend, so she wouldn't miss any school."

Zoe sucked in a breath.

"Son of a bitch." Erica fidgeted on her seat, then her eyes widened. "Dr. Lansing wouldn't have done an abortion on Ashley at the clinic, would he?"

"Oh, my God." They all turned to find Ashley's mother standing over them. She was an older version of Ashley, with sky-blue eyes and streaked blond hair. Her lower lip trembled as she spoke. "Ashley had an abortion at the clinic?"

Zoe heard a startled gasp from the woman at the reception desk. "No, of course not."

"Is…was…is my daughter pregnant?"

Zoe faced the overwrought mother. "Yes."

"And you knew?" She scanned the group. "You all knew?"

"No, not all of us," Zoe said. "But she confided in me."

Mrs. Emerson's eyes filled with tears. "In you? Not me?"

Reaching out to the mother's arm, Zoe squeezed it and began to speak just as Kurt strode through the swinging doors. His face was pale but composed, and he looked strong and dependable. He gave Zoe a grateful look as he approached them.

"Kurt, this is Ashley's mother."

He addressed the woman. "Mrs. Emerson, I'm Kurt Lansing, director of the clinic."

The worried mother nodded.

"Ashley's had a miscarriage. She was ten weeks pregnant. Apparently, she miscarried this afternoon."

"Miscarried? Not..." The mother of four girls, her hand slid to her stomach. "Not an abortion?"

"No."

Mrs. Emerson swayed and gripped Zoe's arm.

"Here, sit down." Zoe indicated the vinyl chair, but Mrs. Emerson resisted.

"Is she all right?"

"Yes."

"I want to see my daughter."

"You can go back momentarily. They're prepping her to go upstairs for a D&C."

The woman sank onto the chair. "A D&C?"

Kurt explained the necessary procedure to rid the uterus of what it didn't expel by itself. Julia and Shondra went white, Erica listened intently and Rachel's eyes clouded.

Kurt glanced at the clock. "Come on, I'll take you back."

As she walked toward the patient area, the mother asked, "How could I not know about all this?"

"My question exactly," came a voice behind them.

Pivoting, Zoe stared into the mottled face of Jerry Bosco.

JULIA STUDIED the man. He looked like Ernest Borgnine, but even uglier and all puffed up with self-importance. He watched Ms. C with a look that chilled Julia.

"What the hell is going on here?" Bosco asked.

"What are *you* doing here, Jerry?" Ms. C wanted to know.

"I was alerted by the ER receptionist to a situation

involving the clinic and a student from our school. As a member of both the town council and school board, I came to investigate.''

Cowed, Julia stepped back. So did Rachel and Shondra. Only Erica stood by Ms. C's side without shrinking from the pushy man. Ms. C faced him squarely. ''I can't imagine what you hope to accomplish coming here like this.''

''That fancy clinic of yours performed an abortion on one of your students. This is sick. *Sick.*''

''Jerry, you have totally incorrect information.''

The outer door to the ER flew open, interrupting them. In rushed Evan and Rob. ''Oh, God, what happened?'' Evan asked. ''Did she...did she something go wrong with the abortion?''

Bosco whirled on Zoe. ''Incorrect information?''

Ms. C said, ''Yes, it's incorrect.'' She grasped Evan's hand and spoke directly to him. ''Ashley had a miscarriage.''

''Is she all right?'' the boy asked.

''A lot you care, you bastard.'' This from Rachel, who dragged Evan around. ''You wanted her to get rid of it. You wouldn't stand by her.'' She accented each accusation by pounding her fists on his chest. ''This is all your fault.''

Gently Rob pulled Rachel back. She turned, crying, into his chest.

Julia pivoted in time to see Dan enter the ER.

''I just finished at the nursery and came right over.'' He stared at her for a spilt second, then drew her to him.

Erica watched Julia and Rachel for a minute, then faced Bosco, Ms. C and good old Evan. Her hands began to shake uncontrollably, so she stuffed them in the pockets of her skirt.

"This is a zoo," Bosco was saying as he scanned the kids.

For once Erica agreed with the jerk.

"Jerry, you've walked into a very difficult situation. You're just making it worse."

"Worse?" His voice raised. "You think this is bad? You haven't seen anything yet. I'm going to close down this damn clinic."

Erica caught sight of Dr. Lansing coming through the gray doors again. For a minute he blurred, then came into focus again.

"You say one false word against my clinic," he told Bosco, "and I'll sue you for slander."

Way to go Dr. L, she thought. She didn't know he could be so tough, but she liked it.

Even Bosco stepped backward. "I'll consult the town's lawyer first, then." The creep scanned them all. "Meanwhile, I'll have the board yank these students from working with you."

Ms. C stood up as tall as she could get, which wasn't much. "And if you do that, Jerry, you'll have me to contend with. I'll fight you with every resource I have."

Well, well, well, everybody was getting tough today. It was kinda cool to watch.

Dr. Lansing came up behind Ms. Caufield and placed a hand on her shoulder. "I suggest you sit down with us or with the ER doctors and get your facts straight, Mr. Bosco. Don't cause unnecessary trouble."

Bosco's beady eyes leveled on him. "I haven't even started yet, Dr. Lansing. I haven't even started."

The asshole stomped out of the emergency room.

Erica watched Ms. C lean back into Dr. Lansing and release a huge breath. He squeezed her shoulder and said, "Whew."

Erica shook her head. She sank onto a vinyl chair, thinking about Ashley's miscarriage and Dr. Lansing touching Ms. C. She wondered how soon she could have another upper. She knew she shouldn't take more, for she'd been overstepping the limit she'd set for herself. Also, she'd gone to great lengths to hide any symptoms from Ms. C & Dr. Lansing, so she shouldn't pop one now when they were around. But she needed a pill. And she'd cut back just as soon as things got better in her life.

"ARE YOU SURE you still want to do this?" Cassie's face was drawn with fatigue as she asked the question. Zoe noticed again that her friend had lost weight since September, the pressures of school and raising a family obviously wearing on her. "What with Ashley's miscarriage and Bosco's being on the warpath?"

Behind her, Mitch placed his hands on Cassie's shoulders and sighed. His green eyes were weary. It was clear they both needed this weekend away from their kids.

"I'm sure. It'll take my mind off what happened with Ashley yesterday." *And off Kurt.*

Cassie shrugged. "There's more. Alexandra's got a cold. She slobbers all over Camille, so the baby might come down with it, too."

"I think I can handle the sniffles." Scowling, Zoe teased, "Doesn't she want to go away with you, big guy?"

Mitch looked a little lost. "Sometimes I wonder. These kids take up so much time."

To Zoe's shock, tears formed in Cassie's eyes. "No, of course it's not that." She turned Mitch. "How could you think that?"

Rolling his eyes, he pulled her close. "I don't, really. We're both drained. We need to get away, love."

"Uh-huh," Zoe said dryly, "you do. Look I can handle the girls. Did you leave medicine for the cold?"

"Yes, along with the pediatrician's number. And a letter authorizing you to seek medical treatment."

"I'm sure that won't be necessary. Now go. The girls are down for a nap, so this is a perfect time to escape." She gave the couple her best stern-teacher look. "After the great friends you guys have been to me this last year, I'd like a chance to do something for you."

"You're a godsend." Cassie scrubbed at her face impatiently, leaned over to hug Zoe and started out.

Mitch hugged her, too. "Thanks, Zoe. I want her to get away, get some rest and some perspective."

"Then go," Zoe whispered. "We'll be fine."

"If you need any help, my brother's great with the girls."

Zoe eyed Mitch. *"Go."*

The Lansing children slept another hour. Zoe wandered about the house, glad to give her friends the opportunity to spend the weekend in the city, envying them their bond and the life they'd built together. In the living room, she picked up a picture of them on their wedding day.

On either side of them, she and Kurt smiled glowingly.

I was going to tell you that night…I was going to ask you to marry me.

Sighing, she sank onto the couch, picture in hand.

She hadn't allowed herself much time to think about Kurt's admission that he'd wanted to marry her the night they found out about Ashley's pregnancy. And for the intervening two weeks she'd buried the notion she could be pregnant, although her period was two days late. Not uncommon, she thought. She'd be fine.

You want to be pregnant, a voice inside her accused. Zoe gripped the picture. "Of course I don't."

It would give you an excuse to let him back in your life.

"I don't need an excuse. If I wanted him back, I'd—"

The Banshee wail interrupted her. Quickly she replaced the picture and mounted the steps two at a time, hustling into Camille's room. Zoe had helped Cassie pick out the yellow-daisy wallpaper and matching green-with-daisies quilt and bumper for the crib. The baby was alternately crying and sucking her thumb.

"What's the matter, love?" Zoe asked as she picked up the child.

Camille quieted and stared at Zoe with huge green eyes. When she realized her rescuer wasn't Cassie or Mitch, she started to wail again, big tears rolling down her cheeks. "Come on, sweetie, it's Aunt Zoe. You know me. I'm your godmother. We're buddies."

The baby continued to cry.

"Hey," Zoe said as she placed her on the changing table, "we're gonna have a great time when you get older—reading books, watching movies, playing games." As she changed Camille's diaper, Zoe noticed she felt warm. But babies often woke up from naps warm, she remembered Lacey saying. Just to be sure, she found a thermometer in the girls' bathroom and took Camille's temperature—a feat in itself. It read ninety-nine. Juice would help, Zoe thought, trekking downstairs with the now-whimpering child.

Camille fussed through the bottle of juice. Zoe walked her, sang, "I'm a Little Teapot" in French, then headed upstairs again and rocked her.

Until Alexandra woke up. The four-year-old wandered into Camille's bedroom.

Zoe gave her a big smile. "Hi, Alexandra. How are you?"

Cheeks pink, her braid messy, the child rubbed her eyes. "Don't feel good."

"Uh-oh," Zoe said, and got up to find the thermometer again.

At ten o'clock that night, Zoe called the pediatrician's after-hours number. She spoke with the doctor on call, who assured her both girls sounded as if they had symptoms of the flu he'd seen lately, but to bring them in the next morning. Meanwhile, she should give them lots of liquids and a pain reliever every four hours.

The medicine had a marginal effect; Alexandra didn't go to sleep until midnight. Zoe rocked Camille till 2:00 a.m., when the baby finally conked out.

Zoe fell asleep on the twin bed in Camille's room, surrounded by a veritable zoo of animals. A huge giraffe stood guard over her head.

She was awakened four hours later by a soulful cry. Bolting up, she rushed to Camille. The infant felt hotter than last night, Zoe noted as she struggled to change her diaper. "Come on, love," Zoe said, holding her while she fixed a bottle of formula. "Please drink some." Camille took about an ounce, then spit out the nipple.

Just then Alexandra entered the kitchen, dragging a

teddy bear by the arm. Fortunately her forehead seemed cooler. "Want juice. And Cheerios," she said, climbing onto Zoe's lap. Zoe blew her hair out of her eyes and sighed heavily.

By the time she reached the pediatrician's, Zoe was exhausted and frantic. Camille's temperature had soared and she cried all the way to the medical building.

Struggling to open the office door, she hoped like hell she could handle two sick girls for three whole days. A class of At Risk kids never caused her to bat an eyelash, but this was something else.

Leaving the office armed with prescriptions for more medicine—Camille had an ear infection on top of whatever flu she had—Zoe prayed she could get the antibiotic and make it back home.

Never in her life has she experienced anything like dragging two little ones into the drugstore, waiting interminably for the pharmacist to dispense the drug while she held Camille and kept an eye on a restless cranky four-year-old.

When she pulled into the driveway with both girls crying loudly in the back seat, she felt like joining them.

At eight that night, with no end in sight, she gave in. She picked up the phone and dialed a number beside it. After two rings, it was answered. She said, "Kurt, this is Zoe. I need some help."

HE'D NEVER SEEN HER so disheveled. Grateful brown eyes locked on him. "Thanks for coming." In her arms she held a sleeping Camille; at her side was a pale Alexandra. He leaned over immediately to lift his niece into his arms and cuddle her against the sweatshirt he'd hastily thrown on with jeans and sneakers. He'd still been dressed from work when Zoe called. "What's the matter baby? You don't feel good?"

Alexandra whimpered, "I want my mommy."

"What's this? My best girl doesn't wanna be with her favorite uncle tonight?"

That made Alexandra smile, and Zoe give him a weak facsimile of one.

The four of them traipsed into the living room. Zoe took the rocker and Kurt sat on the couch. "What did their pediatrician say?"

"Mild flu for Alexandra. But she's a bit better tonight. Camille has the flu *and* an ear infection. I stopped to get the antibiotic at the drugstore, and I'd rather have my fingernails pulled out before I'd repeat that experience. I thought Cassie and Mitch were exaggerating. I had no idea these two could be so..." She stopped, realizing Alexandra was listening intently.

"We was bad, Aunt Zoe?" the little girl asked.

"Oh, honey, you were fine. Aunt Zoe's just new at taking care of children."

Kurt leaned over and took the book Alexandra held, then pulled her onto his lap. "Aunt Zoe might be learning how to take care of children quicker than she thought," Kurt said mischievously.

"No, she won't be." Zoe's tone was confident.

Damn. Though he knew, logically, chances were slim, he'd hoped... "Got confirmation already?" he asked as lightly as he could.

Zoe stared at him blankly. "Confirm... Ah, no, not yet."

He frowned. "Shouldn't you know by now? It was a couple weeks ago that we..." He let the words hang.

"I don't want to talk about it now."

"Just answer that."

"All right, I'm late, but only by a couple of days. It's not unusual for me."

That little piece of news cheered him. He read *Good Night Moon* to Alexandra while Zoe rocked Camille, part of his mind on the possibilities. When the baby started to cry, he watched Zoe try to calm her, then eased Alexandra off his lap and stood. "Let me see her." Taking Camille in his arms, he felt her face and neck. "When did she have the last analgesic?"

"Two hours ago."

"She's hot. I think I'll give her a tepid bath."

Alexandra's eyes brightened. "Me, too. I wanna bath, too."

"Camille's too fussy for you two to bathe together, honey. But Aunt Zoe can give you a bath in the big tub in Mommy and Daddy's room."

"With bubbles?"

"Sure." He winked at Zoe. "Aunt Zoe likes bubbles."

What are you doing? she'd asked once in his bubble-filled Jacuzzi.

Making pyramids on you.

You're crazy, you know that?

Crazy about you.

Kurt banished the memory and concentrated on the child. Upstairs in the girls' adjoining bathroom, he drew the water, whipped off his sweatshirt and bathed the sick baby. When he was done, he wrapped her up in a big towel, dried her gently, dressed her in clean pajamas and headed downstairs. At the master bathroom, he realized Camille was almost asleep. "I think Camille feels bet—" He stopped midword. What he saw took his breath away.

The big tub was indeed filled with bubbles. In it was Alexandra, covered from head to toe in froth.

So was Zoe.

He gaped at the luscious picture she made, unable to take his eyes off Zoe. Part of one shoulder peeked out of the soap, and freckles dotted it. He remembered kissing them one night.

"Wanna come in, Uncle Kurt?" Alexandra asked. "Sometimes Daddy does when Mommy's in the tub."

Zoe sputtered, "Ah, no, honey, that's not a good idea."

Kurt gave Zoe his full masculine perusal. "I think it's a great idea."

"Kurt!"

"Unfortunately Camille here is pretty possessive." He patted the baby's back as she cuddled into him sweetly. "I can't abandon my charge."

Zoe shook her head, but the corners of her mouth turned up. "Get out of here."

"Why? It's nothing I haven't—"

"Don't say it. Just leave."

He chuckled all the way to Camille's room.

"THEY'RE BOTH ASLEEP, finally." Kurt dropped onto the couch next to her, stretched his legs in front of him and closed his eyes.

"Thank God."

He opened one eye. "I can't believe how demanding they are. Just when one quiets, the other wakes up. This is as bad as the night shift in the ER."

She sipped her sparkling water, unable to remember ever being so tired in her life.

"I think you should go to bed down here in Cassie and Mitch's room," he said after a moment.

She thought about the king-size bed. And Kurt. "What about you?"

"I'll bunk in Camille's room on the twin bed. That way, I'll hear either of them from there."

"No, I can—"

His raised his hand to her mouth. His fingers stopped her words. They felt soft and comforting against her lips. She wanted badly to kiss them, feel them all over her.

"How much sleep did you get last night?" he asked.

"About four hours."

"And today they ran you ragged. You need rest."

"What about you?"

"I'm a doctor. I'm used to going without sleep."

"I think—"

"Look, we'll rest in shifts. This—" he nodded upstairs "—will most likely continue into tomorrow and maybe into Sunday. We need to be sensible, sweetheart."

"Oh, God." She sipped her water.

"Besides," he said, his eyes twinkling like dewkissed grass, "I won't be able to sleep, anyway, after seeing you in the bathtub."

She'd forgotten how good Kurt's flirting felt, how playful their life together had been. It was a stark reminder of all they'd lost. And it angered her.

"What is it?" he asked.

"Nothing." She stood. "You're right, we need to be sensible about this. About everything. I'll turn in now. Wake me early so I can relieve you."

"All right."

"Sleep well."

Don't bet the farm on it, she thought miserably.

KURT WAS DIMLY aware of a movement on his chest. He slept lightly on the twin bed, holding the baby clasped to him, but he knew intuitively Camille wasn't waking.

Slitting open his eyes, he saw Zoe lean over him and ease the child out of his arms. "Shh, go back to sleep."

She lifted Camille away from him, soothed her back, then placed her in the crib. Clothed in blue satin pajamas, Zoe looked wonderful as she returned to the bed and stared down at him. "Since you're awake, why don't you go into the guest room and get some good sleep?"

He stretched. "What time is it?"

"Seven. Alexandra's not up yet. What time did Attila the Hun go down?"

"The last time she woke up was about five." He yawned. "She fell asleep again about six-thirty."

"You need more sleep," she said, wrapping her arms around her waist. The action pulled the pajama material tight over her breasts, and he could see the outline of her nipples.

"I need *you.*" Defenses down from lack of sleep, he didn't censor his words or actions. He reached up and tugged on her arm.

She fell on top of him. "Kurt!" she whispered fiercely. "What are you doing?"

He tunneled his fingers through her tousled hair. He loved the way she looked and smelled in the morning. "I'm taking advantage of the situation."

She giggled. "Let me up."

His hands left her hair and trailed down her back to her bottom. He squeezed her gently there. She was soft and supple, and his body responded immediately. "In a minute. You feel too good."

"Kurt." She moaned his name.

"Don't you miss us, love?"

"You're not being fair."

"Don't you?" His hands inched under her top and met skin smoother than satin.

She closed her eyes. "Please."

"Answer me and I'll let you up."

"All right, I miss you." Her middle bumped with his. "I miss this. A lot."

"Kiss me."

"No. I've got to see to Alexandra."

"Please."

Zoe swallowed hard. Stared at his lips. His hand came up to coax her head down.

She ended up going willingly. Her mouth met his, gently at first. Then hungrily. Her whole body pressed into his as she consumed him.

He angled his head to get more of her. Their legs tangled together and his hands gripped her bottom reflexively.

Mumbling—some kind of noise—came from the doorway.

Zoe drew back. "Wh-what?"

"What're you doing on top of Uncle Kurt, Aunt Zoe?" Alexandra must have repeated the question.

Zoe's forehead met Kurt's. She said softly, "Good question, kiddo," and tried to pull away. He held her for a minute, relishing the sight of her flushed and breathing hard from his kisses. Then he let her go.

Though his body ached with fatigue, his heart felt lighter. He turned over and buried his face in the pillow. The last conscious thought he had was that he was making progress with the woman he loved.

THAT EVENING, Zoe stared across the kitchen at Kurt, and her heart turned over. He stood at the wide expanse of window, just as he had on moving day. He was freshly showered and shaved, and his hair was slicked back and still damp. He was dressed in one of Mitch's sweat suits; its deep green turned his eyes the color of the forest. They'd had a hectic day, with two cranky little girls to entertain. Fortunately Camille had taken a miraculous turn for the better about four that afternoon, and Alexandra was almost completely well.

"How long did I nap?" Zoe asked.

"A few hours. It's eight o'clock." He smiled. "Feel better?"

"A little. I wish you'd slept more today."

"I got a good three hours this morning after…" He let the thought trail off.

She blushed. *After they'd kissed.* She'd dreamed about him the entire time she slept. She'd awoken aroused.

Damn it.

Glancing at the clock, she asked, "The girls asleep?"

"Uh-huh. They went down easily just a few minutes ago. My guess is they're out for the count."

Zoe smiled.

"Hungry?" he asked.

"Have we eaten today?" she joked.

"Some leftover pizza for breakfast, I think. The rest is a blur."

She sank onto a chair and sniffed something spicy. "What do I smell?"

"I ordered takeout from that new seafood restaurant in town." He grinned and joined her at the table. "Lobster thermidor." Her favorite.

"Wow!"

"Hey, we deserve it after the weekend we've had." He shook his head. "I forgot how exhausting dealing with sick kids for an extended period of time is."

"What I can't figure out is how Camille got better so fast. Before I took a nap, she was cooing like an angel."

"The antibiotic kicked in." He grinned. "Boy, am I glad."

"Thanks for coming to help, Kurt. I couldn't have done it myself."

"Cassie'll have a fit when she comes home, especially about how you lied to her on the phone."

Zoe shrugged. "I didn't want to spoil their weekend."

"They've got the best marriage I've ever seen, and still it's strained by daily life, isn't it."

Swallowing hard, she said, "Nothing's perfect."

"Relationships take a lot of work." He stared at her intently. "We could have made it, Zoe."

"Don't."

"All right. I'm too drained to argue, anyway. Let's call a truce. No discussing the past or the future. Let's just enjoy tonight." He glanced at the ceiling. "Alone. Hopefully."

"I'd like that."

They ate lobster and twice-baked potatoes and white asparagus. Periodically they checked on the girls to make sure they were all right. She and Kurt sat side by side and watched an old Humphrey Bogart movie on TV. At midnight Zoe felt her eyes closing.

"Here," Kurt said, raising his arm, sliding it around her and tugging her close. He was slouched on the couch with his feet on the coffee table. "Put your head here and sleep."

"...should go to bed," she mumbled against his chest.

She felt his mouth in her hair. "In a bit. Sleep."

The next thing Zoe knew, birds were chirping. She stirred and opened her eyes. She was in the big guest room across from the girls' rooms. Kurt lay next to her. Both of them were on top of the covers, dressed as they'd been the night before, with a crocheted afghan pulled over them. They were snuggled into each other, the way they used to sleep together. Zoe lay quietly, once again overcome with a monumental sense of loss.

Her hand went to her stomach. Sometimes she *did* wish, just for a minute, that they'd have no choice but to pick up their relationship again. That the decision would be taken out of her hands.

She listened to his even breathing, inhaling his unique scent, until she yearned so much for him that she had to move. She slipped out from his grasp, tiptoed to the bathroom and closed the door.

A few moments later, her heart breaking, she fished in the overnight case she'd left on the vanity earlier for a tampon. As she stared at herself in the mirror afterward, tears streamed down her cheeks. "You idiot," she said. "So you got your period. So what? It's for the best."

Backing up, she leaned against the wall. Slowly she slid into a slouch on the floor and buried her face in her hands.

KURT AWOKE BY DEGREES in the guest room of his brother's house. Eyes closed, he reached for Zoe, but she was gone. He sat halfway up and scanned the room; he noted the pretty peach walls and white wicker furniture that Zoe had helped Cassie pick out. Last night had been too dark to see the decor.

Last night, when he'd carried a sleeping Zoe in here and couldn't resist the temptation to join her on the bed. He'd held her all night while she'd snuggled up to him as she used to do.

Where was she? Easing out of bed, he headed to the adjoining bathroom; when he opened the door, he was shocked to find her huddled on the floor, her head down.

"Zoe, what's wrong?"

She didn't look up.

"Sweetheart, are you ill?"

Still nothing. He dropped to his knees and pried her face up from her hands. She was crying, soft silent tears. "What's wrong?"

She just shook her head.

"Is it because I slept with you? I'm sorry, baby, I just couldn't resist." He shrugged helplessly.

"It's not that." Her gaze strayed to the counter. He followed it and saw the tampon box sitting there.

"Oh." His heart plummeted. For a second. Then he realized the significance of her tears.

Sitting down, he propped himself against the wall, stretched out his legs and tugged her onto his lap. She resisted, marginally, but then went into his arms. He held her close. "You're crying because you got your period."

Vehemently she shook her head.

"Yes, love, you are."

"I'm tired…"

He said nothing.

"The girls were sick…I was worried."

Still he made no comment.

"It's been a hard few months…"

His hand drew circles on her back, soothed down her hair. He kissed the top of her head. "You know in your heart it's none of those things."

After a long time, she drew back. "All right. It's just a temporary aberration."

He pinned her with an intense stare. "No, Zoe, I won't let you kid yourself about this anymore."

"What do you mean?"

"I mean that we belong together. And you know it. You'd hoped, maybe unconsciously, that the decision would be made for us, that we'd be forced together by a pregnancy, but that's not going to happen. You're going to have to make a conscious choice to try again."

She straightened. "I won't." She bit her lip. "I can't."

"Yes, you can." He stared hard at her, praying he said the right thing. "I'm asking outright for another chance with you. I know I hurt you. Let me make up for what I did. Let me prove our relationship can work."

Fear filled her eyes. "I'm too scared."

"I won't accept that answer. Not anymore. I've let you call the shots because of my guilt. I'm not going to let that go on any longer."

Her face was full of questions.

"I want another chance, and I'm not giving up until I get it." Easing her off his lap, he stood and pulled her to her feet. "Now let's go check on the girls, I'll cook you breakfast and we'll talk about this some more."

He held out his hand.

Her gaze dropped to it, then back up.

''Zoe,'' he said, his voice a little desperate.

Finally, she placed her hand in his.

CHAPTER TEN

As HE DROVE to the Bayview Heights Administration Building at nine o'clock the following Monday night, Kurt was not happy. Irritable from lack of sleep, he struggled for calm. Thinking about the upcoming meeting—instigated by Bosco—made him crazy, and thinking about Zoe didn't exactly help.

Sunday morning had not turned out as he'd hoped...

She'd taken his hand and accompanied him to the kitchen, but over coffee, she patiently explained why she couldn't risk starting a relationship with him again.

Just as patiently, he'd coaxed, cajoled and even got angry. "Tell me one thing. Why didn't you fight for me a year ago?"

"Fight for you?" The color had rushed to her cheeks. "You mean, beg you to stay, not go back to Elizabeth?"

"No, I mean try to talk me out of it. I've wondered. You let me go fairly easily."

"You jerk! If you thought for one minute I'd grovel..."

He'd swallowed hard. "I never wanted you to grovel. But you might have been able to talk some sense into me. I was making the biggest mistake of my life. I've wished a thousand times you'd talked me out of it."

For a long time, she'd been silent, then her face

crumpled and the comment seemed to slip out. "I've wished that sometimes, too. It was pride, I guess. Along with shock."

"Then don't let that pride get in the way now, love."

"It has nothing to do with pride now. It's fear."

"Then don't let fear keep us apart."

After a long day of discussion in between playing with the now-healthy Lansing girls, she'd finally agreed to give them another chance—with lots of conditions. He'd followed her home after Mitch and Cassie's return, and they'd stood inside the foyer.

"So, how do we do this?" he'd asked, his heart thudding wildly in his chest, his hands itching to touch her.

"Slowly." Her voice was quiet. "And very carefully. I'm not diving back into this relationship without caution."

"I guess that means I'm not staying overnight."

"No, you're not." She frowned. "We'll date. And we'll keep it to ourselves."

"I'm not hiding this from anybody, Zoe."

"I wouldn't ask you to. But we don't need to take out an ad in the *Herald*, either." She raised an eyebrow. "Take it or leave it."

He'd grabbed her then and kissed the challenge off her face. "I'll take it."

He hadn't seen or talked to her since.

Frustrated, he parked and met Seth on the way into the building.

"Hi, buddy." Seth clapped him warmly on the back. "You looked pissed off."

"I am."

Seth shook his head. "I'm sorry about this," he told

Kurt. "We should be grateful to you for opening a clinic here, not questioning your ethics."

"It's not just Bosco. But come on, let's go slay this dragon first." He'd take care of his five-foot one later.

They were the last to enter the room. Around the conference table was assembled a wide cast of characters. His gaze zeroed in on Zoe first. The deep pink of her very proper suit highlighted her cheeks, and her eyes were snapping fire. She wasn't happy, either. He wondered if it was just the situation with Bosco, or if she was upset with him, too.

She nodded at him, smiled at Seth and faced Joe Finn. First the superintendent asked everyone to introduce themselves and explain who they were. Bosco preened with self-importance, the mayor sat cozily between two other board members asked to attend, but the people that really snagged his attention were Mr. and Mrs. Emerson. Ashley's father—a small stocky man—introduced them both and held his wife's hand tightly. Their faces were lined with pain. Kurt thought about Lauren and how he'd feel if he'd been the father in such a situation.

Joe Finn began the discussion. "Both the town council and the school board have some concern over the events of this past week. We need to get the facts straight and listen to everyone's version of what happened. But for the record—" he held up a folder "—I have the ER report that Ashley Emerson did indeed have a miscarriage, not an induced abortion."

Bosco sat forward and frowned. "She would have had an abortion if the miscarriage hadn't happened."

Mr. Emerson's face reddened and his wife turned her cheek into his chest. Damn Bosco.

"Jerry, speculation isn't going to help us." Finn's

tone was barely controlled. "Why don't you tell us your concern?"

"The clinic and the course Ms. Caufield teaches encourage immorality among our kids." He held up a thick bound book Kurt recognized as Zoe's curriculum. "There's a whole section in this course outline on tough choices kids have to make. It deals with having sex, birth control, abortion, and gays and lesbians coming out, for God's sake. It's no wonder that young girl ended up pregnant and pursuing an abortion. Our school encourages it."

Seth threw his pen on the table. "We do not, Jerry. We discuss it." He shook his head. "Forty-five percent of all teens report being sexually active. Do you really think *not* talking to kids about these things will make them *not* do them?"

"Talking about them is tacit approval."

"No, it's not." This from Zoe. She slid a newspaper article toward him. "Read this. It's a survey done in upstate New York recently. The kids in it said they want to talk to adults about their relationships with the opposite sex. My course and all the other health courses encourage kids to discuss the pressures and problems they're confronted with every day. Our lessons help them deal better with everything and make informed choices that are right for them personally."

"Oh, Ashley Emerson dealt well with her situation, didn't she. She *told* you she was considering an abortion." His scornful gaze swung to Kurt. "And you were going to help her get it, if not do it yourself."

"The clinic doesn't perform abortions," Kurt said tightly.

"But you counsel kids about them."

Angry at Bosco's shortsightedness, Kurt leaned over

in his chair. "Planned Parenthood offers many forms of counseling—all over the country, I might add. For heaven's sake, Bosco, that organization is an institution in America. It's funded by the United Way. Even your narrow-minded views won't get rid of it."

"Thank God," Zoe said.

Joe Finn shook his head. "Mr. Bosco wants the clinic closed. And he wants the health courses dropped," Finn said, glancing at Bosco disgustedly. "As we've won national awards for our innovative health program, I'm not of a mind to alter anything. And New York State mandates that certain things, including AIDS education, be taught in our schools. So he can't get rid of that. Of course, he won't be able to run Planned Parenthood out of town, either. The question we needed to ask is, did the school's Life Issues course and the new teen clinic do anything to give the board or the council grounds to investigate further?"

Zoe shot Kurt an I-can't-believe-this look.

Seth frowned.

"Excuse me," Kurt said, "but this sounds like a witch hunt."

Finn sighed. "I have no choice but to address Mr. Bosco's complaints."

"I think they should be addressed. Zoe and I have nothing to hide. I'm just shocked by this backward attitude."

Bosco straightened to an impressive height. "You should have advised Ashley to tell her parents."

"We did." Kurt's voice was implacable.

"Innumerable times," Zoe added. "She refused. Ashley can confirm that."

"Yet you hid the girl's pregnancy and intent to have an abortion from her parents."

Kurt felt the anger rise inside him, but tamped it down. "It's legal for minors to get contraceptives and abortions without their parents' consent."

"But it's not moral."

Zoe slapped her hand on the table. "And who appointed you the moral watchdog of Bayview Heights, Jerry?"

"I was elected to the board and the council by the citizens of this community."

"Not to decide right and wrong for them."

"I want a board vote on this issue." Bosco's tone was firm.

"No!" All heads snapped around to Mr. Emerson. Ashley's father looked determined. "I want to say something."

The superintendent nodded encouragingly. "Go ahead, Mr. Emerson."

The man turned to Kurt. "Ashley finally talked to us about this. She said she didn't tell us she was pregnant because she was ashamed and didn't want to disappoint us." He slid his arm around his wife. "Isn't that right, Susie?"

Mrs. Emerson nodded. "She also said..." Tears clouded the woman's eyes. "She said that if Dr. Lansing hadn't guessed she was pregnant and convinced her to tell Ms. Caufield, she wasn't sure what she would have done."

"She might have told *you*," Bosco interrupted. "She might have had that child and taken responsibility for her actions, instead of finding an easy way out."

Mrs. Emerson drew up in her seat and faced Bosco, a mama bear defending her cubs. "No, Mr. Bosco, she told us she was thinking about committing suicide. But she said the two adults she confided in helped her to see alternatives." Again the woman's eyes teared. "She says she doesn't know if she would have gone through with an abortion, but she *does* know she didn't harm herself because of Dr. Lansing's and Ms. Caufield's support."

"They should have told you, her parents."

Mr. Emerson sighed. "I'm not as smart as my Ashley, and I don't have a college degree like you, Mr. Bosco, but even I can figure out that if they told us, the next student at the school who faced the same problems wouldn't have told *them*." She nodded at Kurt and Zoe. "And she might do what Ashley thought about doing—hurting herself." His voice broke on the last words. He faced Kurt, then Zoe. "I don't know why my little girl couldn't tell us, but I'm damn glad she could tell you two."

Kurt's heart broke for the parents. "Mr. Emerson, I have a daughter a year older than Ashley. She might not have told me, either. Sometimes kids can't share things with their parents that they *can* share with teachers." He gave them an easy smile. "We're all in this together."

"Then I thank God for teachers and doctors like you."

Kurt breathed a sigh of relief.

Across the table he caught Zoe's eye. She gave him a meaningful smile.

He returned it.

AT HER CONDO DOOR, Zoe watched Kurt park in her driveway and walk up the front path. His shoulders slumped with weariness, and she knew his face would be lined—with fatigue and anger. She still knew him so well.

"Invite me home for a drink," he'd said with a disgusted glance at Bosco, who was conferring with the other two board members at the end of the meeting tonight. "I'm…upset. I need to be with you."

She'd agreed, not only because she could see the need in his eyes, but because she felt the same.

When he reached the house, she stood back from the door; he gave her shoulder a gentle squeeze and stepped inside. He was still dressed in his suit and she in her teaching clothes. They didn't speak as he followed her into the living room. Lowering himself onto the pretty green-and-tan-flowered sofa, he looked big and very male. She'd always thought that about him when he lounged among her feminine things.

She fixed him a Manhattan, poured herself a glass of wine, kicked off her shoes and joined him on the couch. She waited until he took a sip, then said, "That was awful, wasn't it?"

"I felt so sorry for the Emersons. Doesn't Bosco realize how much harder he's making it for them?"

"Bosco doesn't care. He never did, and that's his tragic flaw."

Kurt sighed. "There can't be anything worse than hearing your child is suicidal."

"Mrs. Emerson told me after the meeting that Ashley's seeing a counselor."

"I hope she was just having suicidal thoughts. Those are very different from attempts."

"I know." Zoe sipped her wine. "I've had suicidal students."

"Anybody try it?"

Her heart clutched. "A couple over the years. One succeeded, or at least we think it was suicide. He walked in front of a car on the expressway."

"Traffic accidents are often covers for teenage suicide. Louise has had a lot of sad cases."

"Kurt, you know that the clinic is doing a good job, don't you? That we need it and you're helping the town. And the school."

He leaned back and rubbed his eyes wearily. "I guess I do. It's just that Bosco and his ilk make me question how much good I'm doing."

"Don't. You're working wonders down there."

"Seth seems worried."

Zoe remembered the principal's words of caution. *The issue's been tabled, but we need to be careful that we don't give Bosco any more ammunition.*

"He's supposed to worry about the school. He's got a tough job balancing everything."

"How about you? Does this whole thing make you question your classes?"

"Not a bit. I know Bosco, and I refuse to let him get to me."

As natural as summer rain, Kurt grasped her hand and held it. His was muscular and hard. "Then give me a little of that confidence, will you? My emotional fortitude is depleted."

She said huskily, "You've had a rough year."

He stared straight ahead, then said, "What are we going to do, Zoe? You said we'd take it slow. What exactly did you mean?"

Intuitively she knew he needed something from her tonight. In the midst of Bosco's irrationality and self-righteousness, and the stark desperation of the Emersons' situation, he needed something to hang on to.

"What did we used to do for fun, Kurt?"

He thought for a moment. "We went sailing. We loved picnics. Remember that time we were in Central

Park and it started to rain? We huddled under a tree and watched the drops fall into the pond. I'll never forget how pretty it was.''

"Too cold for both of those things, now.''

"You loved Broadway plays. Have you been recently?''

"Pierre and I spent a week in England over the summer. We saw several shows there.''

He went still.

"Kurt?''

Slowly he sat up, leaned over and set down his drink on the coffee table. Facing her, his eyes were earnest. "I have to say something. I've promised not to push you about the two of us. I'll let you take your time for everything else, but I can't sit by and watch you date other men. Not Pierre, not Alex Ransom, not any of the other of the hordes of guys drawn to you like magnets.''

Zoe sipped her wine, remembering her conversation with Alex after school when he'd asked her to go out next Saturday...

"I can't, Alex.''

Smart in the ways of the world, his brown eyes had narrowed on her. "Lansing's worn you down, hasn't he?''

"Not exactly. But...''

He took her hand. "I don't want him to hurt you again, Zoe.''

"I don't want that, either. It's just that I've never really gotten over him.''

"I know.'' For some reason Alex had rubbed his rib cage. "And it's mutual. Pierre and I watched you two at Hotshots that night and commiserated about it.''

"I'm sorry, Alex.'' She'd smiled at the young boy

she'd watched become a very good man. "Someday you'll find someone. Your own age," she'd joked, breaking the tension.

"Nah, I like older women..."

"Damn it Zoe, this shouldn't be such a big decision."

Zoe hadn't realized she'd been silent so long. She looked at Kurt—it took him a long time to get exasperated, but she could see that his temper had frayed. She thought about how helpful he'd been with Ashley, how he'd taken tender care of the Lansing girls and how he'd stood up to Bosco tonight. In so many ways, he was a man to count on, to believe in.

"It's not that big of a decision." This time she reached for his hand. "I won't see other men. You know it never even got physical with anyone else, anyway."

That statement brought images of Elizabeth and how it *had* gotten physical between her and Kurt. "But I'm not over the hump yet, Kurt. When I think about your sleeping with Elizabeth..." She let go of his hand, stood and crossed to the window. "It hurts so much I can't stand it."

"Do you want to talk about that?"

She whirled around. "Oh, God, no. I couldn't bear it."

Staring up at her from the couch, he said, "All right. Come back here and we'll plan some fun things that we used to do."

It took more courage than she thought she had to cross back to him and sit down.

"Lauren's got a birthday coming up," he said lightly. "And I need to shop for her."

Zoe brightened. "Shop?"

"Thought that would perk you up. Let's go to the mall this week and you can help me pick out some things for her."

"It's a date, Dr. Lansing."

He kissed her quickly on the mouth. "Well, that's progress."

"ARE YOU LEAVING?" Ashley watched Dr. Lansing from the doorway. He was dressed in jeans and a sweatshirt and had just put on his bomber jacket. He looked cool, as he had at the Down to Earth weekend.

He shrugged back out of his coat. "I've got a...something in about an hour. But I always have time for you. Come in and sit."

Hesitating a moment, she entered the room and took a seat. She was feeling a lot better physically, even though her emotions were crazy these days. "I won't hang you up long. We just haven't talked in a while."

"How are you feeling?"

"Fine..." She shrugged.

"Ms. Caufield told me you were seeing a counselor." He watched her. "I hope it's okay that she told me."

Ashley rolled her eyes. "I don't have any secrets from you, Dr. Lansing. I'm seeing Dr. Sheffield."

"Louise is the best."

"She's helping me see things better, understand myself more." Ashley looked thoughtful. "You know, she's starting a program that trains students to act as peer educators and assist your staff at outreach events. For kids who are making choices about birth control and other things."

"You'd be great at that."

"I hope so. I'm joining."

He smiled at her. "Anything I can do for you?"

"Yeah, you can get Evan off my back." She was only half joking.

"Evan?"

She frowned. "He won't leave me alone. He says he's sorry. He wants another chance. That he acted selfish and stupid, but he wasn't thinking straight."

A muscle leaped in Dr. Lansing's neck. He was probably as angry at Evan as her parents were. "He behaved badly, Ashley."

"I know." She smoothed down her new flowered skirt she'd bought on a special shopping trip with her mother. "He says he wants me to forgive him."

Dr. Lansing shifted uncomfortably in his seat. "It's a tall order."

"You're a guy, Dr. Lansing. Do all guys think it's that easy to forget something awful they do to you?"

"No, Ashley, not all guys think that." He cleared his throat. "But everybody wants forgiveness. It's human."

"You think I should give him another chance?"

His eyes narrowed. "No, I don't. Not now, anyway. You need to recover from this ordeal physically. You should talk to Dr. Sheffield at length about Evan and a lot of other things. And you should take your time and search your heart for how you really feel about the boy."

"What if he finds somebody else?"

"Then he wasn't worth it. I'm more concerned that you find *yourself* in all this. Forget about Evan for now. Just concentrate on you."

KURT HURRIED UP to Zoe's door ten minutes late, feeling like the worst hypocrite. The advice he'd given

Ashley had been good, though his own parallel with Evan didn't escape him. It was why he'd stopped to pick up flowers. He was starkly reminded of what he had to make up for with Zoe.

She pulled open the door, dressed like him in jeans and a sweatshirt, though the way the denim conformed to her legs was a hell of a lot different and…arousing. Her face broke out in a delighted smile as he handed her the delicate tiger lilies. "Oh, Kurt, how sweet."

It had been a joy to be able to buy them for her again. The thought choked him up.

"You okay?"

"Yeah, I'm fine." He stepped inside. "Sorry I'm late."

Burying her face in the flowers, she said, "The lilies are worth it. I haven't had any of these since—" She cut off her words. There was that elephant in the room again.

As she was snipping the ends and placing the flowers in a vase, he came up and slid his arms around her waist. She stiffened, so he dropped a kiss on her hair and drew back. "We can't watch every word we say, sweetheart. I'm glad nobody else bought you your favorite flowers, though I wish like hell I'd been delivering them by the truckload for the last year."

Still facing away from him, she said, "This is going to be hard, isn't it?"

He leaned against the counter. "Yeah. It is." He sighed. "I'm sorry."

"You know what?" she said, circling around. "Let's banish those words from your vocabulary for a while. I know you're sorry. What we're trying to find out here is if too much damage has been done to get together again."

The thought sent a bolt of pure panic through him. He quelled it. "All right." He sniffed. "What are we having for dinner? I can't smell anything."

She eyed him up and down. "At least you're dressed for it."

"You told me to wear casual clothes."

Grinning, she went to the refrigerator and pulled out two bottles of his favorite beer, which she topped with chunks of limes. Handing him one, she said, "Come on," and headed for her glassed-in porch.

"Isn't it a little cold to be on the porch this time of year?"

"I put the space heaters out here today so we could use it."

He saw why when he followed her out.

The floor was spread with a plaid blanket. On it were all his favorite picnic foods.

Touched, he smiled. "Is that your recipe for potato salad?"

"None other. And Lacey's recipe for Coney Island sauce." She sank onto the blanket and nodded to the outdoors. Under the deck light was the grill. "You'll have to cook the hot dogs out there, though. I'm glad you brought your bomber jacket."

He smiled, and the knot that had formed in his stomach after he'd spoken to Ashley began to loosen.

For two hours they laughed at funny school stories, talked about clinic events, discussed the Lansing girls and Cassie's reaction when she found out they'd been sick. By tacit agreement they stayed away from personal issues or even difficult ones like Bosco. They joked about the Down to Earth weekend over s'mores and ended the evening on the big rattan couch—where they'd made love more than once—staring out at the bay. The view had always soothed him. Tonight the water crashed on the rocks violently, but there was a raw beauty about it.

"It's getting cold out here," she said, shivering.

He reached behind them for a heavy quilt she kept there. Covering her, then himself, he tugged her close. She stiffened again. He sighed, frustrated.

"I...I don't want you to get any ideas, is all."

"Being *near* you gives me ideas, lady. I just wish you'd stop acting like I'm going to attack you every time I touch you."

"I don't think that."

"You said we needed to take this slow. Obviously you meant physically, too. Though I don't quite understand it, because we already made love last month."

"We weren't thinking straight. It wasn't the best thing to have happened."

Like hell. "Fine, but I'm not some teenage boy who can't control himself."

She looked up at him with wide brown eyes. "I know. Maybe I'm more afraid I won't be able to control myself."

"Would that be so bad?"

"Now I think it would be."

"All right. But come close just for a few minutes. I miss touching you. Feeling you against me." He whispered, "I need to be near you, love."

After a moment she slid over to him; after a while, her whole body nestled into him. He inhaled the perfume that always clung to her hair and skin. "Mmm. That's good."

"Too good," she muttered.

He didn't disagree aloud, just watched the water in the bay and thanked God for this second chance.

HECATE'S PALACE was a cute little shop halfway between New York City and Bayview Heights. Thirteen months ago Julia had found it on a Web site for Wiccans and had driven out to look around; she'd ended up with a job. The store was small, with rows of books, even more rows of herbs and baskets full of stones with mystical properties. The air was filled with the exotic scent of incense.

Dan Caruso walked in and she almost dropped a bag of stones as she was restocking the shelves. Dressed in his trademark black, he'd cut his hair so it only skimmed his collar now. His small diamond stud winked in the overhead lights. Holding his hand was a darling little boy.

"Hi, guys," Julia said. He'd come through for her during Ashley's ordeal, but she'd felt uneasy around him ever since. It had something to do with all the rotten things the guys around her were doing lately, like Evan and even Dr. Lansing.

"Hi." Dan's dark eyes twinkled at her. "How you doin', Sabrina?" He'd been teasing her about being a Wiccan and had taken to calling her Sabrina, the teenage witch.

She bristled. "Did you come to my store to mock me, Caruso?"

"Nah, Jimmy and I are lookin' for a book, aren't we kid?"

"Uh-huh." The boy was a miniature of his brother, with his black windbreaker and jeans, black high tops, longish hair and even a little earring. She knew Dan paid for all his clothes.

Julia was immediately smitten by the child. She hunkered down to face him. "Hi, cutie. I'm Julia."

He studied her the way Dan did. "You don't look like a witch."

"That's because you've only seen storybook ones." She stood. "Come on, I'll show you something."

With a death grip on Dan's hand, the little boy followed her to a section in the back. She pulled out a picture book and said, "We got a great chair over there. Wanna read this with me?"

Jimmy's eyes sought his brother's. Dan nodded and said, "I'll just look around."

"For what?"

"Nothing in particular."

Julia settled down with Jimmy on the big chair and began to read him the children's book *What It Means To Be a Witch*. The boy listened intently and his eyes widened at the pictures. When she was done, she found Dan watching her.

"Can we buy this, Danny?" Jimmy asked.

Julia slid Jimmy to the floor and stood. "Nope, you can't." She leaned down and kissed his nose. "'Cause it's a present from me."

Dan studied her. "I'll buy this." He held up a book.

She moved closer to him, but not too close. "What's that?"

"*Living Wiccan, A Guide for the Solitary Practitioner*. The cover says this book is the best resource on Wiccan."

"Why're you buying it?" she asked as she went behind the counter.

"Because *you're* interested in this stuff. Even if you *have* been treatin' me like crap since Ashley was in the hospital."

"I haven't been…" But she stopped because he was right. She had been avoiding him.

"You know," he said, watching her as she cashed him out, "Vivian asked me to hang out with her Friday night."

"Aren't you working?"

"Till six."

"Oh, so you can be with Vivian afterward."

"I'd rather be with you."

"Dan, look…"

When she hesitated, he looked at her unnervingly. Finally he said, "Never mind." He picked up the package. "I get the picture. I'm outta here." He walked over to the stones Jimmy was perusing. Taking his brother's hand, Dan headed to the door, but turned back to face her. "I thought you were different, Jules, from the rest of Caufield's Chicks. But you're not. You're still afraid to go your own way." He shook his head sadly. "Have a nice life."

And he left.

Julia stared after him, feeling bereft.

"COME ON, WE HAVE stores to visit yet." Zoe yanked on Kurt's arm.

"Only a masochist shops on Saturday." He held up the two shopping bags. "Besides isn't this enough for one kid?"

"She's turning eighteen. It's a big birthday."

"Godiva chocolate, four books and a designer handbag should be plenty."

"One more store." Zoe grasped his hand, relishing the right to touch him openly, to tease him, just to *be* with him. The only drawback was that he was charming her all over again, and she was falling hard and fast.

Which was why she had to keep things light. She

was scared to death of the man who hugged her as they walked through the huge airy mall, of the man who held her hand as if she belonged to him.

"Did you enjoy the play last night?" he asked.

"Hmm. I think Jason Priestly's a doll. He looked so yummy in that bare-chested scene."

"You have no shame, woman." He drew her closer.

"I'll prove that to you right now." She dragged him to the store she'd been saving till last.

He gazed at the window and said, "No way."

"Uh-huh. We're buying her something here. I got Erica's birthday present in this place. Eighteen-year-olds love this store."

"Zoe, I'm liberal, but hell, I'm not getting something at Victoria's Secret for my own kid. What kind of message would that send?"

She rolled her eyes. "That you understand the female teenage mind."

"*That* I'll never do."

"Oh, I don't know. These days Ashley, Julia and even Shondra think you're pretty cool."

"Shondra's totally succumbed to Johnny's charms and sees all of us as saints. Rachel, Julia and, of course, Ashley are grateful that I helped her out." He scowled but Zoe knew he wasn't really looking at the display of demi-cup bras in the window. "Erica's hit a plateau with me, though. We're not making any more progress."

Zoe scowled. "Erica looks kind of pale and thin. I took her out for breakfast this week, and she hardly ate anything. I'm worried about her."

"Can I do anything?"

"No. I got her to talk to the school counselor, Barb Sherman, again, but Barb says she didn't tell her much.

Just like the last time." Zoe shrugged off the worry.
"Come on, no bad thoughts today. We're supposed to
be having fun. Let's go get Lauren some fancy pajamas."

"Well, I can handle pajamas, I think."

He was pretty good with women's underwear, too,
Zoe remembered, but didn't tease. She knew he wanted
to make love, and she wasn't ready yet, so they steered
clear of even the slightest sexual innuendo.

They had fun in the store. He blushed furiously at
the assortment of female "unmentionables," and
groaned at the thought of his daughter wearing the
stuff. He took an interest in the pajamas, though. He
was particularly ensnared by a hot-pink nightgown
which wrapped around a mannequin like a second skin.
She saw him finger it, then check out the price.

"Megabucks, I bet," Zoe said, sauntering over to
him.

"It's pure silk." He cleared his throat. "Worth it, I
think."

"It's too old for Lauren."

He stared at her. "I wasn't thinking of it on Lauren."

Her heart thudded in her chest. "Kurt, I—"

"Ms. C? Is that you?"

Zoe spun around, clutching the dark blue satiny pajamas she'd picked out for Kurt's daughter. "Shondra,
hi."

Julia and Rachel came up behind her. "Hi, Ms. C,
Dr. Lansing." Both girls smiled at her and Kurt. Ashley appeared and greeted them with a smile, too.

Finally Erica came into view. She stared at Zoe, then
at Kurt's hand, resting lightly on the hot-pink silk;
when she looked up, her eyes were a little wild.

She turned and walked away.

The girls exchanged long, soulful looks, and Kurt frowned after Erica.

"MEN ARE ALL SLIME." Erica was pissed off, big time. Caufield's Chicks sat in the food court, munching on junk food. She toyed with a French fry, but didn't eat it. It was greasy and made her stomach turn. She tapped her fingernails on the table, thinking.

"They can be," Ashley added. "God knows, Evan is."

"Jules, you zoned out again," Shondra observed. "You been out of it all day. What's wrong?"

Julia shrugged. "Nothing."

"It isn't about Dan 'the Man' Caruso, is it?" Rachel asked.

"No, why?"

"I saw him last night. At Pepper's."

"Yeah? He usually doesn't hang out there."

Rachel and Ashley shared a knowing look. "He was with vivid Vivian."

Erica scowled at Julia's stricken look. *Freakin' men!* "See, they all *are* slime. Thought you had something going with him, didn't you, Jules?"

"No, Erica, I didn't."

Erica shrugged and let the lie go. She rubbed her temples; the headache, which came with regularity, was returning. And her scalp was starting to itch. Again. It had been happening a lot lately.

Shondra added, "Anyway, they aren't all slime. John Battaglia's a doll."

"Do you have any idea the hell he raised at Bayview years ago when he was a student?" Erica asked. "I hear he was a gang leader." She giggled and did a poor imitation of a motorcycle revving. "I wonder if he had a bike. I think they're sexy."

Ashley frowned. "He was in my sister Mimi's class. She said he was nice but had a big chip on his shoulder."

"All guys got baggage." Erica's tone was surly.

Julia sat up straight. "Erica, what's with you? These days you're so negative. You still uptight about this stuff with Ms. C and Dr. Lansing?"

"There's nothing going on there."

"If you believe that, then you're blind, girl." Shondra rolled her eyes. "What do you think that Victoria's Secret thing was all about?"

"You said they told you they were buying his daughter a present."

"They were eatin' each other up with their eyes."

"I think they might be getting back together," Julia observed.

Erica slapped her hand on the table so loudly the people next to them turned and stared. She didn't give a rat's ass. "No way. She wouldn't forgive him."

Ashley shrugged. "Maybe she would if he makes up for what he did."

"You're not thinking about going back with Evan, are you?" Erica was horrified at the thought. Spots swam before her eyes and the headache became full-blown.

Ashley's face was sad. "No, he wasn't the man I thought he was. I'm done with him, at least for now. But not with all guys. My sisters' husbands are great. Mr. Taylor and Captain Lansing are pretty neat." She eyed Erica. "Since when did you get into this male-bashing, anyway?"

Erica stood. Now her skin was itchy all over. "I'm

not. I need to go to the ladies' room.'' She couldn't get away fast enough.

As she headed for the restroom, she searched her purse and popped an upper in her mouth before she got there. She'd been trying like hell to cut down and usually managed, until things like this happened.

When she walked into the restroom, she felt something crawling in her head.

''Oh, God,'' she yelled, and flew to the mirror. Lice? She checked her hair, though her vision blurred.

Then she felt them crawl down her neck.

''Get them off me, somebody please!'' She shook her head, scratching it with her fingers, flailing wildly at her shoulders and arms. ''Get off me!'' she yelled.

''Erica?'' Julia walked in. ''What are you yelling about?''

''The bugs,'' she screamed, backing up against the wall. ''In my hair. On my neck. Get them off me!''

Julia rushed to her and checked her head. She froze for a minute, then said, ''Erica, there aren't any bugs in your hair.''

Erica stared at Julia until she came into focus. It took a while. Julia called her name several times. Oh, God, what had happened? ''Bugs?'' she finally asked, stalling for time.

''You said there were bugs in your hair. Then you zoned out.''

''Um, I was kidding. Jerking your chain.'' Her hands shaking violently, she turned to the sink to throw cold water on her face.

Julia said, ''I don't believe you.''

The water helped sober Erica. She pivoted around. ''All right, I'm just stressed. I haven't been sleeping and my dad's really on my case.''

"But you're seeing things? This is crazy. We need to tell somebody. Ms. Caufield, maybe."

Erica felt her face flush. "No! She'll get my father involved and he'll keep me locked up so my grades won't suffer." She stepped toward Julia and grasped her arm. "Please. Jules. Say you won't tell Ms. C. We always keep secrets for each other. All six of us."

Julia stared at Erica. After a moment, she said, "All right, I won't tell Ms. C. This time. But if something else happens, I will."

Relief flooded Erica as they left the bathroom. That had been really close.

CHAPTER ELEVEN

THANKSGIVING DAY had been everything Kurt had hoped for. He and Lauren had spent the day with Mitch and Cassie. The midday meal had been wonderful and Zoe's presence had made everything perfect.

Then the Taylors arrived for an evening meal of leftovers and Kurt was filled again with a feeling of warmth. Family, friends and good food. What more could anyone ask? Finally, he'd come into the living room with Mitch to watch the Giants make mincemeat out of the Oilers. His brother had been recruited upstairs to put Camille to bed, while Cassie helped Lacey settle the twins down in the guest room. Before he'd left to tend to his daughter, Mitch had squeezed Kurt's shoulder and commented that it looked like things were working out between him and Zoe. As Kurt half watched the football game from a big overstuffed chair, he thought about his big brother's advice last weekend…

"What are you doing here?" Kurt had asked early Sunday morning when he'd opened the door to his town house and found Mitch on the stoop.

"I decided go running with my brother." Mitch hopped from one foot to the other to stay warm. "Get dressed and meet me out here. I'll stretch while you're gone."

"Yes, sir, Captain," Kurt had joked, but he liked the

idea of an impromptu run with Mitch. They hadn't had much time together.

After about five minutes of companiable silence, Mitch asked, "What's going on, buddy?"

"Going on?"

"Things are different between you and Zoe. Cass and I could tell when we got back from New York."

Kurt smiled in the cool morning air. "You guys couldn't tell *anything* when you got back from New York. A weekend alone made you honeymooners again."

"Yep, it did." Mitch grinned. "God, I love that woman."

"I'm happy for you." Kurt meant it.

"So spill it. You didn't just come over to help Zoe with the girls."

"Actually, I did." Kurt slowed somewhat when they reached an incline. "But you're right, Zoe's decided to give me another chance."

Mitch stopped dead in his tracks. "I thought something was going on. Alexandra said she saw 'Aunt Zoe on top of Uncle Kurt' on Camille's twin bed."

Rather than take the bait, Kurt gibed him back. "Yeah? She told us how you get in the tub with Cassie, too, big brother."

Both men chuckled. Kurt said, "I can't believe I've got another chance with her, Mitch."

Clapping Kurt on the back, Mitch said, "Well, don't screw it up this time, buddy."

"I'm trying not to, but she's put a lot of damn rules on the whole thing."

"Sounds like Zoe. You'll live through it, though you won't like it."

"I already don't…"

"Dad?" Kurt came back to the present to find his daughter beside his chair. "You awake?"

He realized he must have dozed off. "Yeah." He reached out for her hand. "Did I tell you how much it means to me having you here today, Lauren?"

"About a thousand times." Light brown hair—with new streaks of blond, he noticed—brushed her shoulders, and her hazel eyes sparkled. She was dressed in typical college garb—denims, boots and a gray Hartwick sweatshirt that matched his. "It's fun seeing Zoe again." She perched on the arm of the big chair and kept hold of his hand. "I really like her, Dad."

"So do I, princess."

She kissed his cheek. "You're a lot happier than you were last Thanksgiving."

"I was just thinking that."

Last year, they'd eaten a stilted meal at an upscale restaurant with Elizabeth's parents. Kurt had been miserable already, after just months into the reconciliation, but was too proud to admit he'd made a mistake.

Just then two boys appeared in the archway: Joe Taylor, Seth's son, and Johnny. They were roommates at Columbia University, and Joe put in as many hours at the *Herald* as Johnny did at the clinic. Again Kurt was struck by their contrast: Joe had classic blond good looks and dressed like a kid in prep school, whereas John wore his standard black and was always in need of a haircut.

"Did you ask him yet?" Johnny teased Lauren.

"No."

Joe gave her a mock frown. "Well, do it, girl."

"Go away and I will."

Laughing, Joe dragged Johnny from the doorway.

"What was that all about?" Kurt asked.

"I know we don't have a lot of time together, Daddy, but I want to do something tonight."

"*Daddy,* huh? Must be something big."

"I'd like to stay here tonight. While we were watching *The Lion King* downstairs, the kids asked Johnny if they could have a sleepover. Alexandra, little Philip, Josh, Johnny, Joe and me in Johnny's rooms."

"Are you kidding? I'm surprised you didn't come screaming upstairs after two hours with those three little ones."

"Josh and Philip are angels." She gave him a Lansing grin. "Alexandra's a handful. But she and Camille are the only cousins I have. I'd like to spend time with them."

He nodded to the doorway. "And those two handsome hunks have nothing to do with it?"

"Johnny's practically family, too, Dad. And Joey's a regular Sir Galahad, so he's nothing to worry about."

"Sure, honey, you can stay here. I'll come back and get you tomorrow."

Her huge hug warmed him. When she left, he remembered how difficult it had been arranging today. As always, Elizabeth's timing had been horrible. Zoe had met him at the clinic last Tuesday to go to dinner, and they were about to leave when the phone rang. He'd punched in the speaker phone as he packed his briefcase.

"Lansing."

"Kurt, it's Elizabeth."

Zoe's eyes had widened. In them he saw surprise change to anger, tinged with a little fear. She started to back away.

He caught her arm and shook his head vehemently. "No, don't go."

"Kurt, are you there?" Elizabeth's voice was slurred.

"Yes, what do you want, Elizabeth?"

"You can't have Lauren for Thanksgiving."

"It's all arranged."

"Sorry."

"So am I. But she's old enough to make her own choices. I promised her we'd spend the day at Mitch's. And we're going to celebrate her birthday on Friday."

"I'll make a stink."

"Try it."

"You'll be sorry."

"Elizabeth, what's this all about?" No answer. "Have you been drinking?"

There'd been a studied pause. "I want to be with both of you, that's all." Her tone was whiny. "Let me come to Mitch's, too."

"Absolutely not."

"Kurt I—"

"I'm not listening to you anymore. Goodbye, Elizabeth."

After he'd disconnected, he and Zoe stared at each other. For a long time. Finally he said, "I've learned my lesson with her, Zoe."

"She hasn't given up, has she?"

"Apparently not. But it doesn't matter."

Zoe had walked into his arms then and hugged him tightly.

"Come to Mitch's with me," he'd said.

"All right. Cassie was elated when I told her we were trying this again. She asked me to dinner, too…"

As if his thoughts had conjured her, Zoe appeared in the doorway. He loved the way she was dressed today, in snug red jeans, a candy-striped sweater and heeled black boots. "You asleep in here, old man?"

"Nope. Just resting."

"Well, perk up, because we're ready for charades. Boys against the girls."

He groaned. "I hate charades."

"Oh, Lord, how can anybody hate charades?"

"Kiss me first."

She eyed him from the doorway. Then she tossed her head and walked toward him, her curvy hips swaying as she came close. He patted his lap. "Sit here." Her gaze narrowed, then she gave him an exotic smile and straddled him.

She'd been noticeably less wary of him physically since the phone call from Elizabeth, even instigating a kiss here and there. "You look great in this sweatshirt, you know that?" she told him, her breath fanning his ear.

"Great? Not yummy? Like Jason Priestly?" His hands flexed on her waist.

"Mmm, yeah, yummy, too."

She lowered her head and took his mouth in a searing kiss.

"Happy Thanksgiving, love," he said against her lips.

"Happy Thanksgiving," she whispered back.

FROM HER POSITION on the floor leaning against the couch, Zoe slid to the rug, holding her sides, which hurt from laughing so hard. "You guys are pathetic. I've never seen such dumb clues."

Giving her a disgusted look, Mitch, who'd just blown the title *My Best Friend's Wedding,* marched over to her, reached down and scooped her up in his arms. He was as tall as Kurt and muscular. "Take it back, lady."

She hung on to his neck. "Never."

He strode to the front door and opened it easily with one hand. It was pouring rain outside. He began swinging her back and forth. "I'll count to three. If you don't take it back, you're getting soaked."

"You wouldn't dare." She watched him, then called over his shoulder, "Cassie, help!"

Cassie came running out and leaped onto Mitch's back. "Leave her alone, big guy."

Dragging Cassie along, Mitch stumbled back into the living room, dropped Zoe into Kurt's lap and tackled his wife to the floor, where he began to tickle her.

"Just because you're such poor losers," Lacey said as she returned from checking on the kids.

Mitch glanced up at her and gave her a say-more-and-you're-next look. She scurried to the couch.

"Don't worry, Ace, I'll protect you." Seth pulled her onto his lap and cuddled her close.

She laughed and whispered something in his ear.

When things quieted down, it was the girls' turn to guess. Zoe drew a scrap of paper from their pile with flourish. In front of a red-faced Cassie and an unusually spunky Lacey, she read it and said, "Piece of cake."

The men booed.

Cockily Zoe held up her hand and spread her fingers.

"Five words," Cassie called out.

Zoe raised her index finger, then touched it to her thumb.

"First word, a small one. The?" This from Lacey.

Zoe nodded and held up two fingers twice.

"Second word, second syllable."

Zoe patted her back.

"Back." Lacey's guess again. "Okay, back is part of the second word."

Watching Zoe's next gestures, Cassie concentrated with the intensity of a brain surgeon. "Third *and* forth words?"

Vigorously Zoe nodded and made a half circle with her hands.

Cassie said quickly, "The whole concept."

Zoe folded her hands, prayer-style.

"Praying?"

She shook her head.

"Religion?"

She shrugged.

"It's religious." Lacey began to brainstorm. "A person. A backward religious person?"

The guys guffawed.

Zoe rolled her eyes.

"Not a person." Cassie frowned. "A thing." Zoe nodded. "A church? The back of a church?"

Lacey stood up. "I know. *The Hunchback of Notre Dame.*"

All three women jumped in the air when Zoe said, "Yes!"

"That's it." Lacey grinned.

"We win," Cassie boasted.

"Damn," Mitch said. "I hate it when women win. They gloat."

"Watch it, mister, I'll throw *you* out in the rain," Zoe told him.

"Yeah, half-pint, you and who's army?"

It was just like old times.

The doorbell pealed. Mitch looked at his wife. "You expecting somebody, Cassie?"

"No, but I'll get it. Maybe it's for Johnny."

Still smiling, she hustled to the door. When she returned, she wasn't smiling anymore. "Kurt, I think you should…"

"Hello, darling." Behind Cassie stood Elizabeth. Her tall model-thin frame was cloaked in an expensive mauve raincoat, her hair curled around her shoulders in studied disarray. Her makeup was exquisitely correct. But she swayed slightly on her feet. "Happy Thanksgiving."

Kurt paled; his gaze swung to Zoe. She looked shell-shocked.

Everyone in the room rose. Cassie crossed to stand next to Mitch, and Lacey sought out Seth. Both couples flanked Kurt, forming a solid wall of support. Zoe nudged up behind him.

"Elizabeth," Mitch said frostily, "what are you doing here?"

"I've come to see my family on Thanksgiving." Glittering eyes scanned the room. "Where's Lauren?"

"She's—" Cassie began.

But Kurt interrupted. "Elizabeth, you smell like gin. You've been drinking."

"Some." She arched a brow. "It's Thanksgiving, darling."

"Look, you don't belong here. I told you that when you called last week. It'd be best if you left now."

Lazily she unbuttoned her raincoat. "I belong with my husband and daughter on a holiday. And you know it." Her glassy gaze zeroed in on Zoe. "Or at least you would if certain home wreckers would leave you alone."

As before, this was too much for Zoe. She wanted no part of it. "Excuse, me," she said, and started to back away.

Kurt reached for her and caught the sleeve of her sweater. "No, you're not going. The only person leaving this room will be Elizabeth." Kurt slid his arm around Zoe, anchoring her to him. "It's over, Elizabeth. There's no chance for you and me. We tried to reconcile and it didn't work."

"We would have stayed together if it wasn't for her." She pointed an unsteady finger at Zoe. "You could never stop thinking about her."

Zoe cringed. Oh, God, she hated this. She wanted to run, but Kurt's arm was like steel around her. He stared down at her with bleak eyes.

Suddenly she remembered what he'd said last week. *Zoe, tell me one thing. Why is it that you didn't fight for me a year ago?*

She looked around—Seth, Lacey, Mitch and Cassie had no intention of leaving Kurt alone with Elizabeth. Only *she* had thoughts about getting away. The idea spun around in her brain. Oh, God, hadn't she learned from the past? Would she really let Elizabeth waltz right in again and take the man she loved?

Shaky, but determined, Zoe faced Kurt's ex-wife. "I'm sorry you're without your family, Elizabeth, especially today. But you were wrong to come here. Kurt isn't yours anymore." She slid her arm around his waist. "And you're just embarrassing yourself by making a scene."

For the first time the woman's cool demeanor cracked. Her gaze flew from Zoe to Kurt. She sent Kurt a sickeningly sweet smile. "I took the train out from the Hamptons and a cab here. You'll need to drive me back."

"No." Kurt's tone was implacable.

Mitch stepped forward. "Come on, Elizabeth. Seth and I'll give you a ride back to the train station."

Seth nodded.

Haughtily Elizabeth surveyed the six people before her. Then, without another word, she turned and walked to the foyer. Mitch and Seth followed her.

When the outer door closed, Cassie cast a worried glance at Zoe and said, "Come on, Lace, let's go get some drinks." Both women squeezed Kurt's arm on the way out.

Once alone, Zoe turned to Kurt. His face was ravaged and full of questions.

In that instant Zoe realized she'd taken one giant step toward cementing her new relationship with Kurt.

KURT PULLED ASIDE the sheers and stared out the window of Zoe's bedroom—where he never expected to be again—at the bay. The water was calm tonight, lazily lapping against the dock and kissing the shoreline. He turned back to the room. It carried her scent of lotions, perfume and soap. He'd always thought the room very feminine—perfect for Zoe—with its creamy walls, wrought-iron bed, ruffled pillows and blue-and-beige coverlet.

And now he was back here...

"Come in," she'd said after they'd left Mitch's house and Kurt had driven her home, the slap of the windshield wipers broken only by an occasional innocuous comment.

"I don't think so, sweetheart. I'm raw. I..." He'd raked a hand through his hair and shrugged. "I don't have much control tonight."

She'd stood on tiptoe and kissed him. The way she used to kiss him when she'd believed he was a man she could count on. "I've changed my mind about taking this slowly," she'd said simply, grasped his hand and, after shedding wet coats and shoes, led him up here to her bedroom. He was still reeling from the impact of her actions...and her decision. What had brought this on?

The door to the bathroom opened and all questions fled. She stood in the half light of a muted corner lamp, clothed in the pink nightgown he'd admired that day at Victoria's Secret; it dipped low in the front and skimmed her thighs. Slowly, as if she was savoring the moment, she moved toward him. Her head was high, and confidence brimmed in her huge brown eyes.

Straightening, he said, "You take my breath away." He nodded to her outfit. "You went back and got that?"

"Uh-huh."

"For me?"

"Yes."

"I'm glad." The significance of the gesture touched him, deep inside.

She stepped closer, gave him a siren's smile. "It's been too long," she said, sliding her hands up his chest, around his neck, whispering against his jaw.

Intuitively he understood what she meant. Their, intense mating a month ago had been frenzied and desperate, the fulfillment of a need clawing at them both. Tonight, in the dreamy intimacy of this room, a new kind of bond would be formed, even better than the one he'd so foolishly destroyed a year ago.

He skimmed her cheek with his knuckles. "Zoe," he whispered, "I love you so much." They were words he'd never said directly to her before.

She startled and he felt the delicate connection between them change, as if a bolt of reality had struck it. She turned her face into his palm. "Come to bed."

He ignored the stab of pain her response, or lack of it, caused. He knew deep in his heart she loved him; if it took her time to rebuild her faith in him, he could wait.

With Circe's smile, she reached for the hem of his sweatshirt and drew it over his head. A clumsy lassitude overcame him as he unbuttoned his shirt, shrugged it off and let it fall to the floor. She leaned over and placed her mouth on his chest. Gently she grazed her lips back and forth.

"I missed this so much," she told him, stopping to kiss his pectorals. His body lurched when her tongue circled his nipple. "How you taste." Her hand came up and threaded through the springy hair on his chest. "How you feel." She stood on her toes again and buried her nose in his neck, inhaling him. "How you smell."

His hands dropped to her waist and flexed there. He tried to still his trembling fingers, calm his thrumming heart, but he'd wanted this for so long he was overcome with emotion.

Her fingers were sure as they tugged at his belt, pushed down his slacks and boxer shorts. Slowly she ran her palms up and down his hips, refamiliarizing herself with his body. She slid them to his buttocks, caressed him there, then around front, and cupped him boldly.

"Oh, baby, no, no, not yet."

He drew back.

It was his turn.

She felt as if she were weightless when he picked her up. Snuggling against him, she steeped herself in the play of his muscles against her limbs and the erratic tempo of his breathing.

It was unlike the last time. Then, their lovemaking had been an explosion. This was more like a smoldering flame. She tingled with a craving so intense it consumed her.

He placed her on the bed and ran his hand down her hip, then up to her breast, which he cradled in his palm. He sat beside her, leaned over, and through the silk, took a nipple into his mouth. She arced off the mattress and grasped his shoulders.

Bracing his arms on either side of her shoulders, he asked, "Do you have any idea how many times I've dreamed about this?"

"Yes." She had, too.

Even his smile was sexy. He tracked little kisses from her neck down to her chest, nosing the fabric of her nightgown away. The hot brush of his lips on her skin made her tense.

"Shh. Easy," he said as he drew down the straps. His eyes narrowed on her as he bared another inch. And kissed what he exposed. He bared another inch. Kissed that, too. He repeated the ritual all the way down her body until she was writhing.

"Kurt, I need you."

"I need you, too, love."

His caresses became bolder, but no less gentle. She closed her eyes and allowed herself to feel what she had missed more than anything else in her life: the rasp of his knuckles over her nipple, then the scrape of his teeth; the curving of his palm over her, then his fingers sliding into her.

"Please," she whispered when his mouth met hers with edgy need.

He drew back and stared down at her. Never unlocking his eyes from hers, he fumbled on the dresser, found a condom she'd put there, sheathed himself and finally, finally stretched out on the bed.

She felt the tears come. Her eyes closed as he slid into her. Then he stopped, leaned over and sipped the moisture off her cheeks. "Ah, love," he whispered. "Don't."

"I've missed you so much," she said against his skin.

Burying his face in her neck, he said, "I've missed you, too." He began to move inside her. "I love you, Zoe. Love you...love you."

KURT ROLLED OVER in bed and opened his eyes. Bright sunlight peeked through the curtains, disorienting him. Then he remembered and reached for her.

She was gone.

Sighing, he settled back into the pillows and glanced at the pretty teakwood clock on the wall. Nine. He hadn't slept this well or this long in fourteen months. They'd made love last night, exquisite, tender, all-consuming love.

And she'd cried.

And she hadn't said she loved him.

He'd brushed aside the disappointment then; he'd been on fire for her. Now, in the brittle light of day, it hurt.

Be thankful for what you have.

Things were going to be all right, he told himself as he got out of bed. Nothing mattered except that they were working their way back together. He was still chanting that mantra in his head when he went downstairs a few minutes later, dressed in the navy terrycloth robe she'd left out on the bed. It was his; obviously, like the flannel shirt, she hadn't thrown it away.

She stood by the kitchen window sipping coffee. He smiled at the picture she made. She wore a long thermal yellow one-piece pajama thing, so different from the silk of the night before.

"Hi," he said softly.

She turned. "Hi."

He'd slept deeply, but she obviously hadn't. There were circles under her eyes and a weariness about her mouth. He crossed to her. When he reached her, he cradled her cheek in his palm. "Didn't sleep?"

Her eyes wide and sad, she shook her head. "You did, though."

"Do you want to talk about it?"

She shook her head. "Nothing to talk about. Just a bad night." She poured him coffee and added some milk. When she handed it to him, she smiled. It was a strained smile. "What time do you have to pick Lauren up at Mitch's?"

"Eleven."

"Well," she said, glancing at the clock, "I have to be at school by ten."

"School? The day after Thanksgiving?"

"Uh-huh. We're setting up for the festival on Saturday."

"The festival?"

She busied herself like little Suzie homemaker, straightening the dish towel, wiping up the counter. "Yes. We started it last year. The festival's a whole day of carnival-like activities. Teachers and kids volunteer to man the booths. The idea behind the project is to raise money for the Good Deeds Christmas project."

Cautious, he leaned against the counter and sipped

his coffee. "Will you be able to celebrate Lauren's birthday with us tonight?"

"No, I don't think so. I promised to take the girls out to dinner afterward, and I told Erica we could see a movie. You know how worried I am about her."

"What about tomorrow? Will you be busy all day at this festival?"

"Yes, I think so. It's, um, been planned for a long time."

"And Sunday? Have you found something to do so you can't spend the day with me?"

"You'll be taking Lauren back to—" She stopped when she must have realized what she'd admitted. Her eyes flicked guiltily to his. "I'm not searching for excuses…"

He stared at her intently. "Making love with me scared you last night."

She nodded, looking so much like a lost little girl that his heart broke. The sun slanted in through the blinds, highlighting some red streaks in her hair and accenting her luminous eyes.

"Why did you do it, then?"

For several seconds she said nothing. Just watched him. "I wanted to. I remembered what you said, about not fighting for you before. When Elizabeth barged in, I decided to fight."

His smile was loving. "Thank you for that."

"I thought I was ready to break the rules, Kurt." She turned to rinse out the perfectly clean sink. "But now I'm confused. And frightened."

He came up behind her. "Is that why you cried?" he asked gently.

She shook her head but didn't face him.

"Zoe?"

At last she pivoted around. His hands loosely

grasped her hips. "I cried because it hit me how much we'd lost. How much time had passed and how much damage we'd done to what had once been so perfect."

"It can be rebuilt."

"Can it?"

Stark fear hit him like an emotional sledgehammer. "You haven't changed your mind, have you?" Now that he'd had her again, he didn't think he could let her go.

Again the delay in answering was long and disconcerting. "No," she said at last. "I haven't changed my mind. But…"

"You don't trust me yet."

She was silent for a moment, then said. "All I know is I'm afraid. I need to step back a bit."

"I see." He strode to the counter and picked up his coffee.

She said, "Look, I have to go shower. I'll be late meeting the girls." As if she knew she was dismissing him, she added, "Don't hurry. You can let yourself out."

He said nothing.

With a torn look, she studied him for a minute, then headed for the door. When she reached it, he called out to her. "Zoe?" She turned. "Would it be all right if I attended the festival tomorrow?"

The flicker of unease in her eyes told him she didn't want him there. "Of course. We're hoping the whole community comes."

That zinged his heart. But he only nodded, and she left then.

He tried to talk himself out of being hurt, that he'd made more strides, more quickly, than he had any right to, that she was just trying to protect herself.

But it didn't work.

She wasn't the only one who was terrified of getting hurt in this relationship. Not by a longshot.

CHAPTER TWELVE

FROM HER PUBLIC-RELATIONS booth in one corner of the gym, Zoe surveyed the Thanksgiving Festival with pride. The gym was filled with the mouthwatering smells of the freshly baked goods being sold at the food concession. Several booths lined the perimeter, some staffed by her kids. Julia, assisted by Rachel, operated a tarot-card-reading booth decorated with stars and moons. Julia looked sad today, and last night, too, when Zoe had seen her. Zoe guessed it had something to do with Dan Caruso.

A giggle drifted from the roped-off area next to the tarot-cards booth. Zoe smiled at Shelley Marco, who laughed as Alex Ransom threw her a basketball; they were running a free-throw game and were shooting some hoops themselves as they waited for customers.

Across the gym was the children's area, a new addition to the festival aimed at enticing parents with small kids. Dan was patiently helping Josh Taylor make sand art, but both boys were getting more colored crystals on themselves than in the bottle. Ashley and Shondra supervised another activity for youngsters—face-painting. Currently Shondra worked on Alexandra Lansing, while Johnny held the little girl on his lap. Shondra laughed girlishly at something Johnny said. Joe Taylor, who was covering the festival for the *Herald,* looked on.

As she watched them, Kurt entered her peripheral vision. Though she tried to stop herself from staring at him, from *drooling* over him, she couldn't. He'd arrived with Mitch, Lauren, Johnny and the Lansing girls shortly after the festival opened at eleven. Leaning against the wall, he sipped coffee and talked with his daughter.

He was dressed in tan jeans and a light green chamois shirt she'd bet made his eyes glow like marbles. Where yesterday morning, fresh from her bed, he'd been rested and happy, today his shoulders slumped with fatigue. She hadn't seen him since she'd left her place yesterday morning.

I want to be cautious.

By closing yourself off so I can't hurt you?

Disgusted with herself, she turned away to fiddle with some papers. She'd never realized she was such a coward. She'd been totally unable to contain her fear of getting close to him again. And he'd been hurt. Damn.

Her gaze drifted over to Erica, who was also working the PR booth. There was another problem. Zoe knew Erica's friends were worried about her, too. Julia, especially, had dropped some broad hints that Zoe should talk to Erica, but when pressed, Julia wouldn't come right out and tell Zoe why.

She and Erica had gone to see an old Robert Redford film last night, then stopped at Pepper's where they'd arranged to meet the other girls for something to eat.

Again Erica hadn't ordered food...

"All right, something's got to be done about your not eating," Zoe had said. "And not sleeping. You know I'm worried about you."

Erica had stared at her with sad blue eyes. "I'm having a rough first semester, is all."

"Why?"

"I'm worried about getting into Georgetown. My dad says it'll be a disgrace if I don't, since all the Cases went there."

"Well, first off, your chances of getting in are astronomical. And second, you've applied to other good Ivy League schools that have indicated they'd take you in a minute."

Erica had only shrugged.

"Look, I know you're not telling me everything. And that's okay. But I think you should talk to a professional counselor. Dr. Sheffield, maybe."

"Maybe." The other kids had come into Pepper's then, and she and Erica hadn't had a chance to resume the conversation...

"Ms. C?" Zoe turned to face Erica. Today she wore the deep-rust T-shirt all the workers had donned; it had been designed, surprisingly, by Dan Caruso. Zoe had had no idea the boy had artistic talent. The front read, "Be thankful for what you have." On the back it said, "And give some of it back to others." Children of various ethnic origins composed a sea of faces under the sentiment.

"You did a good job with the Down to Earth display, Erica," Zoe told her.

"Did I?"

Zoe scowled at the unusual lack of confidence. "Uh-huh."

The girl scanned the gym. "A lot of people are here already. Why'd Dr. Lansing come, do you think?"

To see me. But she didn't say it. Again, *coward* came

to mind. "Because of his brother. And his daughter's visiting for the weekend."

"She nice?"

"Very."

"Did you see them this weekend?"

Zoe sighed. "Erica, I don't really—"

"—want to talk about this. I know. Hey, I gotta pee. I'm going to the bathroom."

As Erica trotted away, Zoe had a fleeting sense of foreboding, and it shook her. Preoccupied with the feeling, she set out course descriptions and thought about Erica's behavior over the past couple of months. Which was why she didn't see Kurt approach her table.

"Hi." The low baritone of his voice curled through her. She loved how it sounded in the morning—a little hoarse, a lot sexy. "Hi."

"This is great." He waved an arm to encompass the gym.

"Yeah."

He nodded to the TV. "Down to Earth?" Up close, his eyes were bloodshot.

"Uh-huh. Franz videotapes it for us every year."

Kurt moved in front of the set. He stared at it as he sipped his coffee. They were as awkward as two strangers forced to share the same space on a train. She hated this wall between them, but didn't seem able to scale it.

He shook his head. "Oh, Lord, is that what I looked like?"

Zoe turned to the TV. On the screen was Kurt dangling from the harness. Her breath caught in her throat, just as it had that day.

"Better not let Bosco see that," he joked.

Zoe didn't respond.

"Zoe?"

She faced him, knowing the color had drained out of her cheeks.

"Sweetheart, I was okay."

"It makes my stomach flop whenever I see that."

He reached out and squeezed her arm.

"Hi, guys." Erica returned, looking bright-eyed.

"Hello, Erica." Kurt's tone was friendly.

"You all right?" Zoe asked.

"Yeah." The girl frowned at Kurt's hand on her arm. "I'm going to check out the kiddie area, okay?"

"Sure, I can handle this."

"So I see." Giving Kurt a long look, she stalked off.

"Something's wrong with her," Zoe said.

"I know."

"More than just us."

"Is there an 'us,' Zoe?"

"What?"

"Never mind. This isn't the place. I think you should try to get Erica to see Louise for some counseling."

"I told her exactly that last night."

"Well, we always were on the same wavelength." He scanned the gym. "I'm going to go get Camille from Mitch so he can help Cassie at the casino."

She swallowed hard. "Will you be here all day?"

He shrugged. "That depends."

Jerry Bosco approached from behind Kurt. "Hi, Jerry," Zoe said stiffly. "Are you enjoying the festival?"

He carried a spiral notepad in his hand. "Some of it." He underlined whatever he'd written. "Those tarot cards are inappropriate. So is the casino ring."

"It's all for a good cause, Jerry. We've used both at our senior bash," she said, referring to the drug-and-alcohol-free activity the school put on after the senior ball. "For fifteen years now." Not that he'd ever helped or even bothered to attend.

"Harrumph." He studied the two of them, then turned and left.

"I'll see you later," Kurt told her, and headed out after Jerry.

She nodded and watched him walk away, a sense of loss engulfing her.

"I GOTTA SAY, Ms. Jacobs, I'm disappointed to see there's no kissing booth." John Battaglia's eyes twinkled as he watched Shondra paint a dragon on Alexandra's face. Since the little girl insisted on sitting on his lap, Shondra was inches away from John; she'd never been this close to him before. He smelled like a man.

"Shush." Her hand trembled a bit.

"People kiss lots in our house," Alexandra proclaimed.

John rolled his eyes in silent communication with Shondra. Off to the side, Joe Taylor chuckled.

"Mommy and Daddy."

Shondra laughed.

"Yeah, they're regular lovebirds," John said.

"And Aunt Zoe and Uncle Kurt, too. They were kissing on Camille's bed."

"Oh, jeez, kid," Joe said, sputtering. "You don't have to broadcast that piece of news."

Shondra turned to see Erica approaching the children's area. She hoped Erica hadn't heard Alexandra telling tales. All the other Caufield's Chicks had decided Erica had done some serious flipping out about Ms. C and Dr. Lansing. And none of them agreed with her attitude. Besides, she was acting weird about everything. Julia was particularly worried about her, though Shondra didn't know why.

Erica stuck her hands in her pockets. "Hi, guys."

"Hi."

"Lookin' good?" Shondra asked her.

"Huh?"

"The dragon, silly."

Erica studied Alexandra's face. "A little grown-up for her, isn't it?"

"Alexandra wanted it, didn't you, baby?"

"Nothing wrong with that." John kissed the top of Alexandra's head.

Dan Caruso came over from the sand-art side. "Shondra, I'm takin' a break." He nodded to Joe and John, then said hello to Erica, who gave him a disgusted look.

"Sure." Shondra poked Erica in the ribs. "Be nice," she whispered to her friend.

As Dan walked away, Erica said, "Look, he's heading right for her."

"Who?" John asked.

"Julia."

But he wasn't, Shondra noticed. Instead, he made a beeline for Vivian's craft booth and stood talking to her for a few minutes. He appeared to be flirting with her.

Shondra's eyes darted to Julia. Her face crumpled as Dan leaned over and whispered something in Vivian's ear, then headed for the refreshment stand catercorner to Julia's booth.

Julia watched Dan saunter up in the loose-limbed way he had of walking, buy a soft drink and lean against the wall next to the food booth. He was only ten feet away. She couldn't tear her eyes off him. Discarding his usual black for the T-shirt he'd designed, his face glowed with health and…masculinity. It made her heart rattle.

"What you starin' at, Sabrina?"

Smiling at the name, she nodded at his handiwork. "Your shirt. It looks great."

She thought he mumbled, "Looks better on you," but she wasn't sure.

"What?"

"Nothin'." He drained the cup, crumpled it and pushed away from the wall.

Oh, God, he was leaving. Julia had been miserable since last week at Hecate's. And when Erica had flipped about the bug thing, Julia had desperately wanted to talk to Dan about it, but Erica had sworn her to secrecy. So she hadn't contacted him. And she was blowing her chance to talk to him now. "Dan, wait," she called when he was several feet away.

He pivoted. "Nope, I'm not waitin'. No more."

"Please don't say that. Let me read your cards." Smiling in the most flirtatious way she knew, she slipped a ticket out of her pocket and stuffed it in the box. "My treat."

His chocolate-brown eyes flared with anger and…interest.

He glanced over his shoulder at the kiddie area. "I only got a few minutes."

"I'll do a short reading." She shuffled the cards fast and divided them into three piles. "I'm all set up." When he still stood there, she said, "Please?"

His shoulders sagged and he sauntered over. Dropping into the chair, he said a little sulkily, "Go ahead."

She turned over a card. "Well, look at that. It's the Hermit."

"What does that mean?"

"It's the past card. It means you've been alone for most of your life."

He grunted.

She flipped over the Death card. "Ah, this one says you want some changes. Something different."

He eyed her warily.

Quickly she turned the Empress face up. "Oh, some good woman's going to be a big part of your life."

"She is?"

"Yeah. She has blond hair." Julia smiled at him. "And blue eyes."

Dan folded his arms over his chest.

Staring back down at the cards, Julia whispered, "And she's sorry for being such a jerk about things."

He leaned over and grasped her chin. "Jules?" She looked up at him. "I been tellin' you, you don't need roles to get me." He nodded at the table. "You don't need tricks."

The moment of truth. She asked, "What do I need? To get you?"

His Adam's apple bobbed. "Just be honest."

She held his gaze, then glanced over at Rachel, who was busying herself so she didn't eavesdrop. Julia looked at Shondra and Ashley and Erica, then Shelley. Finally she faced Dan again. "We're all going over to the Spaghetti Warehouse tonight after the festival. Wanna come with us?"

"Who's goin'?"

"Caufield's Chicks. And Shondra was gonna ask John Battaglia."

"I don't know."

"Come. With me, Dan." She cocked her head. "There are some things I need to talk to you about…but mostly I just want to be with you."

Like a little boy just discovering girls, he shook his head. "You get to me, you know?"

"I do?"

"Yeah," he said, standing, "and I don't know why. But I'll come."

As he turned to leave, Ashley plowed right into him. "Oh, sorry," she said.

He steadied her. Julia guessed Ashley didn't know Dan had been at the hospital the day of her miscarriage, and to spare her more embarrassment, no one had told her.

Ashley said, "Hi, Dan." Her gaze swung to Rachel. "Rach, I need to talk to you."

Dan Caruso walked away, murmuring to Julia, "See you later."

Despite her agitated state, Ashley smiled at her friend. "See you later?"

"Yeah. I invited him to the Spaghetti Warehouse with us."

"Cool," Ashley said.

"What's wrong?" Rachel asked, coming up to them.

Ashley nodded to the doorway. In it stood Evan Michaels. Wrapped around him was a cute dark-haired sophomore named Tiffany. For a minute Ashley thought her heart was going to pound right out of her chest.

"Isn't he working today at the festival?" Julia asked.

"No." Ashley watched the only boy she'd ever been with hug the pretty cheerleader.

"He dropped Ms. Caufield's class before vacation, too," Ashley said.

Shelley, who'd jogged over to them, put in, "Dropped it? This late in the semester?" She scowled. "He's even stupider than I thought."

That brought a smile to Ashley's face.

"You wanna split for a while, Ash?" Rachel asked.

Evan noticed her. She could tell by the smirk on his face as he grasped Tiffany's hand. Then he started toward Julia's booth.

Ashley squared her shoulders. "No. I'm not running away."

When Evan reached them, he slid his arm around his date's waist. "Well, well, well, if it isn't Caufield's Chicks. All lined up in a row, as usual."

Ashley could smell beer on him. "You been drinking, Evan?"

"He isn't driving," Tiffany bubbled. "I just got my license and my dad gave me his Lexus for today."

"How nice." This from Rachel.

Evan shot Ashley a see-what-a-good-catch-I-am look and faced Julia. "I wanna have my fortune read."

"I'm not a fortune-teller. Tarot-reading is an ancient art going back to—"

"Whatever." He plunked down onto the chair and pulled Tiffany close. From the corner of her eye, Ashley saw him nuzzle his nose in her stomach for a second.

The sight of such an intimate gesture hurt, and she remembered their first time together. *It's just you and me, babe.* How complimentary he always was. *Oh, God, Ash, you drive me wild.* But then she remembered other things. *How could you be so stupid...? Get rid of it now!*

Signaling Rachel to come around the table, Ashley started to leave. But she turned back. "Have your cards read, Evan, but you don't really need to. Anybody can see you're heading nowhere. Thank God I'm not in the equation anymore."

As she walked away, she heard Evan say, "Bitch."

And Tiffany added, "She's just jealous."

Then the shuffle of a deck, accompanied by Julia's lilting voice, "Oh, gee, look at this card."

"What is it?" Evan asked.

As somber as a judge, Julia said, "It's the Fool."

ERICA PICKED AT her pizza, ripped off a small piece of crust and munched on it. Its garlicky taste made her stomach queasy. She squirmed in her seat, feeling her skin itch beneath the T-shirt and jeans she wore, trying to concentrate on the conversation around her.

"And then he said, 'All right, Mr. Battaglia, let's see if you can manage this time without turning green.'"

Even though John was kind of cute in his dark T-shirt and black denims, Erica thought Shondra was behaving like some medical groupie; all night long she'd been smiling at him adoringly.

"Did you, like, really hurl?" Shondra asked.

Joe Taylor, sitting between Julia and Ashley, very preppy in his blue oxford shirt and crew-neck sweater, grinned. "Yeah, he did. I was there to see it."

"I can't wait to go to college." Shelley stuffed a huge bite of pizza into her mouth.

"Where you going?" John asked. Erica noticed he paid equal attention to all of them.

"I'm still holding out for Penn State. But the scholarship money's got to come through."

"You guys live in a dorm?" Dan asked Joe. He sat with his arm loosely draped on Julia's chair.

Who cares? Erica thought as Joe and John described their apartment in the city near Columbia. This conversation was making Erica edgy. As was the pretty brown-haired girl sitting across from her.

Lauren Lansing. Erica had heard John ask Shondra if he could bring along his two friends, Joe Taylor and Dr. Lansing's daughter, Lauren. Erica had tried to beg off after hearing that, saying she had a paper to write. But Rachel had thrown a fit, insisting Ashley needed them all there, though Ashley was flirting big time with Joe. Lauren sat quietly listening, cutting her pizza into small pieces with a knife and eating it with a fork.

When she looked up and caught Erica staring at her, she smiled weakly.

Feeling she had to say something to break the awkward moment, Erica asked, "Having a good time?"

"Yeah." Lauren smiled more genuinely at the opening. "Do you like working with my dad?"

"Um, yeah, sure."

"He said you're really smart."

"Did he?"

"Yeah, and you're going to Georgetown."

"Maybe." Erica sipped her soft drink. "Last time my father checked, they were still undecided. I should hear soon, though." She studied the other girl. "Did you come out here to spend Thanksgiving with your father?"

"Yes."

"How come you're not with him tonight?"

Lauren shrugged. "Family togetherness wears thin after a while, know what I mean?"

No, I don't. Erica and her father had gone to his

partner's open house for Thanksgiving two days ago. She would have loved to spend the holiday just with her dad; she'd even offered to cook. "Yeah, sure."

John, who was playing big brother to Lauren, smiled at her. "Since you ditched him, your father's probably working at the clinic right now."

"Maybe," Lauren said. "I was kinda hoping he'd have another date with Zoe."

"Another date?" Erica asked.

Lauren shrugged, totally unaware that everybody at the table had stopped talking. "Yeah, she spent Thanksgiving with us at Uncle Mitch's."

Erica remembered Mrs. Lansing's little girl saying, *Aunt Zoe was on top of Uncle Kurt on Camille's bed.*

Suddenly it became crystal clear. They were getting back together! Shit!

She stood abruptly, tipping her chair back so it teetered and fell with a thud. "I'm going to the bathroom." She grabbed her purse, planning to split for the night. As she turned away, she saw Dan lean over and say something to Julia.

But Erica didn't look back. Her whole body tingled and her palms got sweaty. Her head started to pound. Then her heart. Did she have more pills in her purse? she wondered as she entered the coat room, grabbed her leather jacket and shrugged into it. She'd already taken two today and wouldn't sleep tonight, anyway. What was one more?

You're overusing, big time, Pike had told her, *if you need more already. Even one a day's too much.*

Erica swore aloud when she bumped into somebody as she hurried out of the coat room.

Big hands steadied her. "Watch it."

She looked into Dan Caruso's face.

"Excuse me." She tried to brush past him, but Julia grabbed her purse strap. "Erica, wait."

Erica swung around, spilling the contents of her purse onto the ground.

Dan dropped to one knee. "Sorry, I'll get this." He found lipstick, her wallet, a hairbrush.

Then he grasped the small white paper packet, out of which fell three black capsules.

He frowned at them. Picked one up and studied it.

Erica made a grab for the pills, but he was quick and gathered all of them into his hand.

"What're those?" Julia asked.

Erica froze.

Dan looked at her. "Black beauties." At Julia's puzzled frown, Dan said, "They're uppers."

ZOE WALKED INTO HER HOUSE and threw her coat onto the chair in the darkened living room. What a mess she'd made of things. Stomping into the kitchen, she poured herself a glass of wine and caught sight of her face in the glass above the sink. *Coward. You should have made some overture to Kurt today.*

But she hadn't. She'd watched as he strolled around the festival with Lauren, introducing her to the girls, buying her a beaded headband; she watched as he'd swung Alexandra up on his shoulders while Mitch carried Camille; and she'd watched how his muscles had rippled when he'd shot the basketball and won a fuzzy lion, which he presented to his daughter with courtly flourish.

Sighing, Zoe wandered back into the living room, put an old Beach Boys CD on the player and sat on the couch. Why wasn't she with Kurt? This was so stupid. Where was he...?

"I'm leaving," he'd said at about four.

"Oh. Did you have a good day?"

"Good enough."

When she didn't say any more, he gave her a sad smile, turned and, ten feet away, pivoted and came back. "What the hell," he said, dragging something out of his jacket pocket and slapping it in her hand.

Then he'd walked out of the gym.

She hadn't read it. Because she knew what it was. She could tell from the notepaper—it was what they'd used at Down to Earth.

The twenty-four-hours-to-live assignment—*Write a letter to one person in your life, telling them how you feel about them and what they mean to you...you might want to clear up some old baggage between you...*

After a few more minutes of futile debating, she snagged her purse off the table and fished out the letter. Flicking on a light, she held the note tightly for a moment, then opened it. Her heart thudding in her chest, she read his words:

Dear Zoe,

I write this letter to you knowing full well it's not something I have any right to do. Like everything else I've done since your birthday last year, I'm being selfish. I just hope I have the courage not to give this to you—unless I really do only have twenty-four hours to live. In that case, I'd want you to know how much you mean to me, how much I regret my decision last year, and exactly how wrong I realize I was.

Mitch has always said I don't like to fail at anything. It's why I went back to Elizabeth. That and because I thought it was best for Lauren.

Though my daughter blossomed, I think she would have been all right even if her mother and I hadn't reconciled.

Why did I do this? You know that I'd dated Elizabeth since I was sixteen—that's a thirty-year relationship. Somewhere in my mixed-up brain, I thought I'd always love her. What I hadn't counted on was the depth of my feelings for you. Even as I went back to my ex-wife, I knew I loved you, I just didn't know how much. Nothing Elizabeth could have done, no matter how much she'd changed, would have made me happy. I was too in love with you for a successful relationship with any other woman.

I discovered how I really felt within weeks of the reconciliation. You say you don't want to discuss this part, but I know how much my sleeping with Elizabeth hurt you and I want to set the record straight. You have to understand that the first time, at my house, just before you and I split, was a knee-jerk reaction. I was caught off guard. So shocked and surprised, I just let it happen. I know this was an unforgivable weakness. After that, when Elizabeth and I were reconciled and we slept together, I blanked my mind, and participated in the act with just my body. Notice I didn't call it making love. It wasn't pleasant, and very soon I couldn't do it anymore. Especially since making love to you was the best thing that ever happened to me. I hadn't realized how intimate it was, how emotional and spiritual it was between us. She never affected me the way you did, sweetheart. I'm convinced no one else ever will.

Elizabeth was livid, and that was the beginning

of the end. I also think my distancing made her more determined to keep me. Suffice to say, those months were horrible.

So if I really had twenty-four hours to live, the one thing I'd want you to know is, ironically, I was more yours that year we were apart than I ever was. When you remember me, remember that.

Kurt

Zoe folded the letter.

And wept.

But once the storm was over, she straightened, scrubbed her face and stood. She was headed to the phone when the doorbell rang. Praying it was Kurt, she flew to the front door.

Outside, she found Julia and Dan.

A BLACK CLOUD of depression hovered over Kurt's head as he studied the request from a group of doctors in Puerto Rico to help them establish a clinic in the vicinity of one of their medical schools. He'd come to his office this Saturday evening after the festival to work, and stayed until—he checked his watch—eight at night. Only a few times had he felt such despondency: when Mitch shipped off to Vietnam, and then when he came back in such rough shape; when their parents died; when his marriage broke up; and finally, when he left Zoe. He'd learned over the years that there was only one antidote to despair—work.

It was so quiet he could hear the heat come on and a car horn outside. Then the sound of scraping near the window. Glancing toward it, he took off his glasses to see if someone was there. Had he left it open?

Slowly Kurt rose and strode to the window. He yanked up the blinds and looked outside. Blackness, broken only by a muted security light. His office was in the back of the clinic off a small parking lot. He could see the outline of his car in the spot labeled Director.

Crossing to the other side of the room, he checked the private-entrance door to make sure it was locked. It was. He chided himself for his skittishness, then sank onto the couch and stretched his feet out on the coffee table.

Damn, things were a mess. He was on the brink of giving up on Zoe. There. He'd let himself have the thought; he'd allowed it into his consciousness. She was never going to forgive him, and he didn't blame her. He'd slept with another woman when he was involved with her. He'd left her for that same woman. No matter that he'd suffered that year, too. He knew it was his own actions that had caused all that pain. Zoe had been an innocent participant.

He'd given her the twenty-four-hours-to-live letter today as a last-ditch effort, but he didn't hold out much hope. They weren't making progress. They took two steps forward, then three back. And yesterday morning, after an incredible night of lovemaking, when she'd still put distance between them, he'd come to understand she would never truly commit to him, never completely trust him not to break her heart. Which was why he believed it wouldn't work between them now. He couldn't settle for half of her.

So he thought practically, *do something constructive. Help those Puerto Rican doctors get their clinic up and running.* After all, medicine was the only thing he had left. Besides Lauren, who was growing up fast and would be on her own all too soon. She didn't even want to be with him tonight.

God, you're getting maudlin, Lansing. She's eighteen. She's out with kids her age. You should be glad the others like her.

I am.

Rising, he strode to the desk, dropped into the chair and put on his glasses.

An hour later he heard a *thunk*. In the parking lot. Remembering his earlier unease he strode to the window to look out. *What the hell?* A small dark sedan had rammed into the back of his car. Their bumpers were crunched.

Go to the phone. Call the cops. Don't open the door.

He grabbed the cordless and, back at the window, punched in 911 as a girl slid out of the dark sedan. In the dim light of the parking lot, he could see it was Erica.

Disconnecting the phone, he rushed to the back door and flung it open just as she reached it.

"Erica, my God, what happened?"

She stared at him blankly, her eyes...

Oh, God, how had they missed this? She was *on* something.

"Erica?" He reached for her arm.

Clutching her purse to her chest, she shrank back. "Don't touch me."

"All right. Come in."

She stepped inside and he closed the door. She stood facing the windows, her back to him.

"Were you hurt in the accident?" he asked.

"Accident?" Her shoulders slumped inside the leather coat she wore.

"You hit my car, Erica."

Still, nothing. Kurt considered carefully how to respond. He didn't want to spook her, but she'd obviously come here for a reason.

"Erica, do you want help?"

"Help?" Still her back was to him. He could see her fishing in her purse for something, probably a tissue.

"Do you want me to help you?" he repeated.

She spun around. "No, Dr. Lansing. I don't want you to help me. I want you dead."

It was then that he saw the gun in her hand.

CHAPTER THIRTEEN

THE REVOLVER TREMBLED in Erica's hand and the man before her blurred. The headache came back in a blinding flash and the dizziness returned.

"Erica, you don't mean that." Dr. Lansing's voice was calm, the way it got when he was dealing with an overwrought patient.

"It's the only way."

"To do what?"

"To stop you from hurting other people."

He shoved his hands in his pockets. "You mean Zoe?"

"Yeah."

Watching her, he began edging toward the desk.

"Don't move!"

He stopped.

"I know how to use this," she warned. "My father taught me. He made me go shooting at the conservation range forever to learn how." She scowled. "I loaded it with six shots before I left our house."

Fear flared in Dr. Lansing's eyes. "Where is your father, Erica?"

"At his club, where else? It's Saturday night."

"Shall we call him?" He nodded at the phone. "He could come over, help you deal with this."

She laughed, an ugly sound. "He wouldn't come."

"Of course he would. If we told him you were in trouble."

"I don't get in trouble, Dr. Lansing, don't you know that? I'm a good girl. The best little girl in the world."

"What are you on?" he asked softly.

Her eyes narrowed on him. It didn't matter. He was going to die, anyway. It was necessary. "Amphetamines."

"Where did you get them?"

"Don't worry. I didn't get them from your precious clinic. I tried, though. You're security's pretty good." She thought about it. "That's ironic, isn't it? You let me in here with a gun, but your drugs are safe from me."

"You aren't going to hurt me with that gun."

"Yes, I am."

"Tell me why again?"

A streak of pain shot through her head. Her chin jerked up. "Ohh."

"What is it?" He moved forward.

"Stay where you are! I mean it."

He stayed. But he said, "You're ill, Erica. The drugs are making you do this."

"I don't care why I'm doing this. I just am."

"You're going to throw away your whole future. If you stop now, we'll get you help."

"No." She couldn't stop now. Her heart pounded hard. It was too late. She'd never go to Georgetown now. Never become the CEO her father wanted her to be. The minute she'd pulled the gun out, it was all over.

Finally.

The phone rang, startling her. She jumped. Dr. Lansing reached for it.

"Don't!"

The answering machine picked up. His message played short and sweet. Then a voice came on. "This is the supervisor for 911," a female voice said. "We received a hang-up call from you and I decided to follow up on it. Do you need help?"

"I'm going to answer that, Erica. You really want me to. I'm going to put my hand out like this and—"

The shot was so loud it hurt her ears. She recoiled back, gripping the gun. Her eardrums rang.

From the corner of her eye, she saw something move and her head snapped up. Why was Dr. Lansing falling? What—

He slumped to the ground, clutching his chest. The light green of his shirt darkened from the area around his heart all the way up to his shoulder. Through the fingers of his hand, which he'd brought to his chest, she saw bright red blood.

Oh, my God.

THERE WAS ONLY PAIN. It exploded at his shoulder and radiated everywhere. His arm, his chest, his neck. He felt his stomach roil and knew he might vomit.

"He's dead."

Erica. Though the sound was muffled from the loudness of the gun, he knew her voice.

Barely able to move, Kurt opened his mouth to tell her he was all right; he wasn't dead. But then reality dawned.

Erica had shot him.

His mind filled with several images—Columbine and Florida, and the most recent school shooting in New York City, where three teachers and a nurse had died, along with eleven students.

He thought about Seth's statement at the board meeting: *It's disconnecting that leads a kid to bring a gun to school.*

And so he remained still.

Through slitted eyes, he saw Erica sink to her knees. "I killed him," she whispered, her voice thick with tears.

But he couldn't be sure her regret was genuine. If he moved, if she saw he was alive, would she shoot him again? The pictures in the paper of the city teachers and the nurse swam before him.

Kurt knew he didn't want to die. So he lay still and tried to assess the damage. It felt like knives digging into his shoulder. Blood seeped through his fingers, but it didn't gush; clotting had already begun. He wondered if the bullet was still in his shoulder. He'd need help soon, but to get it he had to play it cool—not like he'd done with the phone. God, he'd been stupid.

Again he slitted his eyes; she was staring at the gun. "I don't deserve to live," she murmured.

No! Kurt knew that young shooters often turned the gun on themselves. No, no, he couldn't let her do that.

But if she did, he'd be safe.

He watched her. She was crying hard now, holding the gun, as if she was weighing it, weighing her options.

Stay still. Protect yourself. Don't move.

All of it was sound advice from his instinct for survival. But Kurt had spent a lifetime saving people, a lifetime helping kids, kids like Erica, just as troubled. And he was part of a fraternity of men and women who'd taken the Hippocratic oath to save a life, not allow it to be snuffed out before his eyes.

So he said simply, "Erica, don't. I'm not dead."

ERICA WAS SO STARTLED she almost dropped the gun. Hugging it to her chest, she said, ''W-what?'' Her voice sounded odd as if she was underwater, and there was a ringing in her ears. Too late she remembered her father's advice to use earplugs when she shot a gun.

Dr. Lansing tried to sit up. More blood seeped from his wound, and he flopped back down, half lying, half sitting on the floor. She stared at the blood.

The blood she had caused. Oh, God.

''I...I'm not dead. Don't do anything—'' he took a breath ''—to yourself...with that gun.''

How did he know what she was thinking?

''Don't...hurt...yourself.'' His sentences were broken, his words halting. He was in a lot of pain. ''It's not too late.''

She felt cold all over. ''Of course it's too late. I shot you.'' She nodded to him. ''In the chest.''

''Not...my chest...my shoulder.'' He waited several moments. ''You need to...go into the bathroom...get towels. For the bleeding.''

She clutched the gun. Was this a trick?

''No trick, Erica.'' He shook his head, closed his eyes. ''I'm hurt. I can't do anything to you. I just want to talk.'' He gasped for breath. Waited a moment. ''I need something for this first.''

''I won't give you the gun. I want it.''

''I know.'' He tried to smile. ''Get me the towels.'' Another pause. ''Please.''

The bathroom was only two feet away. She could back in, get the towels and still hold the gun on him.

Oh, she wasn't planning to shoot him again. Not *him*.

It only took a few seconds. He groaned as he sat up and his arm bled more, turning his shirt and his hand a muddy red. But he took the towel and pressed it to his shoulder. He leaned his back against his desk, his face white and drew in more deep breaths.

"It hurts?"

He gave her a sardonic smile. "Yeah. It hurts."

Her eyes filled with tears and she lifted the gun. She couldn't stand to see what she'd done to him.

"You haven't done anything irrevocable…"

"Yes, I have. I shot you." Tears streamed down her cheeks. "I don't deserve to live. I don't want to live."

"I want you to live." He waited before he went on. Seemed to garner some strength. "You'll leave…sad people behind if you do…what you're thinking about."

She snorted. "My father?"

With effort, he nodded. "He's pushed you too much…hasn't given you enough affection, but he'd be sad."

"No way."

"Your friends. Ashley, Rachel, Julia, Shondra…Shelley. How would they deal with this their senior year? The rest of their lives?"

"I don't wanna think about that."

"You have to. Killing yourself is final."

"I don't care."

"I care."

"I *shot* you."

"I still care."

She didn't say anything.

He bit his lip against the pain. "Ms. Caufield? You know…she wouldn't be able to handle it if you hurt yourself. She'll blame herself."

Erica just stared at him. But she saw Ms. Caufield's face, heard her words, *Honey, you need help. We're*

*going to get you some... I should have done something
before...I've made an appointment with...''*

Erica's eyes closed briefly. ''She'll never forgive me
for this. She loves you.''

''She loves you, too. You can forgive somebody you
love...anything.''

Suddenly Erica felt tired. Her shoulders sagged and
the headache started to recede, letting her focus better.
Was he right? Could she—

''I'm right, Erica.'' The towel fell to the floor. He
sat forward, his face tightening with pain. But he held
out his hand and said with surprising strength, ''Give
me the gun.''

She watched him.

''Give me the gun. I'll help you. We'll all help
you.'' After a moment he said, ''Please, honey.''

Erica lowered the gun from her chest.

She came up on her knees.

Slowly she inched over to Dr. Lansing's outstretched
arm.

And placed the gun in his hand.

He shoved it behind him, then reached out for her
and dragged her to the uninjured side of his chest.
Burying her face there, she heard him say, ''Cry it
out...it's all right...everything's going to be all right.''

ZOE HELD BACK her fear until she got to the ER and
saw Mitch Lansing in the waiting area. He was seated
on a vinyl chair, his hands over his mouth, his face
ravaged; Cassie sat next to him, holding on to him, her
head resting on his shoulder. Halting in the entryway,
Zoe clutched Seth's arm. ''I thought you said Kurt was
all right.''

"Cassie told me on the phone he was." Seth took her hand and pulled her toward the Lansings.

Up close, Cassie's face was drawn and mottled. Mitch looked up. Bruised eyes, the exact color of Kurt's, stared at her.

"Mitch? Has he…is he…" She went weak, unable to finish the untenable thought.

Cassie rose. "Kurt's fine."

Zoe glanced down at Mitch, then up at Cassie questioningly.

"Mitch is upset, that's all. Shooting of any kind, let alone Kurt…this is tough for him." Cassie grabbed Zoe's arms firmly. "But Kurt's okay. Honest."

Seth slid his arm around Zoe and inclined his head to the patient area. "What's going on in there?"

"He's getting patched up. The bullet went through the fleshy part of his shoulder and came out the other side."

Though she tried to be strong, Zoe swayed on her feet. *Bullet.* Dear God. She felt her stomach lurch and clasped her hands around her middle. It was unbelievable what Cassie had relayed on the phone—Erica high on drugs had shot Kurt, and they were at the hospital. It was the worst kind of nightmare.

Cassie was distracted by movement behind Zoe. Her hand went to her husband's shoulder. "Mitch, Lauren's here." She bent and whispered something in his ear.

"I know. I'll be fine." Mitch scrubbed his hands over his face, stood and gave Zoe's arm a quick squeeze. He'd straightened and composed himself by the time Johnny ushered Lauren over to them.

"Uncle Mitch? Daddy's hurt?"

The strong adult now, the competent cop, he faced Lauren and Johnny. Both young people were white-faced and grim. "Your father's fine." He looked at Johnny. "Kurt was shot in the shoulder, but the bullet didn't lodge there. He lost a lot of blood, but nothing life-threatening."

"Shot?" Lauren's eyes widened. "I don't understand. Somebody shot my father?"

"Cassie told us on the phone he was at the clinic," Johnny said hoarsely. "Did somebody try to break in?"

"No." Mitch's voice was controlled, and steely underneath. "Erica Case shot him."

Gasps from behind her. Zoe turned to see a group of kids at the door. Julia, Dan, Joe Taylor, Ashley, Rachel, Rob, Shelley and Shondra. She knew they'd gone out together for pizza after the festival, then they'd gone clubbing.

"We don't know exactly what happened, Lauren," Mitch continued. "All we know is he's all right. He's going to be fine. *Fine*," Mitch repeated as if trying to convince himself.

Lauren threw herself into her uncle's arms and cried. Cassie drew a clearly upset Johnny off to the side. Taking in a deep breath, Zoe faced her kids. She knew it was her responsibility to explain things to them; but how could she when she couldn't understand it herself? She'd have to find a way of course, but all she really wanted was to see Kurt.

FINALLY THE PAIN was abating. Kurt knew that the morphine drip they gave him was kicking in. Lauren leaned over and kissed his forehead. "I'll see you in the morning, Daddy."

"Night, honey." He closed his eyes. Even the dim

light hurt them. He ached all over and the intravenous plug itched like hell.

He heard the door close and breathed a sigh of relief. His daughter was reassured. His brother would take care of her. Now he could sleep. He turned his cheek into the soft pillow.

There was a swish of the door again. He pried open his eyes and saw Zoe enter the room. She approached the bed and bent over him, her face stricken.

"Hi, sweetheart." It hurt to talk and he was woozy, but this was Zoe.

"Hi, love." Gently she kissed his brow, her lips warm, her smell familiar. Her touch soothed him.

"I'm fine, Zoe."

She swallowed hard. He knew she'd keep herself together here, then probably fall apart when she got alone. He wondered if somebody could stay with her for a while. "I know. Thank God."

Reaching up with his good arm, he ran his fingers down her cheek. Even that effort was too much and his hand fell. "I blew it with Erica." He could hear how slurred his speech was.

"Don't think about that now."

"I didn't see…the drugs. What kind of doctor am I…"

"None of that matters now. All that matters is that you get well and Erica gets help."

Zoe was a little blurry when he tried to focus on her. "I was too…preoccupied…with my personal life. With us. I lost sight of her needs."

Zoe's face paled, so he dropped the issue. Until later. He struggled to keep his eyes open. "Where is she?"

"Mitch said Hal Stonehouse is holding her at the police station. Her father's with her."

"No charges," he mumbled.

"What?"

"Don't want to press charges."

"Shh," she said, her eyes glistening. "You've got to think about yourself now, no one else."

Tired. God, he was tired.

And wrong. He'd been so wrong.

"Close your eyes. Go to sleep."

He nodded. Later he'd tell her what he'd decided.

She sat in the chair next to him, grasped his good hand and brought it to her mouth. Having Zoe here, next to his bed, with him felt good. Very good.

Even if only for tonight.

"IF I HAVE TO, Hal, I'll say I was confused and that the gun went off by accident." Kurt stood in the police station, staring down both Hal Stonehouse, Bayview Heights's police chief, and Mitch. Kurt's arm was in a sling and his shoulder hurt like hell. He didn't need this battle.

"That would be perjury," the older man said.

Kurt arched a brow. "Maybe I *was* confused. I was gravely wounded."

"I already released her into the rehab program on your insistence. We aren't letting her off, Kurt."

"She won't be let off. She's got a long treatment to go through, and the scars afterward will be punishment enough."

Hal's gaze flew to Mitch.

"Don't look at me," Mitch grumbled. "I can't knock any sense into that hard head of his. He'd only stay with us for two days after he was shot, and then he went into the clinic on the third morning." Mitch leveled angry eyes on him. "He's a pigheaded son of a bitch."

"I get it from my older brother." Kurt turned to Hal. "Look, the girl was on drugs. Uppers, which in huge quantities cause personality disorder. In the end the *real* Erica gave me the gun willingly. She isn't going to jail, Hal. I mean it."

Thoughts of the incident still haunted Kurt's dreams. God, what if he hadn't been able to talk her down? She'd be dead now. He hadn't told anybody the exact progression of the events of the night, though both Mitch and Zoe had tried to wring it out of him.

Zoe.

He wouldn't think about Zoe.

"You're feeling guilty." Mitch prowled the office. "Just like Zoe. This is so stupid."

Kurt folded his arms over his chest. "I seem to remember some stupid guilt on your part over Johnny Battaglia a few years back, big brother. People in glass houses…"

"Yeah, but—"

"No buts. We missed the signs. We were too caught up in our own problems. We should have helped her."

"Oh, so it's Zoe's fault, too?"

Kurt didn't answer. He knew she felt the same grinding guilt that he did. He could see it every time he looked into her eyes.

Thoughts of those eyes, and what was still between him and her, weakened Kurt. He sank wearily into a chair. "I'm not backing off. So let's find a way to do this."

As Mitch and Hal exchanged frustrated glances, but began to brainstorm how to handle the situation, Kurt thought about Erica. She'd come to see him at

Mitch's—he'd refused to stay with Zoe—two days after the shooting. She'd crept into the guest room, small and fragile. Her father stood at the doorway, like a guard unwilling to let his charge out of his sight. It was about the only good thing that had come from this whole ordeal—Mr. Case's realization of his daughter's needs.

Erica's eyes were sad. "Hi."

Immediately he'd reached out to her. Stunned, she stared at his outstretched arm, then tears filled her eyes. "I don't deserve this." But she put her hand in his, anyway.

"Yes, Erica, you do." He smiled. "Sit with me."

She perched on the edge of the chair. Head bent, she stared down at their clasped hands. Finally she faced him. "I know what you did for me."

"Did?"

"You kept me...you stopped me from..." She bit her lip. "I would've used the gun on myself. You stopped me even though you didn't know whether I'd shoot you again."

Again Kurt smiled. "I knew I was safe."

"You didn't know that for sure at the time."

"I had a pretty good idea, honey."

She'd put her head down on the bed and cried then, big wrenching sobs that he knew were good for her, but only increased his guilt. Gently he stroked her hair. How had they let her get to this point?

His own feelings of remorse were mirrored on Jackson Case's pained face when the man stepped into the room. Case had said simply, "Thank you, Dr. Lansing, for saving my little girl."

Kurt nodded. He knew the father would be there now for his daughter...

The discussion finally ended. After more than one hour, Hal Stonehouse finally relented and agreed to reduce the charges against Erica. Kurt knew that without his testimony, there would be little chance of a conviction. This way, Erica's lawyer would be able to plea bargain. Most likely she'd get probation, in-house drug rehabilitation and mandatory counseling.

"Let's go, Kurt."

He looked up at his brother.

"You should go home and rest. It's only been a few days."

He had no intention of resting, but he was going home. He needed to do some things before he left.

So he stood—thanked Hal Stonehouse for his concessions about Erica—and followed his brother out of the police station.

ZOE SAT AT HER DESK in her classroom trying to grade papers, unable to concentrate. She'd been unable to sleep or eat or do her schoolwork ever since the shooting. Throwing down her pen, she rose and went to stare out the window. It had started snowing, and the glass was icy with December weather.

Her last conversation with Kurt haunted her...

"It's not your fault," she'd told him once he was settled at Mitch's. That he'd refused to come home with her had hurt, but she'd squelched it and concentrated on what *he* needed.

"Yes, it is. I missed the signs."

"So did I."

He shook his head. "And you feel guilty, too. Don' tell me otherwise." She started to protest, but he'd held up his hand. "Don't say you don't, Zoe. I can see i in your eyes. Hear it in your voice. We blew it with her.''

"So you want me to feel guilty?''

"No. I want you to work it out. Just like I will.''

"Together?''

"What do you mean?''

"Will we work this out together?''

"I don't know. Look, I'm tired.''

"Kurt, we need to talk about this. We need to talk about *us*.''

"Not now. Later…''

That had been his mantra for the entire week, and Zoe had been beside herself with worry. Tracing her finger over the cold glass, she stared at the school parking lot. It was hard enough trying to deal with the kids here. The events of Thanksgiving weekend had rocked Bayview Heights High School to its core.

Counseling sessions had been set up, renewal of the Say No to Drugs efforts, and Seth was also meeting with topnotch counselors to create groups for kids like Erica who felt too much pressure, were depressed and didn't know where to turn.

"Zoe?''

She pivoted, shocked to see Kurt in the doorway.

"What are you doing here? Should you be out of bed?''

He nodded. "I'm fine.''

Feeling wobbly all of a sudden, she crossed to him and perched on top of a desk. She nodded to one next to her. "Well, at least sit down.''

He leaned against her desk, instead. "I can't.'' He checked his watch. "I've got a plane to catch.''

"What?''

"I'm going away for a while.''

"Going away? Where?"

"To help open that clinic in Puerto Rico."

"I don't understand." But somewhere inside, she did. Ever since the shooting, Kurt had completely closed himself off from everybody. Especially her. Stalling for time, scrambling for something to say, she took in his navy sport coat and gray slacks, his arm still in a sling.

Well, she wasn't giving up without a fight. She eased off the desk and stood. "How can you just leave like this?"

Reaching out his good arm, he placed his hand at her neck and clasped it gently. "Don't you see, love? I can't stay. I blew it with Erica. I missed all the signs, and she almost died."

"You could have died."

He ignored that. "I was too caught up in what was happening in my personal life. I let it distract me from my work."

"The same is true for me."

"I know, sweetheart. We both made mistakes. You should get some help dealing with your own feelings."

"Stay, and we'll get help together."

"No."

"Kurt, I lo—"

He silenced her with his fingers on her lips. "Don't tell me that. You're riding on adrenaline now. Your emotions are high. You don't know how you feel."

"Of course I do."

He shook his head vehemently and stepped back. "I don't want to hear it, Zoe. I don't need to hear it."

His words hurt. She tried again. "You need me, Kurt. I can help. We can help each other."

"Nothing can change the facts. What I need is to go away. Do some good somewhere else. Clear my head."

"What about the clinic here?"

"It's closed until the court date is set and the plea bargain's accepted. There's no way the place will open before Christmas. If the town council allows it to open at all." He scowled. "Louise has agreed to run things if it does open."

Zoe's throat felt as if it was filled with cotton candy. "After *Christmas*? How long will you be gone?"

"A couple of months, I think."

"Oh, Kurt. Why are you doing this?"

"I need to get away." Again he smiled sadly. "I'm not the man you think I am. You can't count on me, Zoe. Like you've said so many times."

"I was upset. I was figuring things out. I didn't know what I wanted."

"I know. But I'm figuring things out now. Let's leave it at that." He glanced at the clock behind her. "I've got to go."

Tears clouded her eyes. "Please, Kurt, don't leave."

Grasping her chin, he brushed her lips with his. "I have to."

He straightened and walked toward the door. Zoe watched helplessly, hoping he'd turn around, wishing for some sign of hesitancy, of doubt.

Because it never came, she let him go.

CHAPTER FOURTEEN

"WHY WE DOIN' this semester wrap-up today, Ms. C?" Dan Caruso asked the question as he winked at Julia, who stood at the board, ready to write. The boy was slouched in a beanbag chair, more at ease than Zoe had ever seen him. "How come we aren't waitin' till tomorrow?"

Zoe smiled at Dan. "Oh, I don't know. I thought maybe little elves might have planned something for the last day of the semester that could interfere with our closure."

"There's only one elf in this room, Ms. C," Rob Mason said. "And we're looking at her." Rachel turned around and shushed him, then gave him a peck on the cheek.

"In any case," Zoe said firmly, "let's list the ways we grew this semester. Let's talk about the things we learned." She smiled at the group. "We've been through some pretty heavy stuff together in the past five months."

A thoughtful silence. Then Shondra said, "I'll start. I think we got our heads on straighter about what we want in life."

"You can say that again." This from Julia as she wrote the suggestion on the board.

"Yeah, can you see Jules as a psychologist?" Shelley asked. "I always thought she'd *play* Sigmund Freud, not *be* him."

"Don't let them tease you, Sabrina. Juillard's loss is Binghamton's gain." This from Dan. Julia had indeed been accepted at the prestigious school, but had decided to study more than acting.

"Yeah, and it doesn't hurt that Dan the Man's going there, too," Rob teased. He and Rachel were attending Geneseo together.

"Actually I'm not." Dan smiled at Julia and she smiled back. "I'm staying here and takin' courses at Teachers' College in the city. I, um, want to be with my brother."

As had been the case ever since Thanksgiving, Julia only had eyes for Dan. "I'll just be a couple of hours away," she said softly.

"Oh, jeez. Don't let them get lovey-dovey on us." This from Ashley. "Really, Jules—" she looked askance at her friend "—you *need* to join the Girls' Concerns group. Ms. Sherman's continuing it next semester."

"Yeah, and Caruso can join the Guys' Concerns Mr. McKenna's running." This from Rob.

One of the ways the school was trying to reach all kids in all areas was by forming support groups during study-hall time and after school. So far they'd been successful, and Zoe had attended several sessions with the girls during January to help facilitate the group.

Kurt would have been wonderful with the guys.

"Let's continue the list," she said with as much enthusiasm as she could muster.

"I think we're more honest," Madison Kendrick put in.

In a surprise move that had been precipitated by Erica's secrecy and the stress it caused, Madison had discussed openly what it felt like to be on the outside of a group like Caufield's Chicks. The others had listened intently.

"You go, girl," someone said, and they all laughed.

Shelley spoke. "I think we learned how to get along with adults better." She rolled her eyes. "Even Bosco."

"Bosco's coming around," Maddie said. "I'm working on him."

Zoe had to laugh as she remembered Madison taking on Jerry Bosco at a board meeting. She'd boldly stood up to him about the health courses and Down to Earth. And for some reason Jerry had backed down. Madison confided later that she'd gone to see him at the town hall one day, too, and they'd actually talked for some time. Whatever they'd shared must have been good, because Bosco had been willing to visit some of the support-group sessions to experience firsthand what was going on with them.

And he'd stopped attacking the clinic after Mr. Case, Erica's father, had had a talk with him and with the rest of the town council. It was tough to argue with Case when he contended that the clinic had saved his daughter's life.

Kurt would have been happy about that.

"My mom and I are making progress, too." Shondra shrugged a little self-consciously. "You know, after Erica."

"We can mention Erica," Zoe said easily, though her heart tripped a little. "She's been in to see us. And she might stop in at the end of class today to say goodbye."

Erica had finished her mandatory in-hospital rehab

and was now an outpatient at the clinic. She'd been assigned community service by the court as part of her probation and had more counseling sessions during the week.

"I'm glad she's comin' back to school," Dan said.

"Me, too." Zoe zeroed in on Shondra. "We're happy things are better with your mom."

Erica's breakdown had affected many parents in the community, Shondra's mother included. Zoe knew one of the hardest things Shondra had ever had to do was tell her mother about her own experience with uppers. And her mother had listened. It still made Zoe shudder to think of her girls experimenting with drugs. But no longer did she feel so guilty.

Does Kurt? she wondered for the hundredth time.

He was still in Puerto Rico with no plans to come home. She'd heard nothing from him, but the news from Lauren, who'd gone down for semester break, was that his shoulder had healed completely. Cassie and Mitch, who'd spent a week with him at Christmas, reported that he was feeling better about everything. People thought he'd come back when the clinic reopened at the first of the year, once again having the town council's suport, but he hadn't.

The holidays had been a nightmare for Zoe. She'd gone home to Boston to be with her parents, who always unnerved her. When she'd bumped into her ex-husband at the country club and he'd wanted to talk about renewing their relationship, she flew back to Bayview Heights.

"Ms. C?"

Zoe looked up. "What'd you say, Shel?"

"I asked what good things you feel came out of the course. What you learned."

Forgiveness, she thought ironically. *And that you shouldn't waste second chances.* "I learned that you have to look below the surface, that you can't take things for granted, and you can't take the people in your life for granted." She smiled. "We learned a lot about each other and ourselves this semester, didn't we?"

The kids rumbled their agreement.

Glancing at the clock, Zoe said, "One more thing before you go." She held up a packet of letters. "These are the twenty-four-hours-to-live letters that you wrote in October." The class groaned. "I know, you're different now, but you'll want to look at them, anyway. I've saved time for you to talk about them with one another. Read them over, see if you still feel the same way about the person you wrote to and, if you want, give the letter to him or her."

How can I read mine? she thought as she distributed the envelopes. But she'd never cheat the kids by asking them to do something she wasn't willing to do herself.

Hers was the last. With shaking hands she took it to the back of the room and opened it up slowly.

Dear Kurt.

Just reading the salutation hurt. How could she possibly have lost him? *Read it, Zoe. Just read it and get it over with.*

What would I tell you if I had twenty-four hours to live? I'd tell you that I love you, more than I've ever loved a man. I'd tell you that I'm sorry we lost so much time together. I'd tell you that I wish I had fought for you back when you reconciled with Elizabeth. I'd *like* to tell you that I forgive you. But I haven't. To use the kids' phrase, doesn't that suck? That I have only twenty-four hours to live and I can't forgive the man I love?

I need to get over this. I need to work at forgiveness and peace. How can I do that, though? By spending time with you? It hurts just to see you. By talking this out? Maybe we should have an honest conversation with each other. Maybe I need counseling...

Because her eyes filled with tears, Zoe stopped reading. Oh, God, she'd known back in October what she'd needed to do, and she hadn't done it. Eventually she and Kurt had talked about the breakup, but she hadn't gone for counseling until it was too late.

After Erica's incident, Zoe *did* see Madelyn Foxborough, a therapist from the city that Louise had recommended. Zoe had talked through her guilt over Erica, but they'd also discussed Kurt. It had helped.

But it had been too late.

She looked up when the door opened, surprised to see the kids were in groups, discussing their letters.

Alex Ransom stood in the entrance, young and handsome as ever. Zoe had heard he'd started dating the new social studies teacher. "I've got a visitor for you," he said, smiling.

Erica stepped into the classroom. No longer as thin as she'd been, or as sad, she looked young and innocent in jeans and a simple BVH sweatshirt. She smiled at the class. "Is it okay if I come in to say goodbye?"

Several kids got up and rushed to her. Not only Caufield's Chicks, but others, like Madison and Dan Caruso. The thirteen kids left in this class had become tight.

"Hey, aren't you coming tomorrow for the party?" Rachel asked.

The party tomorrow! Zoe rolled her eyes. She knew these kids so well.

And despite what had happened, she loved them—and teaching—every bit as much as she ever had. Perhaps more.

ERICA WATCHED as Ms. Caufield tried to pull herself together. The letter she'd been reading and stuffed in her pocket had made her cry. It was hard to witness, knowing that Erica herself had been responsible for mega tears on everybody's part. But she was done with that. Completely done.

"Ms. C?"

The teacher smiled bravely and came toward her. They hugged, and the class visited until the bell rang.

"Can you stay a minute?" Ms. C asked.

"Sure I can stay. My dad's picking me up at three-thirty."

"It's going well with him?" Ms. C sat down at a table.

Erica rolled her eyes. "Didn't I tell you the latest?"

Ms. C shook her head.

"He's running for the school board. He wants to keep in place some good programs we have here."

"We can use an advocate." Ms. C smiled. "So, you ready to come back next week?"

"Yeah, I can't wait to be in class again. I got credit for most of my first semester courses because of the tutoring, even phys ed for the kick-boxing classes I took at the rehab."

"I'm glad, honey." Again the fake smile. "So everything's back on track."

"Well, I'm not going to be valedictorian." She shrugged. "But I *will* graduate with my class." Sighing, she gave Ms. C. a wise-in-the-ways-of-the-world smile. "And no Georgetown, of course."

"I'm sorry you didn't get in."

"It wasn't the place for me. My dad and Dr. Lansing wanted to pull some strings, but I wouldn't let them." She sat up straighter. "I'm going to take courses at Columbia until I decide what I really want to do. Shondra's mega jealous."

"Because Johnny's there?"

"Uh-huh."

She noticed Ms. C didn't react to her comment about Dr. Lansing. As she'd learned in therapy, she was going to have to take the bull by the horns. "I hear from Dr. Lansing at least once or twice a week."

Ms. C's jaw dropped. This was something Erica had kept from her. "Really?"

"Uh-huh. We've become e-mail buddies." Erica cocked her head. "He's a good writer."

"Is he?" Ms. C cleared her throat.

"Yep. His letters have really helped me come to terms with everything that happened. We talk a lot about forgiving. You know, like forgiving yourself and each other."

"Oh, Erica, I hope he's forgiven himself for what happened." Ms. C's voice was passionate.

"Have you?" Erica asked the woman she loved like a mother.

Ms. C reached out and squeezed Erica's hand. "Yes, I think so."

"Good. Because it wasn't your fault. I did everything I could to hide my habit from you. And I got myself into the drugs and let myself get messed up.''

''The pressure was too much.''

''Uh-huh. It was.'' She raised her chin and grinned. ''But I got myself out of it, too.''

''I know you did, honey.''

Erica checked the clock. ''Well, Dad's meeting me out front. I'd better go.'' She stood. ''We still on for the movies Friday?''

''You bet.''

Erica hugged Ms. C. Damn. This just wasn't right. But she turned to leave, anyway. You could only help people so much, and she'd been giving the pair of them her best shot.

When she got to the door, she heard Ms. C call out, ''Erica?''

She pivoted.

''You didn't answer me. Has Dr. Lansing forgiven himself?''

Hmm, maybe this wasn't a lost cause. And maybe they needed a little nudge. Dr. Sheffield said nudges and interfering were different things. ''I think he's almost there. But he could probably use a push.''

''Your e-mails help, I'm sure.'' Ms. C had stuck her hands in her pockets.

''My e-mails aren't enough.'' She smiled. ''See ya Friday.''

FEBRUARY BLEW into New York with typical midwinter vengeance. Having dealt with the heat and humidity of Puerto Rico for two months, Kurt pulled his wool coat closer around him as he made his way from his car into his office. The whipping wind stung his cheeks, and a few flakes of snow landed on his face. Hesitating only briefly at the door, he unlocked it and stepped into the memories. For a minute all he saw was Erica, holding the gun. Then he felt the impact of the bullet. He smelled the sickening scent of the blood seeping through his fingers to stain the floor. He looked down. New carpet. Louise had told him she'd had it installed. He was thankful for that.

Louise had told him a lot of things in the frequent phone calls they'd exchanged during the six weeks she'd been running the newly opened clinic. *We're fine but we need you... You can't stay in Puerto Rico forever... I never knew you to run away, Kurt...*

Coming inside, he peeled off his overcoat and shrugged into the white lab coat hanging on a hook near the door. His brother had been a lot less kind than Louise when he'd come down to visit at Christmas...

"What is this, some form of self-flagellation?" They'd been in the modest—well, actually, stark—little apartment one of the doctors had found for Kurt. In truth, Kurt hadn't cared a whit about his surroundings. He spent most of his time at the clinic.

"It's fine for me."

Mitch was persistent. "How long are you going to be in exile?"

"I'm not in exile." Kurt had stood and gone to the tiny fridge for a beer. "I need time to think."

"You've had time to think."

His nerves taut, his temper frayed, he whirled around. "Back off, Mitch."

"Not on your life. People need you in Bayview."

"You have your family."

Mitch had sworn then, vilely, and Kurt had tried to mollify him with a beer.

"I'll be back soon. I promise. I need more time."

His brother had played his trump card. "Zoe's sad. All the time. Just like when you went back to Elizabeth."

"I can't see her, Mitch. Not now. I just can't…"

Ironically it had been Erica who'd worn him down. As Kurt sat at his desk and found his calendar, he thought about the girl's tactics. At first her e-mails had been newsy—what was happening in rehab and with her father and at school; he'd responded with stories about the new clinic. Then her posts had gotten philosophical about life. She'd started ending each of her letters with one of the "quotes for the day" her therapist used in rehab. But that wasn't as bad as when she started to fill him in on Zoe—what she was doing, how she was faring. He'd asked her gently not to write about her teacher, but Erica ignored him.

As Kurt pulled out monthly report folders, he recalled some of Erica's specific e-mails. Subtlety wasn't her strong suit…

I saw Ms. C tonight," she'd written. "We went to the movies. She's lost a little weight. I don't think she needed to, do you?" Erica had ended that post with "The three essentials of happiness are: Something to do. Something to love. Something to hope for. I'm gonna get all three, Dr. L. What about you?"

Kurt remembered shrugging off her question and thinking about Zoe losing weight. Every inch of her was perfect. He hoped she didn't get skinny. That night he'd begun dreaming about her—the smell of her just after a shower, the feel of her skin when he touched her and how he always raised gooseflesh…what she sounded like when he made love to her.

Eventually he'd started heading right for his computer each day when he got to work to see what news Erica had about Zoe...

"I went back to school today. Ms. C had lunch with me. She asked about you. The only time her eyes light up is when she talks about you. Our quote today was 'Life consists not in holding good cards, but in playing well those cards you do hold.' What kind of gambler are you, Dr. L?" Erica had asked.

Kurt had spent that entire night wrestling with the bedcovers, remembering how Zoe's eyes had clouded with desire when he was inside her.

The e-mails continued, getting more and more pushy. "Mr. Ransom has a new girlfriend, but we got this hunk of a substitute teacher who moons over Ms. C like Rad Ransom used to. You know, she's really a catch. I saw her laughing in the hall with the new guy. He looks like Pierce Brosnan." Erica's quote for that day was also pointed. "'Nothing is gained without risk. You can't make the basket if you don't take the shot.'" She'd ended with "I know you're a pretty good b-ball player, Dr. L."

Kurt had heard Zoe's laugh for a full day after that, every time he turned a corner...

And so he'd come back. It was time to play his cards, take his shots...hell, the metaphors all said the same thing. He was ready to get on with his life.

He'd told Louise he was returning, of course. And Mitch. But no one else. And he'd purposely come back when Zoe was in Antigua for winter break, so he could get his bearings and work up the courage to face her. But the thought of her in a bikini and all those single guys on the make in the tropical playland bothered the hell out of him.

A knock on his door.

"Come in," he'd said evenly.

Louise poked her head in the office. "Welcome back."

"Thanks."

"You look good with the tan, but tired."

"How are things here?"

She rolled her eyes. "Frantic already. And it isn't even noon."

"I can help."

"I was hoping you'd say that. I told Johnny to let you know what you can do."

He smiled.

"It's good to have you back."

"Thanks. It's good to be here. Leave the door open, would you?"

Kurt had just started making notes on the monthly reports when Johnny appeared in the doorway. Kurt stood and Johnny gave him a big hug. Kurt had missed a lot of people when he was away.

Johnny said, "I wish we had time to catch up, but there's a patient you should see. Dr. Frank is busy with an emergency and I can't do this one." He held up a chart. "A woman with chest pains."

Kurt grabbed his stethoscope and other instruments from his drawer. "Serious?"

"Don't know. She's been having them for a while." He shrugged. "You know how people are. They don't do what's best for them, and they wait until things get so bad they can't stand it."

Kurt stared at Johnny's back as he followed him out the door. Something about the flicker in his eyes reminded Kurt of when Johnny was a street kid... But the boy was heading down the hall, chart in hand. It wasn't until they reached the examining room that Kurt said, "Johnny, I need to see the chart."

"What? Oh, sorry. We're swamped. And I was up late studying." He nodded to the door. "Think you could do this on your own? Dr. Frank asked for my help."

"Yeah sure, but send in a nurse." Kurt shooed him away.

"Glad to have you back, Kurt," Johnny called over his shoulder, again a strange note in his voice. Humorous, almost.

Shaking his head, Kurt studied the chart. Forty-one-year-old woman. Chest pains for weeks. He checked the name. Johnny's scribble was worse than usual. He couldn't decipher it. Jeez, it looked like nobody had even taken her vitals. Knocking briefly on the door, he was still staring at the chart when he stepped inside. "Good morning," he said, taking out a pen. "It seems I can't read your na—" Then he looked up.

Seated on the examining table, dressed in a faded hospital gown that skimmed her thighs, was Zoe. Behind her, the fickle February weather changed dramatically, and the sun made a rare appearance and streamed in the window, bathing her in its warm glow. In that moment he knew in his heart that she was the love of his life.

Shoulders back, she cocked her head. "Good morning, Doctor." Her eyes devoured him, as his did her. She *did* look a little thin, but so good he was immobilized for a minute.

Finally he said, "Good morning. What can I do for you?"

She cleared her throat. "I'm, um, not feeling well," she said softly. "I really need your attention."

His heartbeat hit double time at the meaning of her words. Slowly he walked toward her and pulled a light out of his pocket. "Fine. Let's check your vitals. Look at my nose," he said as he turned on the light and stared deeply into her eyes. "Eyes seem fine. More than fine. Beautiful as ever."

His gaze roamed over her face. "Good color. Maybe a little pale." Then, for the first time in almost ten weeks, he touched her. "What did you say was the problem, miss?" he asked hoarsely, his hand on her throat.

She grasped his wrist and slowly drew his hand down to her chest. "Right here," she said, achingly. "My heart. It hurts. Badly."

His eyes locked with hers. He opened his palm and pressed it against her. "How long has this been going on?"

"Nine weeks, three days and—" she checked the clock "—a few hours."

The corners of his mouth turned up, and simultaneously he felt a hurt so deep it stunned him.

He untied the gown and slid it gently down her shoulders. The freckles he bared beckoned him. Leaning over, he placed his lips on a little patch he was particularly fond of. She startled, then grasped his shoulders. "Oh."

"Something wrong, miss?"

"I'm, um, feeling weak," she whispered.

"Then hold on to me." He slid the stethoscope to the area over her heart as she clutched his upper arms.

"Hmm. Your heart rate's up." He studied her face again. "I'll bet your blood pressure's right off the charts."

"I wouldn't be surprised."

"I wonder what's wrong with your heart."

"I know what's wrong with it."

He arched a brow.

"It's broken."

His throat clogged. "Zoe—"

She raised her hand and stopped his words. "The man I love broke it when he left me. And—" she smiled, though her eyes clouded "—I've found I just can't live without him. Nothing's the same. Everything I always loved—teaching, spending time with my friends, even shopping—aren't any fun."

"Wow, even shopping?" He picked up her hand and cradled it against his chest. "This is a very serious symptom." He kissed her fingers.

"But I'm not sure I can help you. I haven't been very reliable in that…field lately. Maybe you need someone else. I can re—"

She leaned into him and looped her arms around his neck. "I don't want anyone else," she whispered. "Ever. I want you."

There was only a moment's hesitation before his arms closed around her. Both their hearts beat with a dangerous arrhythmia.

He buried his face in her hair. "I missed you so much."

She hugged him to her. "I missed you, too. I need you, Kurt. Please give us another chance."

"I can't bear the thought of hurting you again. Letting you down."

"None of that matters," she said. "We just need to be together."

Brushing back her hair, he asked, "Are you sure?"

She brought his hand to her heart again. "I'm sure. I love you. I'll always love you."

"I love you, too," he whispered, his voice catching on the last syllable.

They held each other for long moments. Then she drew away. "So, are you going to take my case, Doctor?" Her brown eyes, shining with moisture like his own, were also filled with devilment.

"It looks that way." Without releasing her gaze, he stepped back to the door and snicked the lock behind him.

Those eyes of hers danced.

"But I'll have to spend a lot of time with you, miss."

She shrugged, letting the gown slip an inch. "How long?"

"Oh, the next fifty or sixty years ought to do it."

"Sounds good to me."

He came closer. "Mmm, me, too. We'll start with a thorough examination." He reached for the gown.

"Now?" she asked huskily.

"Now," he whispered in her ear. "And forever."

"Can I count on that?"

He drew away. Looked deeply into her eyes. "You can count on that. And on me."

"That's all I need," she said as she pulled him to her.

Special Deliveries

Experience the joy of parenthood,
delivered by two of your favorite Harlequin authors

Janice Kaiser
THIS CHILD IS MINE

Pain can be the midwife of joy...
That's what Lina's fortune cookie tells her.

Beverly Barton
CAMERON

What's in a name?
Everything, if it's all you've got to offer.

Coming April 2001
By Request 2

2 IN 1 VALUE PACK

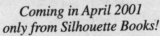

INDULGE IN A QUIET MOMENT
WITH HARLEQUIN

Get a FREE
Quiet Moments Bath Spa

with just two proofs of purchase from y of our four special collector's editions in May.

Harlequin® is sure to make your time special this Mother's Day with four special collector's editions featuring a short story *PLUS* a complete novel packaged together in one volume!

ollection #1   Intrigue abounds in a collection featuring *New York Times* bestselling author Barbara Delinsky and Kelsey Roberts.

ollection #2   Relationships? Weddings? Children? = *New York Times* bestselling author Debbie Macomber and Tara Taylor Quinn at their best!

ollection #3   Escape to the past with *New York Times* bestselling author Heather Graham and Gayle Wilson.

ollection #4   Go West! With *New York Times* bestselling author Joan Johnston and Vicki Lewis Thompson!

Plus Special Consumer Campaign!
Each of these four collector's editions will feature a
"FREE QUIET MOMENTS BATH SPA" offer.
See inside book in May for details.

Only from

HARLEQUIN®
Makes any time special ®

on't miss out! Look for this exciting promotion on sale in May 2001, at your favorite retail outlet.

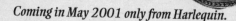

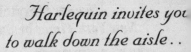

Harlequin invites you to walk down the aisle..

To honor our year long celebration of wedding we are offering an exciting opportunity for you t own the Harlequin Bride Doll. Handcrafted i fine bisque porcelain, the wedding doll is dresse for her wedding day in a cream satin gow accented by lace trim. She carries an exquisi traditional bridal bouquet and wears a cathedra length dotted Swiss veil. Embroidered flowe cascade down her lace overskirt to the scallope hemline; underneath all is a multi-layered crinolin

Join us in our celebration of weddings by sending away for yo own Harlequin Bride Doll. This doll regularly retails for $74.95 U.S./appro $108.68 CDN. One doll per household. Requests must be received no later th June 30, 2001. Offer good while quantities of gifts last. Please allow 6-8 weeks delivery. Offer good in the U.S. and Canada only. Become part of this exciting offe

Simply complete the order form and mail to:
"A Walk Down the Aisle"

<u>IN U.S.A</u>
P.O. Box 9057
3010 Walden Ave.
Buffalo, NY 14240-9057

<u>IN CANADA</u>
P.O. Box 622
Fort Erie, Ontario
L2A 5X3

Enclosed are eight (8) proofs of purchase found on the last page every specially marked Harlequin series book and $3.75 check money order (for postage and handling). Please send my Harlequ Bride Doll to:

_____

Name (PLEASE PRINT)

_____

Address   Apt. #

_____

City   State/Prov.   Zip/Postal Code

_____

Account # (if applicable)   098 KIK DAF

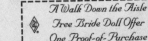

Visit us at www.eHarlequin.com

PHWDAPOP